THE WRONG MAN

A SLATER AND NORMAN MYSTERY

P.F. FORD

To my amazing wife, Mary – sometimes we need someone else to believe in us before we really believe in ourselves. None of this would have happened without her unfailing belief and support.

PROLOGUE

Diana Woods looked at herself in the mirror and was pleased with the reflection she saw. The new underwear she'd been given looked good on her, but then she had known it would. She worked hard to make sure that even at forty-five she still had the sort of figure that made everything look good. She did another twirl so she could catch a view of her backside. *Yes,* she thought, *I feel good in this stuff. He'll be drooling next time he watches me undress.*

Then the doorbell rang and she wondered who it could be. *Probably Laura from next door. But she's not supposed to come round until six. Couldn't she have waited? I've only been home from work five minutes.*

She ran through to the front bedroom and looked out of the window. She could just see the roof of a small, white van parked outside. This was a nice surprise. She really hadn't expected him to call round today. It was a pity she was going out in half an hour, but there would still be time for a little fun before she went.

She slipped a slinky, black negligee on over her new underwear and then padded down the stairs in her bare feet. She smiled to herself as she realised he had bought the negligee for her as well. It seemed as if he was all around her already, and soon she'd have him all to herself anytime she wanted.

The doorbell rang again.

'Alright, I'm coming,' she called, quickening her pace.

She threw the door open.

'Oh. Hi. This is a surprise. You didn't say you were coming round, did you? Well, come on in, but you'll have to be quick. I wasn't expecting you and I'm going out at six.'

She turned on her heel and started walking towards the kitchen at the back of the house, well aware that she was leaving little to her visitor's imagination. But then, that was all part of the fun.

'I was just going to make a cup of tea,' she called over her shoulder. 'Come on. I'll make us both one.'

She heard the front door close behind her as she picked up the kettle and walked across to the sink.

'Why on earth have you got gloves on?' she asked. 'It's not cold, is it? Or, are they your fancy driving gloves?'

There was no reply, and as she turned on the tap to fill the kettle she suddenly became aware that something wasn't right. But by then it was too late, and her eyes widened in pain and shock as the blade of a knife was driven deep into her back.

It would be hard to say if the blow had been delivered with great accuracy or if it was just luck, but whichever was the case, the blade struck at the perfect angle to slip neatly between her ribs and plunge straight through her heart. She didn't even have time to scream before she slumped forward across the sink and then her knees buckled beneath her. By the time she was sprawled face down on the floor, she was dead.

The killer watched in fascination as blood seeped from the wound, creating a widening red patch around the knife handle as it soaked into the flimsy fabric of her negligee. But there wasn't time to linger. There was still work to be done, although it wouldn't take long.

In less than two minutes, the front door was quietly pulled closed and the killer was gone.

CHAPTER ONE

The Bishops Common had been given to the townspeople of Tinton back in ancient times to allow the commoners to graze their animals without cost. Very few of the present day commoners were actually aware of this privilege, and none of them possessed livestock in need of grazing.

They *did* have a rather exclusive enclave of ten homes all to themselves. The houses had all originally been hovels, but it was impossible to tell now. Over the years they had been restored and extended by their various owners and now formed a collection of desirable homes, in an equally desirable location.

'So where is this place?' asked DS Norman Norman. 'I never heard of this Bishops Common before.'

'That's because it's a rather exclusive, and sought after, area,' replied his friend and colleague DS Dave Slater, from the driving seat. 'It's the epitome of peace and tranquillity where nothing ever happens and the police never need to set foot.'

'So this isn't a regular event then?'

'If you mean do they normally find dead bodies lying around, then the answer is no. I believe this is a first.'

'I didn't even know there were any houses down here,' said

Norman, as they turned off the main road and onto the track that led down to the common. 'You *are* sure there are houses here, are you? Only I don't see any.'

'That's because they're down the lane here and round the corner,' replied Slater. 'That's part of the attraction for the people who live here. It's the seclusion that makes it such a sought-after spot. That and the fact all the houses are detached.'

'Well I think it's a crappy place to live.' As a native Londoner who loved the place, Norman found it difficult to see the attraction of living in the countryside. 'You couldn't pay me to live out here.'

'Trust me,' said Slater, smiling, 'the likes of you and me couldn't afford to live out here. Anyway, I don't understand this aversion you have to country life. You spent three years in Northumberland, and you've been here over a year now. Surely you can't still hanker for the noise and pollution of London?'

'You're never going to convince me the smell of horse shit and cow shit is better than diesel fumes,' said Norman. 'No way.'

'All that crap floating around in the London air is taking years off of everyone's life.'

'It's an acquired taste, I'll grant you that.'

'The smell of farm animals doesn't kill your lungs.'

'But this hankering for the smell of cow shit just isn't natural,' said Norman. 'If we were supposed to like it we would have been born cows, right?'

'You need to see someone about your logic.' Slater laughed, shaking his head. 'There is absolutely nothing natural about breathing air filled with diesel fumes.'

They rounded a bend in the lane.

'Here we go.' Slater took one hand off the steering wheel and pointed. 'Crime scene up ahead.'

They could see houses now, to the right and left of the lane. Some were set well back with hedges and trees out front, and one or two were much closer to the lane. The one they were looking for was about fifty yards up on the left hand side. It was easily identified by the blue and white cordon tape and the police vehicles parked outside.

'What time is it?' asked Norman, squinting at his watch.

'Eight-thirty,' said Slater. 'So we had a whole two hours between finishing our normal day's work and getting dragged back out for this.'

'D'you think this is what they meant when they said we should make better use of our own time and our opportunities to relax and sleep in between shifts?' Norman smiled wryly.

He was referring to a recent memo that had been sent round to every department, advising officers they could become more efficient if they made better use of their own time and made sure they had sufficient rest and sleep.

'Just having some of my own time would be a start. Do you get any time of your own?' asked Slater as he parked the car.

'I know what you mean.' Norman let out a laugh. 'But right now you need to put Mr Negative to bed and slip on your positive head. Can you do that?'

Slater had a natural tendency to focus on the negatives. Norman had made it his personal goal to instil in Slater a much more positive attitude in line with his own. It was very much a work in progress, and he still had to remind Slater sometimes, but he saw hopeful signs in his colleague.

Slater fixed a stupid grin on his face and turned to Norman.

'There you go,' he said. 'I'm happy. Okay?'

'That's a very insincere smile. Which, in itself, is indicative of possession of a negative attitude.'

'Oh nuts,' said Slater, swinging his door open. 'The use of over-wordy pronouncements indicates the desire to appear superior, which surely, in itself, is a negative trait.'

Norman tried to think of a smart remark of his own, but Slater was out of the car and the moment was gone.

As this was the scene of a murder, it was necessary for anyone entering to don one of the all-in-one paper 'romper' suits provided by the forensics team. Slater headed into the tent that had been erected in the front garden. Getting into these suits had always been something of a challenge for the rather portly Norman, and was often a source of great amusement for his colleagues; Slater chief among them. Fortunately, Norman didn't seem to be offended by this and there had been more than one occasion when he had played to the gallery and gone out his way to make everyone laugh. Slater knew Norman was of the same opinion as him: sometimes a little humour, in the right place and at the right time, was essential to help everyone cope with some of the darker stuff they had to deal with.

Recently the forensics department had invested in the latest design of the offending suits. No one seemed to know the official name, but because they were blue, the general consensus was they made anyone wearing one look like a smurf. Norman had somehow managed to keep back a personal supply of the older white suits but these all now seemed to be gone, as Norman had showed up empty-handed.

Slater put his own suit on in less than a minute and was ready to go, but Norman seemed to be having some sort of problem. Slater folded his arms and watched patiently as his friend struggled.

'No, it's okay,' said Norman. 'You go on. I'll catch you up in a minute. Some joker seems to have given me a small size. I distinctly said large.'

Slater winked at the PC who was responsible for signing in and handing out suits. He put his finger to his lips to indicate the PC should say nothing.

'Perhaps they didn't bring any of the larger size,' he suggested, smiling broadly. 'I'll go on ahead.'

He didn't bother to tell Norman they were 'one size fits all' just like all the old white suits used to be. He figured his partner would find out soon enough.

He made his way through the open front door, stopped, and looked around.

'Hello?' he called. 'Eamon? Where are you?'

'Through here, in the kitchen.'

A familiar collection of noises told him there was a forensic photographer somewhere nearby, and as he followed the voice through to the kitchen, he could see the accompanying flashes as the cameraman did his work.

Dr Eamon Murphy, the pathologist, was kneeling over the victim's facedown body, directing the photographer. He looked round when Slater came into the room.

'I'm glad I'm not the only one who's been dragged away from his dinner.'

'Ah yes,' Slater said, grinning at him. 'These unannounced informal gatherings are one of the joys of police work.'

'But I don't work for the police.'

'Only because we can't afford to pay your exorbitant salary. Anyway, I thought you were on the payroll now.'

An agreement had recently been cobbled together with the local hospital whereby Murphy could be contracted out to the police as and when necessary.

'I'm not actually a full time employee,' said Murphy. 'I'm supposed to be contracted on an ad-hoc, consultant, basis.'

'So you get to choose how much you get paid? Now that's a novel idea. Maybe I can try doing that.'

Slater squatted down near to the body, but not too near.

'So this situation is just about perfect then,' he continued, his grin becoming even wider.

Murphy raised a quizzical eyebrow.

'Well, you couldn't get much more ad-hoc than this, could you? And it just so happens I need to consult your considered opinion as to this unfortunate lady's death.'

'I suppose I asked for that,' said Murphy, with a rueful smile.

'You did once tell me you'd like to get out and about more often,' said Slater.

He waited while Murphy directed the photographer to take one last shot for him.

'So, what have we got, Eamon?' he asked, once the photographer had stepped away.

'Diana Woods. Forty-five years old, stabbed in the back with a wide-bladed knife, possibly the one missing from the knife block up there.' He pointed to a knife block on the kitchen side. 'I won't know for sure until I do the PM, but it looks like the knife went straight into, and possibly right through, the heart.'

'Would you like to guess a time?'

'I estimate she's been dead no more than three or four hours at most. So my best guess at this stage is that she died somewhere between four thirty and six-thirty. I can't tell you much more at the moment.'

'That's okay,' said Slater. 'It's a start. Are we sure she was murdered in here? The body hasn't been moved or anything?'

'I think she was stood at the sink, filling the kettle when it happened.'

'Really?' Slater was impressed. 'Filling the kettle? How do you know that?'

'It's in the sink, it's full, and the lid's on the side,' said Murphy. 'Simples, as they say.'

There was a commotion from the front of the house and Norman arrived on the scene. He appeared to have squeezed himself into one suit, but another was draped over his shoulders with the arms tied around his neck, and the legs tied around his waist.

'What happened?' Slater tried to suppress a smirk.

'It seems they don't make these suits with the larger person in mind.' Norman plucked helplessly at the skin-tight suit. 'When I did the zip up the front, the damned thing split up the back. So I had to put another one over the top just to cover the back.'

Slater exchanged a glance with Murphy, who was looking at Norman as if he was something the cat had dragged in.

'Diana Woods.' Slater pointed at the body on the floor. 'Eamon says she was stabbed around five-thirtyish—'

'That's just a guess, and it could be an hour either way,' Murphy said, quickly.

'And it looks like she was stabbed with one of her own carving knives.' Slater indicated the knife block with the missing knife.

'Who found the body?' asked Norman.

'Next door neighbour, I think,' said Murphy. 'One of your officers is with her.'

Ian Becks, the Tinton forensic team leader, appeared in the doorway.

'I thought I heard the cavalry,' he said. 'Late again, mind you.'

'We can't get here until someone tells us we're needed,' Norman said.

Becks took a long, quizzical look at him.

'What the hell are you wearing? Two suits?'

'Yes, about that,' said Norman, frostily. 'You need to order a larger size.'

'That is the larger size. Maybe it's not actually the size of the suit that's the problem.'

'We can argue about that another time, Becksy.' Slater jumped in before they could go off on a tangent about Norman's weight problem. 'What can you tell us about the murder scene?'

'Not much, so far,' said Becks. 'There's no sign of a struggle anywhere else in the house, and no sign of a break-in, so I guess that means she let her attacker in. We've got a couple of smudged foot-prints on the kitchen floor, but they seem to be the same size as the shoes the victim wore so they're probably hers. No murder weapon so far either. We'll keep looking, but I wouldn't raise your hopes.'

'I suppose it would have been too much to hope you might find a nice set of prints or something,' said Slater, sighing.

'I'm just about ready to move the body now,' said Murphy. 'The guys will be here shortly to take her away. The PM will begin at eight in the morning, if that's okay with you.'

'Sure,' said Slater. 'We'll be there.'

'Yeah, great.' Norman looked glum. 'I just love to watch a little slicing and dicing just after my breakfast.'

'Maybe we can toss a coin-,' began Slater.

'And maybe we can't, because you always cheat, and I end up losing. This time we'll both go.'

'Whatever. But I'm sure there's something I have to do first thing.'

'Yeah, there is. Come and watch a PM,' said Norman, with an air of finality.

He took a look around the kitchen.

'It looks like you two have this covered,' he said to Becks and Murphy. 'There's not much we can do here that you haven't already done, so we'll leave you to it and go talk to this neighbour.'

'Yeah, thanks, guys,' Slater said, as he followed Norman out of the room.

Night was on its way, and the light was beginning to fade as they made their way back out of the house and across to the tent, where they handed their suits in for disposal before checking which house was home to their witness.

'Laura Pettit,' said the PC on duty, reading from his notes. 'She lives in the house to the left over there.'

He waved his hand in the general direction just in case they were in any doubt.

'In my experience,' said Norman, as they made their way towards the neighbour's house, 'that nice, neat murder scene, with no obvious clues, tends to suggest this murder was planned, and not some random attack.'

'Yeah,' said Slater, heavily. 'That's what I was thinking. And it looks like she probably let the killer in, led them through to the kitchen, and was comfortable enough to turn her back on them to fill the kettle.'

'Or the killer could have had a key and let himself in.'

'But if she was at the sink wouldn't she have heard the key in the lock?'

'Not necessarily. Maybe she had the radio on and didn't hear anything.'

'Either way she probably knew her killer.' said Slater.

'Looks that way,' said Norman, nodding.

They were outside the house now and Slater rang the doorbell. The door slowly opened to reveal the smiling face of PC Jane Jolly.

'Why if it isn't Jolly Jane, Tinton's favourite PC.' Norman beamed fondly at her.

Jolly was probably the most well-liked officer at Tinton, and everyone who met her tended to fall under her spell. There was nothing glamorous about the hard-working mother of three, but she had an inherent goodness about her, and a winning smile that was readily shared with everyone she came into contact with. And if that wasn't enough, she was also a very efficient, and highly valued, member of the team. Norman had a particularly large soft spot for her.

She stepped outside and pulled the door behind her.

'Mrs Pettit's still a bit upset,' she explained. 'She had a nasty shock, finding her friend like that.'

'Can we speak to her?' asked Slater. 'Is she up to it?'

'You can try. But it would probably be better if you could wait until the morning.'

'This is murder, Jane,' said Norman. 'We can't afford to sit back and do nothing. Even if we get just five minutes, it's better than nothing.'

Jolly nodded her head slowly.

'Yes, of course,' she said. 'Come on in.'

They followed her into the house and through to a huge country-style kitchen, large enough to accommodate a large pine table that dominated one end of the room. The forlorn figure of Laura Pettit sat on a chair at the table, head bowed. She didn't even look up when they came in.

Jolly had obviously been sitting with Laura, her empty chair now pushed back from the table.

'I'll make a fresh cup of tea,' she said, crossing to the table and collecting the two cups from the table.

'Laura,' she said, gently. 'This is DS Slater and DS Norman. I know you've had a nasty shock, but do you think you might be able to answer some questions?'

She looked up at the mention of her name, her face tear-stained and snotty from crying.

'Yes.' She nodded. 'I'll try.'

Jolly carried the cups over to the other side of the kitchen and made herself busy while Slater and Norman made their way over to the table and sat down. Slater was painfully aware how difficult this must be for their witness.

'I'm really sorry for the loss of your friend, Laura,' began Slater, quietly. 'I'm not going to insult you by pretending I know how you feel. It must be very difficult for you, but we need your help. Do you think you can tell us what happened?'

'She was such a lovely person,' said Laura. 'Beautiful and bubbly, she really had it all, you know? How could anyone do something like that to her?'

'I'm afraid there's no real answer to that,' said Norman. 'I guess you could say some people are just plain evil.'

'We like to go out together, when we get the chance. My husband's taken our two girls to a concert tonight, so we thought we'd have a girl's night out. Eat out early and go on to the cinema. It was my turn to drive. I was ready to go at six as we had arranged, but by ten past there was no sign of Diana so I went to see where she was. I knew she was in because her car was there, but when I rang the doorbell there was no answer. I could hear the radio was on so I went round the back, but the back door was locked, so I looked through the window and that's when I saw her.'

This prompted a burst of tears and Jolly was quick to step in and comfort her. Norman made space for her and went off to finish making the teas. It took a couple of minutes before Laura managed to compose herself again.

'So this would have been about ten past six?' asked Norman, as he placed the tray of teas on the table.

'Certainly no later than six-fifteen. And then I ran back here and called the police.'

'You didn't see or hear anything?' asked Slater. 'Say from about five onwards?'

'I'm sorry. I was wallowing in the bath with some music on. When you have two young teenage daughters you have to make the most of your chances to relax. I didn't get out of the bath until it was time to get ready to go out.'

'Can you think of anyone who might want to do this to Diana?' asked Norman.

'Everyone thought she was wonderful,' said Laura. 'Well, everyone except that husband of hers.'

'Husband? We need to notify him.'

'His name's Ian Woods. People call him Woody. He doesn't live here anymore. He left her a few months ago. It turns out he was quite a nasty piece of work in private. Diana told me how he used to beat her up and pick on her all the time. You wouldn't have known it though. He liked to pretend he adored her and he would do anything for her. I suppose it just goes to show we don't always see the real person if that person doesn't want us to.'

'Why did they split up?' asked Norman.

'Because he was an idiot,' she said. 'She was the perfect wife, not only good looking and good fun, but she was a fabulous cook, too.'

'Did she ever report his violence to the police?' asked Slater.

'She was much too proud to do that,' said Laura, her lip trembling. 'She just put up with it without complaining, which so many women do, don't they? Anyway, I should think he's the one who stabbed her.'

She dissolved into tears once again.

Slater and Norman shared a look. Slater could see they weren't going to get much more from Laura tonight. They could always come back tomorrow.

'Thank you for talking to us,' said Slater. 'You've been very helpful. But we will need to talk to you again tomorrow.'

'We'll let ourselves out, Jane,' said Norman. 'You stay here with Laura.'

Once they were outside, Slater turned to Norman.

'We need to find this husband.'

'Yeah. He sounds a bit of a charmer, doesn't he?' Norman gave a grim smile. 'Maybe we can find an address in the house somewhere. What about the rest of the neighbours?'

'It's getting on for ten o'clock. Let's check the one on the other side of Diana's house, and then we'll go back to her house and see if we can find an address for this guy.'

The neighbour they wanted to speak to wasn't at home, so they decided to try the next nearest house which was on the other side of the lane, but further down towards the common. The lady's name was Amanda Hollis, and she backed up Laura's view that Diana Woods had been the perfect wife and an all-round good egg. Just like Laura, Amanda claimed to have always had her doubts about Woody because he kept himself to himself.

'You can't trust a man who's too quiet,' she had told them, wagging a finger for emphasis.

'Do I see some sort of pattern emerging here?' Norman asked Slater, as they walked back to Diana Woods' house.

'It seems our Woody's not the most popular guy, is he?'

'But if he's such a nasty bastard why would she let him in the house and then turn her back on him?'

'If he only left a few months ago, he'd have his own key,' replied Slater. 'And Laura said the radio was on.'

'I dunno.' Norman sounded skeptical. 'If this guy had been abusing her for years, surely someone would have seen something, like a bruise, maybe.'

'Yeah, but you know how women put up with that sort of thing.'

'But they're not usually confident, outgoing, bubbly personalities, are they?'

'Not usually, no,' admitted Slater. 'Anyhow, let's not start jumping to conclusions. We don't even know where he lives yet.'

'Right.' Norman clapped his hands together. 'Let's see if we can find an address, or a phone number, so we can talk to the guy before we condemn him.'

'I can't believe a woman like this wouldn't have a mobile phone.' Norman peered down the back of the bed.

'There must be one somewhere,' said Slater. 'Maybe the killer took it.'

'But there doesn't seem to be anything else missing. So if her phone was taken it must have been for a very specific reason.'

'Perhaps there's a message on it that incriminates our killer.'

'That would be a good enough reason,' Norman said. 'But the fact nothing else seems to be missing makes me think this wasn't some robbery that went wrong. It was definitely personal. Whoever it was came here to commit murder, plain and simple.'

'But why would someone want to murder this woman who, according to her neighbours, is some sort of angel?'

'When we figure that out, we'll be halfway to solving this case.'

Slater turned back to his task and slid a drawer open.

'Aha!' He smiled and lifted a diary out. 'Maybe this will tell us something.'

He thumbed through the pages, but to his great disappointment, most of them were blank.

'Oh Diana,' he said, sighing heavily. 'What's the point of having a diary if you're not going to write all your secrets down for me to find?'

'Nothing in there?' asked Norman.

'Just an occasional hair appointment. It doesn't look like there's anything significant in here.' Slater continued to thumb through the pages. 'But at least we have some phone numbers.'

'Anything for Woody?'

'Yeah. There is. A mobile number.'

'Let's try it,' said Norman. 'They're still married, at least on paper, and his wife's dead. Someone should tell him.'

'There's one here for her parents, too,' said Slater.

'They've already been told. Better not call them again at this time of night. But let's try this Woody guy. I'll speak to him.'

Slater carried on with his search while Norman dialled Woody's number. He listened for a couple of minutes and then hung up.

'It's gone straight to voicemail. Do you think I should leave a message?'

'Try again,' said Slater. 'If he still doesn't answer, leave a message.'

Norman dialled the number again.

'This is DS Norman from Tinton police. I need you to contact me as soon as you can. You can reach me on...'

Slater had found something interesting and he tuned Norman out as he read what was written on the sheet of paper in front of him. The writer had obviously had second thoughts and scored through the words, but they were still legible.

'Dear Woody,' it read. 'I can't tell you how much I miss you. Please, please, come and see me so we can talk about this situation and sort things out. I don't want it to end like this.'

'Here.' Slater held out the piece of paper to Norman when he'd finished his call. 'What do you make of this?'

Norman took it and read the words.

'You'd think she'd be glad to see the back of him if the guy was such a shit,' he said. 'But this seems to say the exact opposite.'

'She never sent it, though. And it's dated over two months ago.'

'Maybe this was a draft copy. Or perhaps she changed her mind.

Only Woody can tell us if she ever sent him anything like this. If he doesn't call back by about eight tomorrow morning, I think we need to find his address and pay him a call.'

'It's nearly midnight,' said Slater. 'Let's call it a day for now, shall we?'

'That's the best idea you've had all day,' said Norman. 'Let's do it.'

'You'll be pleased to know I am the proud owner of a new mobile phone,' announced Norman, five minutes later, as he struggled to lower his rather large backside onto the passenger seat without dropping into it.

'Mind my springs,' said Slater. 'That seat has developed a serious sag since you became my partner.'

'Don't nag. We have this discussion every time we use your car, and I maintain it's the seat that's at fault. My driving seat doesn't sag one little bit, and neither do any of the other cars we use.'

He finally succeeded in lowering himself into the seat, and sat back with a sigh.

'Have you fixed this seat belt yet?' he asked.

'It's not a short belt. It's your waistline that's the problem,' said Slater, patiently.

He put the car into gear and began to pull away.

'Anyway, what's with the new phone?' he asked. 'I thought you liked living in the past.'

'Yeah, I know,' said Norman. 'But sometimes even I have to move with the times. I can even get emails with this new phone.'

'My, my,' Slater said, smiling. 'How cool are you?'

'I got a new number, too.'

'Oh, you didn't? You do realise how much hassle that's going to cause, don't you?'

'Actually, yes I do,' said Norman. 'But I have to stop all these damned spam calls I'm getting, somehow.'

'You're a police officer,' said Slater. 'Why don't you just tell them you're going to arrest them or something?'

'Yeah, yeah, yeah. I already tried that. It just didn't work. Now they just won't be able to find me.'

'You hope,' said Slater.

CHAPTER TWO

As usual, it was a very small team that gathered in the small incident room next morning. To be exact, there were just the three of them: Slater, Norman, and PC Jane Jolly.

'Is this it?' a dismayed Slater asked Norman.

'Apparently we might get some more help if the bodies can be spared,' said Norman. 'But don't hold your breath.'

'This is supposed to be a major incident,' said Slater, in exasperation. 'It's a bloody joke.'

'It is what it is. There's no point in complaining about it.'

'If they cut our budget any further, we might as well pack it in and go home. But that's my negative head speaking, and a negative head never solves anything, right Norm?'

'Exactly.' Norman smiled at him. 'So let's do what we can and try to be as effective as we can.'

'Yeah, I know,' Slater said, with a sigh. 'Right, then,' he began after a moment, trying to sound a whole lot more positive than he felt. 'Has Ian Woods called back yet?'

'Not so far,' said Norman.

'First job for you then, Jane. Find out where the guy lives. You've got his mobile number. Find the service provider and tell them we need his address, or else. You know what to do.'

'No problem,' said Jolly, smiling. 'I'll have it within the hour.'

'You can have longer,' said Norman. 'We have a PM to attend at eight.'

'And can you get hold of her phone records?' asked Slater. 'We might not have found her mobile phone, but there's still the landline. We can start with that.'

'I'll get onto it as soon as I've found that address,' she said.

I t's a special (or perhaps strange) sort of person who enjoys watching a post mortem. It could be argued that both Slater and Norman were special in their individual ways, but neither possessed the particular quality that would allow them to watch a pathologist at work without feeling somewhat queasy.

Dr Eamon Murphy was aware that both his guests would be much happier if they could be just about anywhere else that morning. This was his first official forensic post mortem, though, and he was determined to take his time and get it right. He had been working unofficially for Tinton police for some time, but in the past his work had always had to be overseen. Now, at last, he had been officially recognised and was deemed to be up to the required standard.

'I realise neither of you would choose to be here,' he said to his audience. 'So I'll try to be quick, but as it's my first, I also want to make sure I get it right.'

'In that case, as it's your first, I'll try not to spoil things for you by throwing up,' said Norman.

Murphy knew neither of them was likely to do such a thing, but he had prepared for it just in case.

'I've laid out two bowls over there.' Murphy pointed across the room, grinning. 'But if you choose to use one, you have to empty it and clean up behind you.'

'I think we'll be okay, Eamon. This certainly isn't the messiest corpse we've seen,' said Slater.

'It's the slicing and dicing that always gets to me,' confessed Norman. 'I don't know how you can do that.'

'It's the fascination of what a body can tell me,' said Murphy. 'That's what drives me. Without the dissection it would be a bit difficult. I'm sure there are parts of your job that make people feel the same way, but you do them because it's part of the process.'

Silence greeted this remark.

'Right, then,' said Murphy, once he was sure Norman had finished complaining. 'Shall we begin?'

He removed the sheet covering Diana Woods and began his examination, dictating into a head microphone as he worked. An assistant hovered in the background ready to help whenever he was needed. After the initial examination, Murphy undid Diana Woods' negligee. The assistant stepped forward to help him.

'That's odd,' he said. 'She's still got the shop labels attached to her underwear.'

He indicated a label hanging from the bra strap.

'Who keeps the labels on their underwear?' asked Norman.

'Someone who's just bought it and is trying it on for size?' suggested Slater.

'But she would know her own size before she went shopping,' argued Norman. 'And if she was in doubt, wouldn't she try the bra on in the shop?'

'Suppose they were a gift?' said Slater. 'Maybe someone gave them to her and guessed her size.'

'It's an expensive gift,' said Murphy. 'A matching set in real silk, according to this label.'

'So, she likes nice underwear,' said Norman. 'There's no law against it.'

'It could be significant though,' said Slater. 'No one has mentioned a boyfriend so far, and Woody doesn't sound like the sort of guy to buy something like this.'

'Maybe he was trying to win her back.'

Murphy and his assistant got back to work. Murphy suppressed a smile as he saw Norman pale as he got down to the real work. Norman took his phone out, muttering something about checking his emails, and stared at the screen resolutely for the next hour.

'Tea, gentlemen?' Murphy suggested after he had finished. 'We might even have some biscuits if you're really lucky.'

'I'll do a full report for you obviously,' he told them a few minutes later. 'But the gist is she was stabbed, in the back, by a flat bladed knife. Possibly the carving knife from the set in the kitchen. I would suggest the killer was probably, but not necessarily, shorter than the victim. The angle of entry would suggest the knife was pointing upwards as it entered the body, passed through the ribs, and plunged into the heart. Death would have been more or less instantaneous.'

'What about time of death?' asked Slater. 'Is it still the same?'

'I would narrow it down to between five and six pm,' said Murphy. 'The victim had recently had sex, but a condom was used so there were no samples to collect.'

'Definitely not rape?' asked Norman.

'There's nothing to suggest it wasn't consensual.'

'Are the two events related?' asked Slater.

'I can't say for sure at this stage. But I think it's probable she had sex a few hours before she was killed, so it's unlikely they are related.'

'Would it have been the night before?' asked Slater.

'Not that long before,' said Murphy. 'I would guess not more than four to six hours before she was killed.'

'Maybe it was someone at work,' said Norman. 'In the broom cupboard, perhaps.'

Murphy and Slater both looked at Norman.

'What?' he asked defensively. 'Workplace affairs aren't that unusual.'

'Yeah, but in a broom cupboard?' asked Slater.

'Okay, so it was bad taste,' admitted Norman. 'But even so, we can't ignore the possibility of a workplace affair that might have gone wrong.'

'We can't afford to rule anything out,' conceded Slater. 'And we do need to check out her workplace.'

'Obviously blood and toxicology will take a few days,' Murphy said. 'I'll let you know as soon as I know.'

He looked at Slater and Norman in turn.

'Well,' he said. 'How did I do?'

'It worked just fine for me,' said Norman.

'We already knew you could do the job, Eamon,' said Slater. 'You don't have anything to prove to us.'

Murphy tilted his head in acknowledgement of the compliment.

'That's good to know,' he said. 'Thank you.'

'Anyway, we need to get on,' said Slater. 'Thanks Eamon. We'll speak soon.'

'Yeah, it's been a blast, Eamon,' said Norman. 'It's a really great way to start my day. I'm really sorry I can't stay for the encore.'

'I hope you don't mind,' said Jolly, when they got back from the PM. 'But I've taken it upon myself to have someone call on Mr Woods.'

'But we need to interview him–' began Norman.

'Yes, I know that, but he lives in Wales. It would take you the best part of four hours to get there. You'd be tied up for a whole day, and we don't even know if he's going to be there. Can we afford to lose two thirds of our team for a day?'

'Ah, right,' said Norman. 'When you put it like that, it's probably not the best use of our time.'

'I've contacted the station nearest where he lives. They're going to send someone round to tell him his wife has died, and to tell him we need to speak to him. I've also asked them to report back on his reaction to the news, and to let us know what he's going to do next.'

'Sometimes I think you should be in charge here, Jane,' said Slater. 'We'd probably be a whole lot more organised.'

'Flattery is good,' she said, smiling, 'but you can still go and get your own coffee and cakes.'

'Am I that obvious?' asked Slater.

'Patently.' Jolly laughed, shaking her head.

She shuffled through her notes.

'Diana Woods' parents are coming in later. They're going to formally identify the body. And don't forget you still need to speak to all the residents of Bishops Common about the murder.'

'We're going back to speak to them this morning,' said Slater. 'And we ought to get a statement from Diana's parents.'

'I can deal with them if you're not back,' said Jolly. 'If it helps.'

'If you're sure,' said Norman. 'It would certainly help if we didn't have to keep rushing backwards and forwards.'

They had started from the main road and called at every house along the lane leading to Bishops Common, working towards Diana Woods' house. Almost everyone had been at home, but so far, Slater was frustrated to admit it had been a fruitless journey. No one had seen or heard anything. There was even one homeowner who hadn't even realised there had been a major incident further down their lane yesterday.

'How could you possibly miss all those sirens and blue lights?' Norman asked Slater, as they walked away from the house. 'And all those vehicles?'

'It's a sign of the times. You've said as much yourself before now. People keep themselves to themselves and only look out for themselves.'

'Yeah, I guess that's so.' Norman sighed. 'I suppose they were glued to their TV set or something important like that.'

The next house they came to was that of Amanda Hollis. She had been the last person they spoke to last night.

'I suppose we'd better call in again,' said Slater. 'She might have thought of something new.'

But, in fact, all Amanda Hollis wanted to do was reinforce what she had told them the previous night. As far as she was concerned, they need look no further than Diana's husband Ian Woods. She had been over to see Laura Pettit just this morning, and they were quite convinced he was the only person in the whole world who could possibly have wanted Diana dead.

'You don't need to look any further,' she assured them. 'And I'll be happy to stand up in the witness box and say whatever you need me to say to convict him.'

Norman and Slater exchanged a look.

'Hearsay isn't proof of a crime, Mrs Hollis,' said Slater, more patiently than he felt. 'Perhaps you didn't realise but we actually prefer to use facts as evidence. That way we know we're convicting the right person.'

'Well, I can assure you you'll find we're right,' she said, adamantly.

'Have you ever done jury service, Mrs Hollis?' asked Norman.

'That's a strange question. No, I haven't. Why do you ask?'

'I just wondered,' said Norman innocently. 'I was just thinking of all the time and money we could save if everyone adopted your approach to justice.'

'I'm sorry, I don't follow you.'

'You don't? Well, if I had all day free and nothing better to do, maybe I'd try and explain it to you, but we're actually trying to solve a murder here so I'm afraid I don't have the time right now.'

'Thank you for your time, Mrs Hollis,' said Slater, stepping in front of Norman. 'But we really must get on now.'

'But what does he mean?' she asked. 'Is he trying to imply something?'

'Good heavens, no,' replied Slater. 'He has a thing about the justice system and how it could be improved. Your trial by rumour suggestion would certainly speed things up. We could do away with the whole criminal justice system at a stroke. Anyway, we must go.'

He turned and ushered Norman from the premises before he really lost it with this stupid woman. He felt Amanda Hollis' eyes boring into his back as they walked back down the path.

'Jeez,' said Norman, when they were out of earshot. 'Listening to that woman slagging off Ian Woods brings a whole new meaning to the expression "witch hunt". Is she for real?'

'She doesn't exactly offer an impartial opinion, does she?'

'That can't possibly be her car in the drive,' said Norman. 'Surely she must be a broomstick user.'

He looked at the next house along the lane. It was that of Diana's next door neighbour Laura Pettit, who'd had the misfortune to discover the body yesterday.

'Oh great. If those two were sharing the same cauldron this morning, I suppose we're going to get a load more of that "it must be Woody" shit here.'

'You're probably right,' said Slater. 'But there's only one way to find out.'

H alf an hour later they were walking from Laura Pettit's house. 'What did I tell you?' Norman shook his head. 'They're almost word perfect too, as if it's all rehearsed. You have to wonder what's going on here. I'm almost beginning to feel sorry for this Woody guy.'

'They've obviously put their heads together and agreed what they're going to say,' said Slater. 'But even so, we can't discount it. If what they're saying about him is even half right, then he's got to be in the frame.'

'The only good thing to come out of this was getting Diana's mobile number. That was good thinking on your part.'

'I figured her friend had to have it. It was just a question of waiting for her to stop talking long enough for me to ask the question.'

They walked on past the scene of the crime and stopped at the one remaining house in the lane. There had been no one home the previous night when they had called, and there was no one in this morning.

'Maybe they're away,' suggested Norman as they headed back down the lane towards their car.

As they walked, another car came around the bend in the lane heading towards them. The car slowed down and pulled up alongside them; its driver's window slid smoothly down and a man's face appeared.

'Are you the police?'

'DS Slater and DS Norman.' Slater flashed his warrant card. 'Can we help you?'

'I might be able to help you.'

The man stepped from his car, closed the door, and then leaned back against it.

'My name's John Hollis.'

'Amanda's husband?' asked Norman.

'That's right,' he said. 'I'm on late shift this week so I wasn't here last night, but I believe you spoke to my wife, didn't you?'

'That's right, we did,' said Slater.

'So you know Woody did it,' said John Hollis with a rueful grin. 'I'm sorry about that. I had it drummed into me all night long, if it's any consolation. I'm afraid my wife and Laura Pettit seem to have got it in for poor old Woody.'

'Why?' asked Norman. 'What's he ever done to them?'

'I think it's more a case of what he didn't do. Woody's quiet and he's shy, and he'd rather stand in the corner than be the centre of attention. That can make him hard to get to know, but when you do get to know him he's a good guy, and he's the sort who would do almost anything to help a friend. The problem is Laura wanted him to help her out in ways that he wasn't prepared to, if you see what I mean.'

'And you know this how?' asked Slater.

'I know this because he told me.'

'If he's so quiet and shy, why would he tell you about something like that?'

'I'm probably one of the best friends he's got,' said Hollis. 'He was actually quite upset about the whole incident, and he wanted to tell someone about it, so he told me over a few beers one night. He didn't want to tell his wife, so who else was he going to tell?

'The thing is, he only ever had eyes for Diana. There was no way he was interested in any other woman, so Laura got the cold shoulder. Ever since she's been waging this campaign to convince everyone Woody's some sort of shit and the world's worst husband. If he was an astronaut, up there in space, orbiting the moon now, she would still tell you he had done it.'

'So why would your wife have it in for him?' asked Slater.

'If you mean did she try it on with Woody, too,' said Hollis, 'the answer's no. She became an anti Woody campaigner when he left Diana, and Diana started spreading all sorts of crap about what sort of husband he had been.'

'Are you saying Laura Pettit and your wife are lying about Mr Woods?' asked Norman.

'I'm saying I think you're being subjected to a considerable degree of exaggeration. I'm sure Woody's no saint. But then, let's face it, none of us are. And, as they say, who really knows what goes on behind closed doors? But he was married to Diana for twenty years, and I know she wasn't the sort of woman to put up with the abuse he was supposed to have been dishing out. There was never so much as a hint about it during all the time I've known them, and even my wife will concede that much, and yet, the moment he left her, she started telling people what a bastard he was. Personally I think it's all bollocks.'

'But why do you think she would do that?' asked Slater.

'To divert attention away from her own behaviour and make herself out to be the squeaky clean victim in their failed marriage, that's why,' said Hollis.

'What do you mean, "divert attention away from her own behaviour"?'

'Have you spoken to Woody yet?'

'No,' said Slater. 'We're hoping to speak to him later today.'

'Well, it's not my place to speak ill of the dead,' said Hollis. 'But when you speak to him, ask him why he left his supposedly perfect wife.'

He checked his watch.

'Sorry,' he said, as he opened his car door and climbed back inside. 'But I've got to go. Work calls and I need to get changed before I go.'

'We may need to speak to you again,' said Slater.

'Anytime I'm not late for work.' Hollis smiled at them through the open window as he pulled away. 'Just let me know.'

'So what do we think so far?' asked Norman as they continued walking back to their car.

'I think we need to speak to Ian Woods, is what I think,' said Slater.

'Yeah,' agreed Norman. 'It looks like one of those marriage break-ups where the friends have taken sides, so there's not much chance of learning anything we can rely on.'

'It's amazing so many people could be at home and yet no-one saw anything,' said Slater.

'But this is a rural area, right? It's not like a busy street where someone might be sitting staring out of the window watching all the people go by. I mean, that would be a seriously boring pastime out here, wouldn't it?'

'I know you're right,' said Slater, 'but it would make our job so much easier if someone had seen something!'

'No doubt about that. But that would be too easy, wouldn't it? Next thing we know you'll be expecting me to buy lunch.'

They had reached their car now, and Slater plipped the locks and they climbed in. He put the key in the ignition and was just about to start the car when he realised what Norman had just said.

'It can't possibly be my turn again,' he said, turning to look at Norman in dismay.

'I left my wallet at home.' Norman grinned sheepishly. 'What can I say? I'm sorry, alright?'

'That's every day for over a week,' said an exasperated Slater, as he started the car. 'Next time we have a night out, I'm going to leave my wallet at home and you're going to have to buy me the most expensive meal I can find. And I'll be drinking champagne.'

As Slater put the car in gear and started to drive, Norman's phone began to ring. It was standard procedure for Slater to point out how bad Norman's ringtone was, but as he glanced in his direction he could see this might not be the right time to do so. Norman was looking at his new phone, shock and dismay all over his face.

'You okay, Norm?' he asked.

Norman dismissed the call and put the phone back in his jacket pocket. He gazed distractedly out of the window.

'Norm,' insisted Slater. 'Are you okay?'

'Yeah. I'm fine,' replied Norman, unconvincingly.

CHAPTER THREE

'Any luck?' asked Jolly, when they eventually got back.
'Nothing we didn't already know,' said Norman. 'What's been going on here?'

'Diana Woods' parents have identified the body.'

'Did they have anything to say?' asked Slater.

'They're waiting to talk to you,' Jolly replied, unhappily. 'I'm sorry. I did try, but they didn't seem to think they should be wasting their breath on a lowly PC. They insist on talking to "the person in charge".'

'That'll be him, then,' said Slater and Norman in unison, each pointing at the other.

'I told them it would be both of you.' Jolly smiled sweetly.

'Where are they?' asked Slater.

'I wasn't sure how long you were going to be, and this isn't exactly The Ritz, so I suggested they go and wait at their hotel.'

'That's okay,' said Norman. 'We can go and talk to them there. Any news on the husband?'

'Yes. They found him at home this morning and told him. Apparently he's on his way here now.'

'He's not on the run, then,' observed Slater.

'According to our colleagues in Wales, he appeared to be shocked by the news.' Jolly thumbed through her notes. 'That was at just after ten this morning. He was going to pack a bag and make his way here almost straight away. It's just after two now, so I guess he could be here by three.'

'Is he coming straight here?' asked Slater, looking at his watch.

'That's what they told him to do. If you want to go and speak to Diana's parents, I can look after him until you get back.'

'That sounds good to me, Jane,' said Norman. 'C'mon Dave, let's go meet the parents.'

The Coach and Horses was more of a big, old pub with a few bedrooms than a hotel, but it was comfortable, had a warm, welcoming atmosphere, and served good food. Norman thought it was infinitely preferable to many of the modern soulless places that were now so widely available.

They found Diana Woods' parents, Mr and Mrs Hanning, in the bar area. They appeared to be in their sixties and were sat together, holding hands and staring at the floor. They seemed to share a sort of caved-in appearance, as if their world had just collapsed around them.

The two detectives had agreed Norman was taking the lead on this one.

'I'm DS Norman and this is my colleague, DS Slater,' he said. 'First of all, let me say how very sorry we are for your loss.'

It was Mrs Hanning who acknowledged them. Her husband didn't even look up when Norman spoke.

'Thank you,' she said. 'It was such a shock to find two police officers on our doorstep, and then to be told our daughter's dead. It doesn't seem possible.'

She squeezed her husband's hand.

'Poor Arthur's taken it very badly,' she continued. 'She was the apple of his eye, you see.'

'She was so beautiful,' said Mr Hanning, still staring at the floor, his voice barely a whisper. 'Perfect she was. Absolutely perfect.'

His shoulders shook as he began to quietly weep, and Norman wished he could be anywhere rather than here, watching this man's heart breaking. He snatched a look at Slater, who seemed equally uncomfortable.

'We really don't want to intrude at a time like this,' said Norman, quietly. 'But we need to ask you a few questions. We can come back later if you'd prefer.'

For a moment, it looked as though Mrs Hanning was going to take them up on Norman's offer, but Mr Hanning was too quick for her. He seemed to summon some inner strength from somewhere and, clearing his throat, he sat up straight and looked at them for the first time.

'Let's get it over with,' he said. 'The sooner we tell you what you need to know, the sooner you can arrest that man.'

'Err, which man?' asked Norman.

'Why that useless bugger of a husband of course,' said Hanning. The sadness was gone for now, and his eyes sparkled.

'You mean Ian Woods?' asked Slater.

'Who else would I mean? He's the only useless sod she was married to. I always knew he was trouble. I told her right from the start she could have done much better for herself, but would she listen? She'd still be alive now if only she'd listened to her old dad.'

'She was an adult, dear,' said his wife. 'She was old enough to make her own choices.'

'But she wasn't old enough to make the right choice, was she?'

'So why do you think Ian's responsible?' asked Norman. He realised this was obviously something the Hannings had been arguing about, on and off, ever since Diana had married Ian Woods all those years ago, and he didn't want it to flare up again right now.

'Have you ever heard of King Midas?' Hanning didn't wait for an answer. 'Everything he touched turned to gold. Ian Woods was King Midas in reverse. Everything he touched turned to dust. He's bloody useless.'

'They seem to have a nice enough house,' said Slater.

'That was all down to her, not him,' spat Hanning. 'She was a shining light and he spent twenty years doing his best to put that light out. Now it looks like he's finally done it.'

'I understand you don't like the man,' said Norman. 'But do you actually have any evidence to back up your assertion that he's a murderer?'

'I'm just telling you, aren't I? The man spent years abusing her and now, after she finally kicked him out, he's come back and murdered her.'

'Did you ever see any signs of abuse?' asked Slater.

'What's the matter with you people? Don't you believe me?'

'I'm afraid we need evidence, Mr Hanning, not just your opinion,' replied Slater.

'No,' said Mrs Hanning. 'We have never actually seen anything to prove he was abusing her, but after she kicked him out she told us how badly he had been treating her.'

'Thank you, Mrs Hanning,' said Norman. 'You say Diana kicked Ian out. Are you sure that's how it was? Only we've been told Ian left Diana.'

'Rubbish!' snapped Mr Hanning. 'She was the perfect wife. No man in his right mind would have walked out on her. I'm telling you, everybody loved her. You need look no further than her husband. He did this to her!'

And so it went on until Norman decided they were wasting their time. He felt genuinely sorry for their loss, but Mr Hanning was so focused on blaming Ian Woods it was ridiculous. If he got his way, they would simply string the man up the moment he appeared.

He made all the right noises to keep the Hannings happy for the time being, made his excuses, and nodded to let Slater know it was time to go.

'If this was the Wild West that guy would have arranged a lynching by now,' said Slater as they left the hotel. 'And good ol' Woody would already be strung up.'

'From what we've been told so far, this Woody guy should be easy to identify,' said Norman. 'He'll have horns and be carrying a trident.'

'Either that or he'll have several knives sticking out of his back.'

'So you don't buy all this stuff about him being an arsehole, then?'

'It's not just that,' said Slater. 'I'm finding it just as hard to believe this idea that Diana Woods was so perfect. Maybe I'm being cynical, but in my experience no one's completely flawless.'

They walked over to their car and climbed inside.

'It was interesting to see Mrs Hanning wasn't quite as forthright as her husband when it came to condemning Woody,' Slater said.

'Yeah, I noticed that,' said Norman. 'But does it mean anything significant? I mean there's often a strong protective bond between a father and daughter, right?'

'That may be so, but I got the impression Mrs Hanning might not be quite so sure about her daughter's perfection as everyone else seems to be.'

'She said they're going to be here for a day or two. Maybe I should come back and see if I can get a chance to talk to her alone. She might let her guard down a bit further if "Avenging Arthur" isn't around.'

'He arrived about twenty minutes ago,' said Jolly. 'I settled him in the interview room with a cup of tea and told him you wouldn't be too long.'

'You're becoming something of a slave driver, PC Jolly,' said Norman, with a wry smile. 'How am I supposed to maintain my energy levels if you don't ever let me stop to eat?'

'I figured you had enough reserves that it wouldn't be a problem.' Jolly pointed at his waistline. 'Of course, if you can't stand the pace, I could always ask for some help on your behalf.'

'Ooh! How could you,' said Norman in mock horror. 'You know how to strike me right through the heart with those cutting remarks.'

'How is he?' asked Slater, ignoring Norman's theatrics. 'How does he seem?'

'He seems genuinely upset,' said Jolly. 'And, in my opinion, for what it's worth, he seems like a nice man.

'But you've only just met him,' said Slater.

'Okay,' she said. 'I'll qualify my statement by saying my first impression is that he's a nice man. Is that better?'

'I didn't mean to question you, Jane,' said Slater hastily. 'Of course we value your opinion. But the fact is you have only just met him.'

'Yes,' she said testily. 'And my first impression makes me feel he's a nice man.'

'Okay,' said Slater, warily. 'Point taken. You think he's a nice guy. I've got it.'

Norman was grinning like the proverbial Cheshire Cat at Slater's discomfort.

'You'll split your face in two if you're not careful,' Slater warned him quietly.

'It could even be worth it, seeing you squirm like that,' said Norman, laughing.

They stopped in the observation room and peered through the window at Ian Woods. He certainly didn't look like a thug, Norman thought. In fact, he looked quite unremarkable in every way, except perhaps in his face. His hair was receding and thinning, and he looked haggard, like a man who hadn't slept properly in weeks. This made him look much older than the forty-six-year-old he was supposed to be. He didn't look a well man, and he appeared somewhat under-nourished too, like maybe he wasn't eating well. Certainly there wasn't an ounce of fat on him.

'What do you think?' asked Norman. 'Does he look upset because his wife's dead? Or because he thinks we're on to him?'

'He didn't have to come here,' Slater pointed out. 'He could have done a runner and been well away by now. And anyway we don't even know where he was at the time. He might have a cast iron alibi.'

'Okay. This is how we'll play it then. You be the good cop, and I'll be the bad cop.'

'Or we could just wing it, like we usually do.'

'I'm sure we'll end up that way,' said Norman. 'But how about we start like we know what we're doing, and then see how it goes from there.'

'Okay, let's do it.' Slater opened the door and stepped aside to let Norman lead the way. 'Lead on, Macduff,' he said, as Norman squeezed past him.

'Yeah. Once more into the breach and all that jazz,' muttered Norman.

He led the way up to the door of the interview room, stopped briefly outside, then swung the door open.

'Good afternoon, Mr Woods,' he said, as he entered the room. 'My name's DS Norman, and this is my partner, DS Slater. We're leading the investigation into your wife's death.'

Woods had jumped to his feet, and was half holding out his hand, awkwardly.

'Please, sit down,' said Norman. He smiled to try and put Ian Woods at his ease, but it was obvious the guy was like a fish out of water.

'I'm sorry,' said Woods. 'I'm not sure if I'm coming or going right now. This is a situation no one ever prepares you for, you know. When the police arrive at your door you think maybe you've been caught speeding or something silly like that. Then they said my wife was dead and, well, it was like getting a kick in the guts. I've just driven two hundred miles to get here, but I don't remember a single thing about the journey.'

He looked uncertainly at Norman and then at Slater. They could see he was all over the place. Norman thought if he was acting, he was pretty good.

'I suppose I shouldn't tell you that, should I?' Woods looked worried. 'About driving like that, I mean.'

'Look, Ian,' said Slater. 'Is it alright if I call you Ian?'

'Sure. Ian or Woody, that's what my friends tend to call me.'

'Okay Woody,' said Slater. 'We're not here to talk about your driving. I understand it must have been one hell of a shock when you found out, and we're sorry for your loss, but we need to ask you some questions about what's happened.'

'Can I see her? Don't I have to identify her, or something?'

'Her parents have already done that,' said Norman.

Woods looked a bit miffed.

'We found your number last night and tried ringing you, but there was no answer,' Norman explained. 'That's why I left a message on your voicemail asking you to call us.'

'Ah, yeah,' said Woods. 'I turned my phone off while I was driving, and there's no signal at home. In fact, the signal's pretty pathetic all around where I live. It's a pain in the backside, I can tell you.'

'Anyway, we couldn't get hold of you, so we called her parents,' said Norman.

'So you were driving yesterday,' said Slater. 'Where did you go? Anywhere nice?'

'I've got a small van. I used to work as a courier for a company based in Tinton, until I split from Diana and moved to Wales. But my old boss called me. He had a pickup in Swansea. Some documents to be taken to Southampton. I'm not far from Swansea so he asked me if I'd like to help him out. It would have taken one of his guys four hours to drive across, you see, whereas I'm less than an hour down the road. I fancied a run out, so I said yes.'

'How come he got hold of you?' asked Norman. 'I thought you said there was no signal.'

'He sent me a text. I got it when I went out to the shops and then I called him back.'

'What's this guy's name?' asked Slater.

'Jim Brennan,' said Woods. 'I've got one of his cards here somewhere.'

He fumbled his wallet from his pocket and found a card which he handed to Slater.

'Okay, so you were doing this job,' continued Norman, 'and you got to Southampton at what time?'

'I can't remember exactly, somewhere between two and two-thirty I think.'

'What did you do after that?'

'I stopped for a cup of coffee, filled up with diesel and made my way slowly back home. I knew I was going to get caught up in the motorway traffic approaching Bristol so I stopped for a meal before I got that far.'

'What time did you reach the Severn Bridge?' asked Norman.

'It wasn't until about nine pm, I think,' replied Woods.

'You must have got home pretty late,' said Slater.

'It was about eleven. There wasn't any need to rush.'

'So, let me get this straight,' said Norman. 'It took you over six hours to get to the bridge, and the another two hours after that. So that's eight hours in all, and yet you've just driven here in four hours.'

'Like I said, I wasn't in any rush yesterday,' said Woods, looking confused.

'Southampton's not far from here, is it? What is it? Less than an hour?'

'I used to reckon an hour and a half to allow for traffic,' said Woods, innocently. Then a look of panic flashed across his face.

'Now wait a minute,' he said. 'What are you saying?'

'I'm just saying you would have had plenty of time to call in to see your wife on the way back, that's all.' Norman smiled at him.

'What? You think I murdered my own wife? Why would I want to do a thing like that?'

'Well, you weren't exactly getting on too well, were you? I heard she kicked you out.'

'What? No. That's rubbish,' said Woods. 'She didn't kick me out. I left her. I couldn't take any more, right? Sure I felt I had to get away, but I would never hurt her. I mean, why would I?'

'The fact you left her suggests to me there were some problems between you. Maybe you needed to fix the problem for good.'

'I did that by moving out,' protested Woods. 'I didn't need to kill her.'

He looked desperately at Slater and Norman. No one said anything for almost a minute until Norman broke the silence.

'Okay, Woody, let me be honest with you,' he said. 'I'm having a problem understanding how it could have taken you so long to get back to Wales yesterday. You see, the thing is, Diana was killed at around five-thirty yesterday afternoon. Now it seems to me you would have had plenty of time to make a little diversion to Tinton on the way home. And that would explain why it took you so long to complete the journey home.'

He stopped for a moment or two to watch the remaining colour drain from Woody's face before he continued.

'What you're telling us about your journey home seems to be conveniently vague, and your version of events that led to you being in Wales seems to be at odds with what we've heard. So now we have to consider why there should be these discrepancies. You're not a stupid man, are you, Woody? I'm sure you can see how we wouldn't be doing our jobs if we didn't look a bit deeper into this. You understand, don't you?'

Woods gulped loudly.

'Help us out here, Woody,' said Slater. 'If you stopped at motorway services we may be able to find you on CCTV and prove it. Where did you stop for coffee and fuel in Southampton?'

'It was just a roadside petrol station. I don't know what it's called but I can show you on a map.'

'Okay. How about the meal? Where did you stop for that?'

'Leigh Delamere services,' said Woody. 'I got there around five-thirty and left at about eight-thirty.'

'Three hours?' Norman whistled. 'You spent three hours in the motorway services? What did you do that took three hours?'

'I took my book. They have some comfy seating in there. I got settled. Like I said, I don't have anything to rush home for.'

Norman was sceptical about Woody reading a book for three hours in the motorway services, but he decided they didn't need to pursue the matter any further right now. They could come back to that later.

'We'll be checking CCTV at all these places,' warned Norman. 'We'll find out if you're lying.'

'I'm not lying. I'm telling you I didn't murder my wife. I loved her!' Woody shouted the last three words and then there was a hushed silence.

'So, if you loved her so much, how come you live two hundred miles away?' asked Norman, breaking the silence.

Woods stared at the table in front of him.

'Come on, Woody,' said Slater, gently. 'If you want us to believe you, you need to help us to understand what was going on between you and Diana. How about you start by telling us why you and Diana split up.'

'If you've met Diana's parents I expect you've already heard chapter and verse about how it's all my fault,' said Woody. 'And if you think she threw me out, you must have believed them.'

A look of comprehension spread across his face.

'Of course,' he said, looking hard at Norman 'Now I get it. I bet he told you I killed her, didn't he? And you believe him. Whatever happened to "innocent until proven guilty"?'

Norman shifted uncomfortably under Woody's gaze. What Woody was saying wasn't exactly correct, but he could see why he would think it was.

'Aren't you supposed to examine all the evidence and work out who did it? So what's gone wrong? Is this some new form of short-cut justice? Because from where I'm sitting it looks like you guys have already made your minds up about who murdered my wife.'

Now Norman felt seriously uncomfortable and he sensed Slater shift awkwardly next to him. Woods had just accused them of doing the very same thing they had accused Laura Pettit and Amanda Hollis of doing.

'Now wait a minute, Woody,' Slater said. 'We're not accusing you of anything–'

'Yes you bloody well are,' interrupted Woody. 'All you've done since you came into the room is suggest I killed her. Perhaps you should remember I'm the husband who's just found out his wife's been murdered. Just because you don't understand why we were living apart, that doesn't automatically mean I killed her.'

There was a brief silence, and then Norman stepped in.

'With respect,' he said, 'you'd be surprised how often it's the husband who's guilty. I would also point out that this is your opportunity to tell us your side of the story, and so far you've been pretty vague about your movements yesterday. I can promise you we will be checking CCTV recordings to see if we can verify what you've told us so far. You need to think about that.'

'And here's something you need to think about, Detective Sergeant Norman. I did not kill my wife, and it doesn't matter if you keep me here for the next ten years, I am not going to confess, because I haven't done anything wrong. Now, unless I'm very much mistaken, I believe I'm entitled to refuse to answer any more questions. Am I right?'

'You're not under arrest Mr Woods–' began Slater.

'Which means I could just walk out, right now,' interrupted Woods. 'I know that, but I'm damned if I'm going to do that and give you lot further reason to suspect me. I'm prepared to stay here as long as it takes. But just so you understand, I'm not saying another word until I've made a phone call and spoken to a solicitor.'

'There's no need for that–'

'I disagree.'

Norman stared at Woods. This wasn't quite the outcome he'd been hoping for, but he couldn't deny the man his right to a solicitor if he insisted.

'Okay,' he said, reluctantly. 'While we get that arranged, let's take a break for a couple of hours. Are you sure you want to stay here?'

'Absolutely.'

'What did you make of that?' Norman asked Slater, after they'd left Woods with the duty sergeant to make his phone call.

'If you mean "how did we do," said Slater, 'I think we made a complete balls-up.'

'Well, yeah. I can't argue with that. I think that was mostly down to me. I messed up good and proper, but that's not really what I meant.'

'Well, he's very definite about what he says he didn't do.'

'He's also very vague about what he says he did do,' Norman pointed out. 'I mean, with the gaps in his story, he had plenty of time to call on Diana after he left Southampton.'

'There's no denying that. But there's a big difference between having the time to do it and actually doing it.'

'Are you telling me you believe him?' asked Norman.

'Let's put it this way,' replied Slater. 'I don't think he's actually lying, but I also don't think he's telling us everything.'

'So, what's he hiding?'

'That's what we need to find out.'

'Do you have a plan?' asked Norman.

'We've got some time to kill now, so why don't we use that time to go and see this Jim Brennan guy and see if he can confirm this stuff about a courier job. In the meantime, we could get Jolly Jane to take Woody his cup of tea and sit with him for a while. Maybe she'll be able to strike up a conversation and learn something that might help us.'

He looked at Norman.

'So that's my plan. What do you think?'

'I think I don't have anything better,' said Norman. 'So let's do it.'

Fifteen minutes later, Jane Jolly knocked on the door of the interview room and pushed the door open. She carried a tray with two cups of tea and a plate of biscuits which she placed on the table between her and Ian Woods.

'I've brought you some tea,' she said, smiling warmly at him. 'Mind if I join you? It's my tea break and there's no one around upstairs.'

CHAPTER FOUR

'We're looking for Jim Brennan,' said Slater. 'Who's we?' asked the man sat behind the desk in front of them.

'DS Slater.' Slater produced his warrant card.

'And DS Norman,' said Norman, showing his own card.

'In that case, you've found him. What can I do for you?'

'D'you know a guy called Ian Woods?' asked Slater.

'Woody? Yeah, I know him,' said Brennan. 'Why? What's he done?'

'No one's saying he's done anything. We just need to know if he was working for you yesterday.'

'That's right. He used to work for me full time, until he moved to Wales. He was one of my best drivers so when I got this job to pick up from Swansea I thought I'd ask him if he was free.'

'How did you get hold of him?' asked Norman. 'Only he says he's got no phone signal at home.'

'We have a system, you see,' said Brennan. 'We've done it a couple of times before. I send him a text, and then he calls me back when he gets it. It's no good for a job that needs doing right now, but this one was arranged a few days in advance.'

'So what job did he do for you?' asked Slater.

'Pick up in Swansea at ten in the morning and deliver to Southampton. It was nothing complicated, but using a guy based in Wales saved a lot of time, and I know I can rely on Woody.'

'What time did he get to Southampton?' asked Norman.

'Hang on a minute and I'll tell you exactly.' Brennan picked up a large diary from the desk in front of him and flipped through the pages.

'Here we go,' he said, running his finger down the page. 'He called in, job done, at two-twenty.'

'Just over four hours,' said Norman.

'Yeah, that's about what I would have expected. Like I said, I know I can rely on Woody.'

'What happened after that? Did you have another job for him?'

'I was hoping he might call in here and say hello,' said Brennan. 'But he never did. When we arranged the Swansea job, he told me he had a load of records and CDs to collect from Diana, that wife of his. Apparently he left them behind when he walked out. She was threatening to chuck them out if he didn't collect them. He said he was going to call in at her place on his way home from Swansea, but I've no idea whether he did or not.'

Slater and Norman exchanged a look.

'What?' Brennan said. 'What did I say?'

'You don't know, do you?' asked Slater, but he didn't wait for Brennan to reply. 'Diana Woods was murdered at around five-thirty yesterday afternoon.'

Brennan's expression told them no, he hadn't known about Diana's death.

'Oh my God! Really?' he said. 'But, what's that got to do with Woody? Surely you can't think he would have had anything to do with that. He might have left her, but he still cared for her. There's no way he would ever hurt her. No, I'm sorry, if you think it was him you've got it all wrong, that's for sure.'

'But you just told us he said he was going round there,' said Norman. 'What if he went round there, they argued, and he lost his temper?'

'What Woody? Nah. No way. With the way she behaves, if he was going to kill her he'd have done it a long time ago, but he's never so much as raised a finger to her.'

'I'm not with you,' said Slater. 'What do you mean "if he was going to kill her, he would have done it a long time ago"?'

'And what does "with the way she behaves" mean?' asked Norman.

'You mean Woody hasn't told you what she's like?' Brennan looked from Norman to Slater, and then back at Norman again. 'No. I can see he hasn't. But I don't think it's my place to tell you. I suggest you ask him why he left her.'

'You could tell us now,' said Norman. 'It would save us all a lot of time.'

'I'm sure it would, but I think you should hear it from him. I will tell you this much, though – if she was my wife I would have booted her out years ago.'

The two detectives exchanged a look, and Norman looked quizzically at Brennan.

'I'm not big on second chances, see,' he explained. 'One betrayal would have been more than enough for me.'

'You mean she–' began Norman.

'Like I said. I think you should hear it from Woody.'

They decided to return to Tinton police station via Bishops Common. The crime scene was cordoned off with one solitary officer occupying a car parked on the drive, supposedly guarding the site. He climbed hastily from his car when Slater and Norman pulled up in the lane.

'I was just having a tea break,' he explained, sheepishly.

'Relax, son,' said Norman. 'We haven't come to check up on you. Just make sure you don't get too comfortable and fall asleep in that car.'

'Yessir,' replied the red-faced PC. 'I'll try not to do that.'

'Do you have a key?' asked Slater.

The young man dug in his pocket, finally producing a key with a huge label attached. He handed it to Slater, who marched up to the door and slid the key firmly into the lock and turned. The door swung open and Norman followed him carefully inside.

They found the box on the dining room table. It was crammed with old vinyl albums and CDs.

'There's some good stuff in here.' Norman flicked through the albums. 'Old stuff, too. Whatever this guy might, or might not, have done, he has pretty good taste in music.'

'I'm sure he'll be gratified to know you think that,' said Slater, looking over Norman's shoulder. 'But I suppose this proves he didn't collect them yesterday.'

'It doesn't prove he didn't come here, though. It just suggests that if he did come here, he left in a hurry and forgot to take this box with him.'

'Yeah, maybe.' Slater admitted, grudgingly.

'Let's go and ask him,' said Norman.

As they left the house, Norman's mobile phone began to ring. He fished the phone from his pocket and looked at the incoming number.

'Shit!' he hissed, quietly.

'You okay, Norm?'

'I just need to deal with this,' said Norman.

'Okay,' said Slater. 'You carry on. I'll lock up and return the key.'

Norman walked off towards their car, keeping his back to Slater and his head down, almost conspiratorially, as he answered the call.

Slater kept his distance as Norman spoke into the phone, waiting until he had dismissed the call and put the phone back in his jacket pocket. When he turned to face Slater, Norman did not look a happy bunny.

'Norm,' insisted Slater. 'Are you sure you're okay?'

'Yeah. I'm fine. Really.'

Slater was unconvinced.

When they got back, Woody was in conference with his solicitor, so they agreed to give them some time to talk. In the meantime, they sought out Jane Jolly.

'So what did he have to say for himself?' Slater asked her.

'Nothing earth shattering, I'm afraid. But enough to convince me he's not your man.'

'You sound very sure of that, Jane,' said Norman. 'How come?'

'I just get the impression he still loves her. He didn't leave her because he wanted to – he left because he had to. I think he adored her, but she didn't care too much for him.'

'So why did he stick around so long?' asked Slater.

'Because when they got married they adored each other,' Jolly said. 'I think he was hoping if he waited long enough she would see what was happening and they could get back to where they were in the beginning. But he couldn't wait forever.'

'Does that sound likely to you?' Slater asked Norman.

'As it happens, yes,' said Norman. 'I can relate to that sort of hopeless feeling.'

Slater didn't labour the point. He knew this was a touchy subject for his colleague. Norman had been happily married for many years until he was wrongly pushed into exile in Northumberland. His wife, a lifelong Londoner, wouldn't leave her family to go with him and, as a result, their marriage had subsequently crumbled. Even today, more than four years on, it was clear Norman still hoped they might one day get back together.

'Come on, Norm,' said Slater. 'Let's go and see what Woody has to say about that box of records.'

Ian Woods' solicitor was called Simon Strong. He looked as if the name was likely to be a good fit. He made it quite clear from the start that his client was here on a voluntary basis and if, at any point, he was unhappy with the way things were going he would insist on leaving. Slater knew this meant he felt they had no hard evidence to arrest his client.

'Okay, Woody,' began Norman, once they were all settled at the table. 'You'll be pleased to know Mr Brennan confirmed your story about working for him yesterday. He says you called in at two-twenty to say you'd finished.'

'That's what I told you.'

'I know, but you understand why we have to check these things. We're just doing our job, right?'

Woody nodded.

'So tell me again, what did you do after you finished?

'I went for a coffee, filled up with diesel and then drove slowly homeward.' Woods sighed impatiently. 'I've already told you all this.'

'But Jim Brennan thinks you might have gone somewhere else before you went home,' said Norman.

Woods' mouth dropped open and the colour drained from his face. He gulped a couple of times.

'What's he been saying?'

'He says you told him Diana had more or less ordered you to come and collect your vinyl records and CDs, or she was going to dump them. According to Jim Brennan, when he told you about the job he wanted you to do for him, you said you were going to call in to Diana's on the way back and pick them up.'

Slater was studying Woody's face. When Norman had told him Brennan said he might have gone somewhere else, he had looked terrified and filled with guilt. Now Norman had told him Brennan had suggested he might have gone to Diana's, almost placing him at the murder scene in the process, he actually looked relieved. This didn't make any sense.

'Yeah, well,' said Woods. 'The day before, when I was two hundred miles away and just thinking about it, collecting my old records had seemed like a good idea. I even drove all the way up here from Southampton, but when I got on to the Tinton bypass, and started to get really close, I chickened out. The chances are she would have just screamed her head off at me again, and for what? A few vinyl records and a handful of CDs? I don't need that sort of hassle. I can always buy them again. So I just kept on going and headed for home.'

Norman said nothing. He just sat back in his chair and studied Woods. Slater was still trying to understand why Woods would look so relieved to be placed at the murder scene.

'Why would she scream at you?' Norman asked, finally. 'You would have been doing what she asked. What would she have had to complain about?'

'You don't know Diana. It didn't matter what I did. It was always wrong. You can only take so much of that and then you have to get away, or...'

'Or what, Woody?' asked Norman. 'You have to get away, or you'd have killed her?'

'Do I need to remind you, Sergeant,' interrupted Strong, 'that my client is here on a voluntary basis to help with your enquiries. I don't think your suggestions are being very helpful, do you? Mr Woods has answered your question, and explained why he didn't go to the house. Now, if you have some other questions, we will be happy to help, otherwise I think we may be done here.'

'Who owns Diana's house, Woody?' asked Slater. 'Is it in joint names?'

'Yes. We hadn't got as far as dividing things financially, yet.'

'Do you have a front door key?'

'I had one.' Woods smiled, ruefully. 'But she changed the bloody locks after I left.'

'Why would she do that?' asked Norman.

'To stop me getting in, of course.'

'But it's your house, too.'

'But I chose to leave, didn't I?' said Woods. 'She seemed to think that meant it was all hers. Like I said, we hadn't got around to sorting out the financial stuff yet.'

'So you actually gain from her death,' said Norman. 'Instead of half a house you now have a whole house.'

'So there's another motive, right? I'm sure if you sit there long enough you might be able to come up with one or two more. Why don't you just charge me if you want to?'

'I warned you, Sergeant.' Simon Strong stood up and started gathering his things together. 'We're out of here – now. Come on, Ian.'

Woods looked uncertainly at Strong, and then began to climb to his feet.

'If you wish to speak to my client again,' said Strong, addressing Slater and Norman, 'you will contact him through me. Is that clear?'

. . .

'I suppose that went about as well as could be expected,' said Norman, once Simon Strong had led his client from the room.

'You think?' asked Slater. 'If you don't mind me saying, you seem to be as convinced he's guilty as those two harpies out at Bishops Common.'

'Well, I'm sorry you feel that way.' Norman crossed his arms and a couple of spots of colour appeared on his cheeks. 'But right now, everything we know seems to indicate he has motive, he had the means and he had the opportunity. On top of that he admits he was in the area that afternoon and he's unable to explain why it took him so long to get home that day. I think that gives me good reason to think he's involved in her death.'

'You didn't think his reaction was a bit weird when you told him what Jim Brennan had told us?'

'I saw the colour drain from his face when he realised Brennan had placed him at the scene,' replied Norman. 'If that's not a sign of guilt, I don't know what is.'

'But that's not what you saw,' argued Slater. 'He wasn't feeling guilty about being at Diana's. He was actually relieved when you said Brennan had told us he was going there.'

'You must have been looking at someone else. I only saw a guy looking guilty.'

'You need to take those blinkers off, Norm. You're so focused on him being the killer you're missing the more subtle stuff.'

'Are you trying to tell me how to do my job?' Norman glared at Slater as he spoke, his lips tight.

'I'm just saying there's more to this than meets the eye. Sure, he's guilty of something, but I'm sure it's not Diana's death.'

'So you think you know how to do this job better than me.' Norman's voice seemed louder, suddenly. 'Despite the fact I've been doing it nearly twenty years longer than you.'

'Aw, come on, Norm,' said Slater, hoping to appeal to his colleague's better nature. 'You know I don't think that. It's just that you seem to have made your mind up already. Let's be honest, we've barely scratched the surface of this woman's life so far. There could be any number of skeletons in the cupboard, and any one of those could be a reason why she's dead.'

'So now you're saying I'm cutting corners.'

'Now you're twisting my words, and applying a meaning that's not there.' Slater held up his hands in appeasement. 'You're not hearing what I'm saying.'

'Oh, I hear it loud and clear,' said Norman, shaking his head and breathing heavily. 'You think you know better than me and that I should do what Detective Sergeant High and Mighty Slater says without thinking for myself, right?'

'Wrong, actually,' said Slater, wondering what the hell had happened to their relationship all of a sudden. 'I've never suggested anything of the sort and you know it.'

'What I know,' said Norman as he stood up, pushing his chair back roughly, 'is that I'm getting pretty pissed off with your superior attitude. And why is it you're always poking your nose into my business? Right now I've had enough. I'm going home.'

He marched from the room. Slater sat, bewildered. What had just happened? They had always been able to kick ideas around before, and they'd even argued before now without falling out. He was quite sure he hadn't done anything wrong, so what the hell was going on?

I t was just gone six as Slater trudged his way slowly back to their incident room via the canteen. He had been quite sure if he arrived bearing coffee and cakes he could make his peace and they could get back on an even keel, but when he pushed his way through the doors, Norman wasn't even there.

'Where's Norm?' he asked Jolly, as he placed the tray of coffees on the nearest desk.

'I assumed he was with you, interviewing Ian Woods.'

'Oh. Right. So he has gone off home then,' said Slater, wearily.

'Has something happened?'

'I'm not quite sure,' he said. 'We seem to have fallen out over this case. Or maybe I should say Norm's fallen out with me over this case.'

'Why?' asked Jolly. 'I've never known you two to fall out before.'

'Yeah. Quite. But now, apparently, I'm suggesting he doesn't know what he's doing, and I'm expecting him to do whatever I say, and if he doesn't agree with me he must be wrong.'

'That doesn't sound like you and Norm,' said Jolly. 'What's brought this on?'

'He seems adamant that Woods is guilty, and I'm saying we don't have enough proof,' said Slater. 'We've had these differences plenty of times before without falling out, but this time he seems to be taking it personally for some reason. And he reckons I'm always poking my nose into his business.'

'Well I know that's not right. I've watched you. You always hang well back if he's making a personal phone call. That's hardly poking your nose in, is it?'

'I don't even ask about his wife these days,' said Slater. 'I know it's a sore point so I avoid it unless he brings it up. I don't know what's going on. Maybe he's just having a crappy time and needs someone to take it out on.'

'Was there anything in particular that prompted this explosion?' asked Jolly.

'It was after we'd finished interviewing Woods. It didn't go well, and I told Norm I thought he was too focused on Woods being the killer. There was one incident in particular that I thought was really strange, but Norm didn't even notice it.'

'And you thought he should have seen it?'

'He told Woods that Jim Brennan had said he'd been going on somewhere after he finished at Southampton,' explained Slater. 'Woods went pale. He looked guilty as hell.'

'Which he would, if he was guilty,' suggested Jolly.

'Right,' said Slater. 'I quite agree. But at that stage he didn't know where Brennan had said he was going. But when Norm told him Brennan had said he was going to Diana's, he actually looked relieved. Now, how weird is that?'

'So he would rather we thought he was at the murder scene than where he actually was?'

'That's how it looked to me. But Norm seemed to miss it completely.'

They both stopped to think and sip their coffee, before Slater continued.

'But what would Ian Woods feel so guilty about that he would rather be suspected of being at the murder scene?' he asked.

'You mean you haven't guessed?' asked Jolly. 'It seems obvious to me. He was with a woman he shouldn't have been with, and he wants to keep her out of it.'

'But he doesn't have a girlfriend.'

'You mean he doesn't have a girlfriend you know about,' said Jolly. 'That's not quite the same thing, is it? Perhaps he's seeing someone's wife. He wouldn't go around telling everyone about that, would he?'

'Of course,' said Slater. 'How could I have been so stupid not to think of that myself? You see, Jane, that's why you're such an important part of this team.'

'I just have a different perspective, that's all,' said Jolly, but she was smiling proudly. 'So all you need to do is ask Ian Woods who she is.'

'We can't even approach him now,' Slater told her. 'After our interview this afternoon went pear-shaped, all future communications have to go through his solicitor.'

He thought for a few seconds.

'But Jim Brennan might know,' he continued. 'I get the impression he's more than just a boss to Woods, and they're actually good friends. Maybe Woods confides in Brennan.'

'I wouldn't rely on Brennan telling you anything if that's the case. Good friends can keep a confidence you know.'

'But a good friend might also feel it's worth sharing a confidence to avoid a murder charge.' Slater began sorting through the papers on his desk. 'I've got his card here somewhere. I'll give him a ring.'

'Right,' he said, five minutes later. 'Jim Brennan will talk to me if I meet him first thing in the morning, so I'll be a bit late getting here.'

'That's fine,' said Jolly. 'I'll be here. Perhaps I can have a little chat with Norm and see what's eating him.'

'Just tread carefully,' said Slater. 'I don't want him thinking I came up here telling tales behind his back.'

'You didn't.' Jolly stepped away from her desk and began gathering her things. 'You came here because you were concerned. That's quite different.'

She slipped a jacket over her shoulders.

'I'll see you when you get here,' she said as she slipped through the door.

'Goodnight, Jane,' said Slater, smiling after her.

CHAPTER FIVE

Jim Brennan didn't make the world's greatest cup of tea, but at seven in the morning, Slater was grateful for anything that was warm and wet.

'There won't be anyone here for at least an hour,' he explained to Slater. 'That's why I come in this early every morning. It's a bit of *me* time. I get a chance to catch up on any outstanding paperwork in peace. Or sometimes I just watch the news on the TV. Anyway, you didn't come here to find out what I do with my mornings, did you? So what can I do for you?'

'It's about Woody. He needs your help,' said Slater.

'From what I hear, all you have is a lot of innuendo, and no actual proof that he'd done anything wrong. If you're looking for me to help you convict him, you're wasting your time.'

'He's not as safe as you seem to think,' said Slater. 'It really wouldn't take much to tip the balance against him, and he's not helping himself with his story. According to what he's told us he had plenty of time to have killed Diana because there's a gap of a couple of hours he can't account for, or rather there's a gap of a couple of hours he won't account for. My colleague thinks it's because he was at Diana's, but I think he was somewhere else. I think it's possible he was with another woman and he's protecting her identity. You're his friend. Has he confided in you about an affair?'

A wry smile crossed Brennan's face.

'I wouldn't be much of a friend if I was prepared to share such things without asking him if he wanted me to, now would I?' he said.

'Look,' said Slater. 'If he was with a woman, she can give him an alibi for that afternoon, and he's off the hook. Right now he's still very much in the frame.'

Brennan was shaking his head.

'You don't know much about Woody, do you? Come to that, you don't seem to know much about Diana, either.'

'So help me out. Tell me about Woody and Diana. All I've heard so far is about how she was a saint and he was a bully.'

'Ha!' said Brennan. 'Yeah. That's the fictional version of their marriage that's been pushed around locally since they split up. You have to remember it's very easy to spread disinformation when the subject of that disinformation is well out of the way and unable to contradict it. Mind you, I think Woody's so glad to have escaped he doesn't really care what she says about him.'

'I'm not sure I really understand what you're saying,' said Slater.

'Then let me make it simple for you. Diana Woods was a lying cheat. She was a slapper who would sleep with anyone who was prepared to buy her a drink. She has all these women friends who think she's such a wonderful person, but what they don't realise is while they're so busy being dazzled by her shining light, she's busy working her way through their husbands. She's shagged half the blokes in Tinton, and she's especially fond of Woody's mates. I suppose it's the excitement of the risk, or perhaps she just can't help herself, like one of those sex addicts.'

'But that's the complete opposite of what her friends have told us.'

'Yes, I'm sure it is,' said Brennan. 'But that's the clever part, see. She was so nice to everybody, they thought she couldn't possibly be anything but an angel, could she? And, of course, none of the husbands were going to tell their wives the truth, were they?'

'Did Woody know?' asked Slater.

'Woody's a lovely bloke but where she was concerned he was a fool.

I'm sure he must have known, but he didn't want to believe it, you know? He loved her, and he had this stupid idea that if he hung on in there she would stop messing around and become the wife he wanted her to be, but all that happened was she got to despise him for being so weak and letting her get away with it. The longer it went on, the worse she treated him. I watched him going downhill for years. If he'd stayed with her she would have broken him completely.'

'But if he was so intent on hanging on in there, why did he eventually leave?'

'Because you can always deny your suspicions as long as you don't actually find any proof,' explained Brennan. 'But once you find the proof on display right under your nose, you can't deny it anymore, and that's when you suddenly realise what a bloody fool you've been for all those years.'

He looked at Slater, but Slater just returned his gaze. He was pretty sure Brennan was just about to fill in the blanks for him, so he didn't feel the need to pass comment.

'It was a few months ago now,' began Brennan. 'We had this special job he was supposed to be doing for me. We sat here all morning waiting for the customer to say they were ready to go, and then at about midday they decided they weren't going to be ready and they postponed the job until the next day. Woody was well browned off having sat here all morning for nothing, so I sent him home for some lunch. When he got there, Diana's car was parked outside. She should have been at work, so he knew something was up.

'He thought maybe she was ill, or something, so he let himself in as quietly as he could. As soon as he went in the front door, he could hear them at it upstairs, grunting and groaning like a couple of pigs. They were so busy shagging they didn't hear him coming up the stairs. The first thing they knew was when he slapped the guy's bare arse as hard as he could.'

'Who was the guy?' asked Slater, wincing at the thought of how much that slap must have stung.

'Her boss,' said Brennan. 'Apparently they'd been at it for a couple of years, but they usually went to his house at lunchtime on the days when his wife was at work. Maybe she wasn't working that day, or

maybe they just couldn't wait, or maybe Diana just got careless. Whatever the reason, it was a step too far, and even Woody couldn't stay in
denial after that. That same afternoon he packed his bags and moved
out. Within two weeks he'd left the area and found himself a place to
live in Wales.'

'So, if anything, the abuse and cruelty came from Diana and not
from Woody,' said Slater.

'I think it's fair to say she was torturing him for most of their
marriage.'

'And everyone thinks she's a saint.' Slater sighed.

'If she's such a saint,' said Brennan. 'Why did she proposition me?'

Slater didn't know what to say to that.

'I'll tell you why.' Brennan was in full flow now. 'It was because she
thinks I've got a bit of money and I'd be prepared to spend it on her in
exchange for a shag. She tends to think just because a bloke has a bit of
cash he's willing, you know? To my mind that's nothing more than
prostitution when you think about it. And before you ask, no, I did
not take her up on her offer.'

'And all this stuff about Woody beating her up-' began Slater.

'Is complete bollocks. That's all rubbish she'd been putting around
since they split up to make sure she looked like the victim and he
looked like the villain. She couldn't have her "Little Miss Perfect"
image ruined by the truth coming out, now could she?'

'Shit,' said Slater, almost to himself. 'Fancy putting up with that for
all those years.'

'Yeah. Not many blokes would, would they?' said Brennan. 'But ask
yourself this – if he was going to kill her, don't you think he would have
done it the day he caught her out? If it was me, I would have killed
them both, I can tell you. But Woody's not like that. He didn't want
revenge. He didn't even tell the other bloke's wife.'

'Your logic is flawless,' said Slater. 'But unfortunately it's not really
much help if he doesn't have an alibi. Are you sure there's not another
woman in his life?'

'In a way I wish there was. The poor bloke deserves a bit of happiness. But even if there is another woman in his life, I can assure you
he's never told me about it.'

As Slater drove away from Jim Brennan's office he felt that, at least now, he'd managed to fill in a few blanks about Woody and Diana's past. But he was still none the wiser when it came to where Woody had been on the afternoon Diana was killed.

'Morning, Jane. Morning, Norm,' said Slater as he pushed his way through the doors into the incident room.

Both Jolly and Norman were at their desks, Jolly looked up and smiled when he walked in, but Norman merely grunted, keeping his head down and his back to the door. Slater's spirits were, in turn, raised by Jolly's smile, and then depressed by Norman's back.

'Good morning,' said Jolly. 'I'm glad you're here. I've got some messages.'

'I hope they're good news.'

'One of the neighbours along Bishops Common claims to have seen a white van in the lane around the time of the murder, and DCI Murray would like an update on the case so far, as soon as you're ready.'

Oh great, thought Slater. *Norman's going to be gloating, and Murray's probably going to be griping because the budget's run out and we haven't made an arrest yet. What a way to start the day.*

'What time does the Old Man want to see us?' he asked.

'Oh you've got a good half hour,' said Jolly. 'I'll go and get some coffees.'

She stopped at the door and, catching Slater's eye, she nodded towards Norman. The message was clear enough.

'I'll just be a couple of minutes,' she said, as she left the room.

Crap, thought Slater. *How do I start this conversation?*

But it was Norman who swung his chair round to face him.

'Err, I think I owe you an apology,' he said awkwardly. 'I was well out of order yesterday, snapping your head off like that. It's just that, well, I have some personal stuff going on right now, and I let it get to me yesterday. It's a piss poor excuse I know, and I'm sorry I took it out on you.'

'It's okay,' said Slater, with a big sigh of relief. 'I can be pretty snappy myself at times, so I can hardly make a big deal if you get your own back now and then.'

'But I've never seen you stomp off home like a five-year-old. That was unforgivable behaviour on my part. I'm sorry.'

'Hey, look,' said Slater. 'It's done, and it's forgotten. If there's anything I can do to help with your problems, you only have to ask. And that's not interfering, right?'

'I know, I know,' said Norman. 'And don't think I'm not grateful for your offer, but this is something I have to deal with on my own.'

'Okay, whatever you say. But the offer stands. You only have to ask.'

Jolly backed her way through the door bearing a tray of coffee and bacon sandwiches. When she turned to face them, she obviously could tell from the look on their faces that they had cleared the air, as she beamed at them both.

'Breakfast is served,' she announced.

'Jane Jolly you're an angel,' said Norman, fervently.

He grabbed a sandwich and a coffee.

'Right,' he said. 'We'd better decide what we're going to tell the Old Man.'

'What about this neighbour?' asked Slater. 'Shouldn't we speak to her first?'

'We don't have time. We'll have to drive out there after we've seen him. I don't wish to gloat, but it looks as if she's going to put Ian Woods at the murder scene. That rather proves it for me.'

'Not so fast,' said Slater. 'There must be hundreds of white vans in and around Tinton every day. Unless she has a registration number it doesn't prove anything.'

'You really don't want this guy to be guilty, do you?' asked Norman. 'I don't see why you're so keen to save him.'

'I've just been talking to Jim Brennan. According to him, everything we've been told about Woody and Diana is arse about face. She was a cheat, and she'd been cheating on him for years. The reason he left was because he caught her screwing her boss, in his own house and his own bed.'

'Okay,' said Norman. 'So there's a lot of mist and fog to fight our way through. But that doesn't prove he's innocent. If anything it just gives him a really good motive for murder.'

'I know how it looks,' said Slater. 'But I still think we're missing something. And now we know more about Diana. According to Brennan she's slept with half the men in Tinton, so there could be dozens of suspects.'

'But only one whose van was at the scene at the right time. Jane told me about your "other woman" alibi theory. Did Brennan know anything about this woman?'

'No,' conceded Slater. 'But that doesn't mean she doesn't exist, does it? Maybe it's someone else's wife and Woody knows what discreet means.'

'Even if it means being discreet gets him accused of murder?' asked Norman, cynically. 'Seriously?'

'Chivalry's not completely dead,' Jolly chipped in. 'There are still some men alive who know what it means.'

'Yeah, but you're biased,' said Norman. 'Your first impression was that he was a nice man. Remember?'

'I'm a good judge. I have woman's intuition on my side.'

'Yeah, but I have evidence on my side,' said Norman. 'And I just keep getting more and more of it.'

Detective Chief Inspector Bob Murray massaged his temples with his fingertips. He was tired, as he always seemed to be these days. The mound of paperwork on his desk seemed never-ending, and he imagined himself suddenly standing up and shoving it all onto the floor, leaving the mess for someone else to deal with. As Norman and Slater stood awkwardly in front of his desk, like school-boys in the headmaster's office, Murray wondered if he would miss any part of this job when he left. If he ever left. He had applied for volun-tary redundancy, but hadn't heard a thing yet. Every morning he woke up wondering if today would be the day he would be free at last.

His thoughts snapped back to the present as Slater cleared his throat.

'So, where are we with this Diana Woods murder case?' Murray asked.

'I think that rather depends on your point of view,' said Norman, cutting off Slater who had just opened his mouth.

'What's that supposed to mean?' asked Murray, impatiently. 'Do you have a suspect?'

'Yes,' said Norman. 'Ian Woods.'

'Evidence?'

'He's the husband. He moved out a few weeks ago after he caught the victim in bed with another man.'

'So that's a good motive,' said Murray.

'Woods was in the area on the afternoon she died, and there's a big hole in his story that would give him plenty of time to have committed the murder,' continued Norman.

'So there's the opportunity,' said Murray. 'What more do you need? Arrest the man.'

'Err, with respect,' said Slater. 'All we have is circumstantial. We have no hard evidence to prove he was even in the house that day. There are no forensics to put him at the scene, and no witnesses.'

'But we do have his boss's testimonial,' said Norman. 'He says Woods told him he was going to see his wife that very afternoon to collect some records and CDs.'

'Yes,' argued Slater. 'But Woods says he chickened out and didn't go.'

'And we've just had a witness come forward to say she saw Woods and his van in the lane at the time of the murder,' said Norman.

'We don't know that for sure,' protested Slater. 'We haven't even spoken to this witness yet!'

'Do you know this man Woods?' Murray thought he might have whiplash from the way the conversation was flying back and forwards between Slater and Norman. 'You seem very keen to argue in his defence.'

'No, I don't know him,' replied Slater. 'I'm just not convinced he's guilty. I admit he looks possible, but I'd be a whole lot happier if we had some real evidence to connect him to the crime scene.'

'It seems open and shut to me.' Murray waved a hand. 'He went to the house to collect his records and CDs, got into an argument with his wife, lost his rag and murdered her. If it was me I'd have hauled him in here and charged him by now. I don't know why you haven't.'

'You're joking,' said Slater. 'We don't have enough evidence to do that.'

Murray looked Slater up and down. He was a good detective, but he had a habit of speaking his mind, which could be quite irritating. Even more irritating if you were exhausted and fed up.

'I'm sorry if things aren't going quite the way you would like, Slater,' he said. 'But I think you'll find I have a bit more experience than you in these matters. I'm not asking you to arrest this man, I'm giving you an order.'

'At least let us speak to the witness who's just come forward,' pleaded Slater. 'She could be wrong.'

'She could be right,' pointed out Norman.

'And if she is,' said Slater. 'At least we'll have some concrete evidence to back up this assumption that he's guilty. Give me that, and I'll arrest the guy myself.'

Murray gave Slater his most intimidating death stare, but he knew from experience that Slater wasn't going to back down.

'Very well,' he said finally. 'You go and see this witness first, and then you go and arrest Woods. And I'm not having you run off doing your own thing, Slater. Do you understand?'

Slater nodded.

'Just in case you don't understand,' continued Murray. 'DS Norman will take the lead on this. At least I know he'll do his duty as directed.'

He returned his attention to the pile of paperwork on his desk. Out of the corner of his eye, he saw Slater open his mouth to speak, only for Norman to shake his head furiously. Murray looked up.

'Are you two still here?'

'Just going,' said Norman. 'Come on, Dave. Let's go.'

'I s he in a good mood this morning, or what?' said Slater as they made their way down the stairs from Murray's office.

'He's a man under a lot of pressure,' said Norman. 'Getting into an argument with him will only make it worse. You should know that by now.'

'Yeah. I know that. But surely we need to make sure we have enough evidence if we're going to charge a man with murder. I want to be able to sleep at night, you know.'

'Let's go and talk to this witness. Maybe she'll provide the proof you need to get a good night's sleep and keep the Old Man happy.'

CHAPTER SIX

'Plum Tree Cottage,' Norman said, checking the address written on the sheet of paper he was holding. 'This is the house.'

'But didn't we speak to her yesterday?' asked Slater. 'Wasn't she one of the ones who said she didn't hear or see anything?'

'We spoke to her husband yesterday. We didn't actually see her. He said she was ill in bed.'

'So how did she see a van driving past?'

'Perhaps she wasn't ill at the time,' said Norman, wearily. 'Or maybe she can see out of the window from her bed. Jeez, how the hell do I know?'

'I just think it's a bit fishy, that's all,' said Slater.

'I seem to recall her husband was no spring chicken. Maybe she's a not so young and her memory's a bit slow.'

'You're not filling me with confidence, Norm.' Slater sighed.

'Instead of trying to second guess what's caused her to remember, why don't we just go and ask? 'Isn't that why we're here?'

'Yeah. You're right,' admitted Slater. 'We have to keep open minds.'

'We?' spluttered Norman. 'I don't think it's a question of "we", do you?'

But he really wasn't in the mood for an argument this morning.

'Look,' he said. 'We're much more effective as a team when we're not arguing, right?'

'Of course.'

'So let's not argue about it. Let's just go and ask some questions and then draw some conclusions. That's what we do best, isn't it?'

'You're right,' Slater said, nodding. 'Come on, let's go.'

M rs Turner was a very old-looking sixty-four. If she hadn't told them, Slater would have guessed she was at least ten years older. She had seemed surprised to see them on her doorstep, and Norman had to remind her she had called the police station earlier that morning.

'Did I?' she asked him in surprise.

'Yes, ma'am,' said Norman patiently. 'You spoke to a young lady officer called PC Jolly. You told her you had some new evidence about the death of Diana Woods.'

'Oh yes,' she said. 'That's right. I remember now. Amanda told me I should call you.'

'Amanda? Do you mean Amanda Hollis?'

'Oh yes,' enthused Mrs Turner. 'She's such a lovely girl. She always looks in to see if I'm alright. She even does a little shopping for me. Diana was the same. Like angels, they are, the two of them.'

Slater's heart sank. It seemed Mrs Turner was confused to say the least, and, on top of that, she appeared to be yet another member of the Diana Woods fan club, so the chances are she was going to be a member of the Ian Woods hate club, too. He thought it would be great if they could find someone who might actually offer some impartial evidence.

'Is Mr Turner here today?' asked Norman.

'Oh no. He only stays home when I'm having one of my bad days. It's the drugs you see. I have chemotherapy to keep the tumour at bay, but the side effects can be dreadful. We're lucky his employer is so understanding.'

Slater felt an immediate stab of guilt for judging her. No wonder she didn't seem one hundred percent.

'Oh, wow,' said Norman. 'I'm sorry to hear that, Mrs Turner.'

'It's a bugger alright. But I've got a saying to help me cope. Don't let the bastard grind you down. That's my motto.'

She gave them a sad smile. Then there was one of those awkward silences when no one really knows what to say next. It was Mrs Turner who rescued the situation.

'Well,' she said, suddenly becoming all business-like. 'You didn't come here to hear about my illness, did you? You'd better come in.'

She led the way through to a spacious lounge. At one end a set of folding doors opened out onto a beautiful garden.

'That's some garden,' said Norman, admiringly.

'Isn't it?' Mrs Turner's voice was filled with pride. 'Being able to enjoy my garden is what keeps me going.'

She ushered them towards two comfortable armchairs and then settled down on one opposite.

'PC Jolly tells me you think you saw something significant at around the time Diana died,' began Norman.

'Yes,' she replied. 'I'd had a bad day, and I spent most of it in bed sleeping, but I woke up at around five forty-five. I was feeling much better so I decided to get out of bed. Our bedroom is at the front of the house so the window overlooks the lane. I heard a car going past so I looked out of the window. Only it wasn't a car. It was a small white van.'

'You're quite sure about the time?' asked Norman.

'I know that was the time because I looked at the clock, wondering where the day had gone. It's become a habit. When you spend as much time sleeping as I do, you really do wonder where all the time goes. You resent it, so you tend to keep a check on it. It's silly I know. It's not as if I can get it back, is it?'

'No,' agreed Norman. 'You can't get it back, but I can see why you'd want to know how much you've lost every time you wake up.'

'When I was talking to Amanda,' she continued, 'she told me I'd seen Ian Woods driving away and that I had to tell you as much.'

'And did you see Ian Woods?' asked Norman.

'Well it must have been him,' she said. 'He killed Diana, he has a white van, and it was the right time. Who else could it possibly have been?'

Slater let out an involuntary, impatient sigh. He really had intended to let Norman do all the talking, but now he couldn't stop himself.

'Did you see the registration number?' he asked.

'Well no,' she admitted. 'But he was driving that van when he lived here. I'd know it anywhere.'

'What make was it?'

'I don't know,' she said, impatiently. 'They're all the same, aren't they?'

'No, Mrs Turner. They are not all the same.'

'But he was driving it.'

'You saw his face?' asked Norman.

'Well, no,' she conceded, reluctantly. 'But it was definitely a man. I could see that much.'

'So you don't really know it was him,' concluded Norman.

'But we all know he murdered her. Amanda told me. And it was a small white van at the right time. I've heard all the things people have been saying about him. It must have been him.'

'Do you know how many small white vans there are within ten miles of this house?' asked Slater.

She said nothing.

'There are well over a hundred,' said Slater. 'We checked, so we know it's right.'

She managed to look indignant they hadn't taken her word as gospel, but again she said nothing.

'You may well have seen a white van, but if you can't tell us the make of the van, and you didn't actually see the registration number, and you didn't see who was driving, you can't say with any certainty that it was Ian Woods, can you, Mrs Turner?'

'It could have been any one of the hundred and odd small white vans that are registered locally,' added Norman.

'But they said...' she began.

'But they were wrong to say,' said Norman, gently. 'We don't know Ian Woods killed Diana. You can't tell us what you think we want to hear Mrs Turner. You can only tell us what you really saw.'

'But Diana was so lovely,' she said. 'Why would anyone else want to kill her?'

'That's what we have to find out,' said Norman. 'But whoever is guilty, we have to be able to prove it with facts, not with guesswork. Now I'm happy to accept you saw a white van, but I can't accept you saw Ian Woods, and I can't accept it was definitely his van.'

She looked distinctly crestfallen.

'Don't feel too bad about it,' said Norman. 'You may well have provided us with a vital piece of evidence, and for that we're very grateful, but we can only accept the facts and not the speculation.'

'I feel such a fool,' she said.

'Don't,' said Norman. 'It's not necessary.'

'That Amanda Hollis is a bloody menace, going around putting ideas into people's heads like that,' said Slater, as they got back into their car.

'I know,' agreed Norman. 'But you can't deny this doesn't look good for your friend Woody.'

'He's not my friend,' said Slater. 'I just don't think he should be the victim of a witch hunt. You agreed with me when we were out here before.'

'That was before we had any evidence to back up their claims. Right now it's getting difficult to see how it could be anyone else.'

'But we've got no hard evidence. It's still possible he had nothing to do with it.'

'We have no hard evidence, *yet*. And if you want to talk about possibilities, it's still possible Tinton Town football club will, one day, reach the premier league, but it's really hard to believe isn't it?'

Slater realised he was wasting his breath so he didn't pursue the point.

'Where to?' he asked, hoping to change the subject as he started the car.

'I think we'd better go back,' said Norman. 'I think we need to talk to your man Woody again.'

'I don't think we should be arresting him.'

'And what if we don't arrest him and he decides to do a bunk?' asked Norman. 'We'll look pretty damned stupid in front of Murray then, won't we?'

'Don't you think he'll have gone by now if he's intending to?'

'We don't know that he hasn't yet.'

'If he's still at that hotel like he said he was going to be,' said Slater, 'it proves he's not going to run, right?'

'It might just prove he thinks we're too stupid to catch him,' replied Norman.

'Oh, come on, Norm. You've met the guy. Did he really come across like that to you? Because he doesn't look like a confident, cocky, killer to me.'

Norman didn't say anything, and Slater knew he was mulling it over.

'We're going to have to bring him in, whether you like it or not,' Norman said finally. 'Let's hear what he has to say when I tell him a white van was seen at the scene of the crime. Then I'll decide if I'm going to hold him or not.'

'I've got the landline phone record,' announced Jolly, when they got back. 'And I've got some CCTV footage from Leigh Delamere services on the M4.'

'Does the phone record tell us anything?' asked Slater, hopefully.

'Not really. I've printed it out. There's a copy on your desk. It looks like she hardly seemed to use it. I suspect it's just there for the broadband. She probably used her mobile more than her landline.'

'Any news on when we'll have that?'

'I'm chasing it,' she said. 'But you know what these places are like.'

Yeah. He knew. He just hoped it wasn't going to take too much longer.

He picked up the copy of the phone records and glanced through it. As Jolly had already said, it looked as though Diana Woods made most of her calls from her mobile phone. There were just a handful of calls made from the landline, and most of those seemed to be to 0800 numbers. But there was one call that appeared to have been made to a mobile number just three nights before she had died.

'We've got Ian Woods' phone number, haven't we?' he asked.

'It's there on your desk, somewhere,' said Jolly.

He sorted his way through his desk until he found the file with Ian Woods name on top. He flipped the file open and ran his finger down the personal information on the first page. Sure enough, it was the same number Diana Woods had called.

'Well,' he said. 'This phone record shows she called Woods three days before she died. It wasn't a very long call, but it would have been long enough to give him an ultimatum about his records going to the tip if he didn't collect them.'

'That call could have been about anything,' said Norman. 'We have no way of knowing exactly what was discussed.'

'You're not going to cut this guy an inch of slack, are you?'

'No, I'm not. At least, not as long as he's our prime suspect. Now where's that number for Simon Strong? I'm going to tell him we need to speak with his client again, assuming the guy hasn't already done a runner.'

Slater looked at Jolly and raised his eyebrows.

'They're going to be here at four,' said Norman, a few minutes later. 'So we've got a couple of hours to kill.'

'In that case I'm going to have a look at this CCTV footage,' muttered Slater, climbing to his feet.

'Have we got Woods' credit card records yet, Jane?' asked Norman.

'Should be here later this afternoon.'

'One more thing,' said Slater. 'We need you to contact everyone who lives on Bishops Common. Did anyone have a parcel delivered late that afternoon, or did anyone have someone working on their house? We're looking for a reason for a small white van to have been down there.'

. . .

'My client has asked for my advice regarding coming here under a voluntary basis to answer questions, and I have advised him he should stop, forthwith,' announced Simon Strong when they were assembled in the interview room.

Norman looked a bit miffed at this, but Slater could understand what Strong was saying. If they arrested Woods, they would have a limit as to how long they could detain him without charging him. If they continued as they were, with Woods here as a volunteer, they could go on forever.

'But I don't have many more questions to ask,' said Norman.

'Well, if you arrest Mr Woods you can ask as many questions as you wish,' replied Strong. 'Otherwise we're out of here, right now.'

'Very well.' Norman climbed to his feet to deliver his speech. 'Ian Woods, I'm arresting you on suspicion of the murder of Diana Woods...'

'Okay, Woody,' began Norman, once the formalities were out of the way. 'This is how it is. We now have a witness who saw a small white van, similar to yours, leaving Bishops Common at five forty-five on the afternoon Diana was murdered. I believe that was your van. What do you have to say to that?'

'D'you know how many small white vans there are on the roads in this country?' asked Woody. 'They're all over the place.'

'But they're not all being driven by you.'

'Well the one your witness saw wasn't being driven by me either.'

'You're quite sure about that, are you?' asked Norman.

'Absolutely,' said Woods. 'I already told you. I didn't go to Bishops Common. I was going to go but I changed my mind and went home instead.'

'Oh yeah, that's right. You chickened out in case Diana shouted at you. That's very brave of you.'

'It's got nothing to do with being brave. I just don't need that sort of hassle. I'm not short of money. I can buy those records and CDs again. Why put up with a load of earache when I don't need to?'

'How come a courier is so well off?' asked Norman.

'I don't see that it's any of your business,' said Woods. 'But I've got nothing to hide so I'll tell you. As a courier you can get lots of down-time when you're just waiting around. I used my downtime to educate myself about the many ways you can make a living online. Over the past three years I've built myself a business. It's how I could afford to walk out and start again. I don't need Diana's money, you see. I earn two or three times what she earns. If she had only taken a little interest in what I was doing she would have known that, and maybe she could even have been a part of it, but she chose not to know. That's also why I don't need her share of our house. I was going to sign the whole lot over to her as part of our divorce.'

They would have to check his bank statements, of course, thought Slater, but if he was telling the truth that was the financial motive crossed off the list.

'Anyway,' said Woods. 'I thought you were going to check the CCTV from the services to check out my story. They will prove I'm telling the truth.'

'Yeah,' said Norman. 'About those CCTV cameras. The footage from the petrol station in Southampton confirms that part of the story–'

'Of course it does. Because I'm telling the truth.'

'But we have a problem with the Leigh Delamere footage,' continued Norman. 'The cameras can confirm what time you left, but they don't show you arriving. For all we know you could have arrived just five minutes before you left.'

'But my credit card receipts will show what time I paid for my meal. I can't fake that, now can I?'

'We've already requested that information,' said Norman. 'It should be here any minute.'

'Well, until you've checked it out,' interrupted Strong, 'I would suggest you have no more questions for my client. I would also like to suggest you have no real grounds for holding him.'

'But that was your idea, Mr Strong,' replied Norman. 'You asked me to arrest him, so I did.'

'It's okay, Simon,' said Woods. 'I'm innocent. If I have to stay in a cell for a couple of nights to prove it, then that's alright. I appreciate these guys have plenty of people telling them I'm responsible so they have to check me out. It's what they do, isn't it?'

Slater wasn't sure if this was just bravado from Woods, or if he really was this laid back about the situation. Either way it was very convincing. He doubted he would have been so calm if the situation had been reversed.

'Okay,' said Norman, after a couple of minutes. 'Let's adjourn this interview until we've had a chance to check out this credit card. Let's reconvene at six o'clock.'

CHAPTER SEVEN

'This guy's way too cool,' Norman said to Slater as they made their way back up to their incident room. 'He knows something we don't.'

'Yeah,' said Slater. 'He knows he's not guilty and that we're wasting our time trying to prove otherwise.'

'He hasn't convinced me yet.'

'What about the fact the pathologist reckoned the killer was short?' argued Slater. 'Woods must be six feet tall. Where I come from, that's not considered short.'

'That's not enough to rule him out.'

'But you'd happily accept it ruled him in, if it was the other way around, wouldn't you?'

'Well, yeah, I guess so,' said Norman. 'But-'

'Never mind but,' interrupted Slater. 'You seem to be trying to make the evidence fit, instead of taking it at face value.'

'Now wait a minute,' Norman began, but Slater was having none of it.

'You know we don't have a single shred of real evidence against this guy,' he insisted. 'But you won't admit it. This isn't like you, Norm. I don't know what your problem is, but it's making you blind to the facts.'

Norman stopped dead in his tracks, but Slater kept on walking. He felt sure they were wasting their time focusing on Woods, but he didn't see what more he could say to make Norman see it for himself.

'D id you find out how long it would take to drive from Tinton to Leigh Delamere services?' Slater asked Jolly.

'About an hour and forty-five minutes,' she replied. 'Of course that's if he stuck to the speed limits, so you could probably knock as much as a half hour off it if he was tearing along.'

'Yeah, but don't forget most of that journey would have been done in the rush hour,' he said. 'I think you'd be hard pressed to save that much time in heavy traffic, so let's call it an hour and a half at best.'

'So, it's just about possible he could have done it.'

'Ah. But only if there were no hold-ups,' said Slater, unconvinced.

'I didn't check. But I can, if you want me to.'

'Yes, please,' he said.

Norman bumped his way through the doors and glared at Slater, but before he could say anything, Jolly defused the situation by thrusting a handful of papers at him.

'Ian Woods' bank and credit card statements,' she said.

'Right,' he said, taking the papers and heading for his desk. 'Now let's see what I can prove.'

Slater's desk phone started ringing.

'There's a lady down here in reception, wants to talk to you,' said the voice of the duty sergeant. 'She says she has some information for you regarding Ian Woods.'

'Let me guess,' said Slater. 'Does she want to tell me what a nasty piece of work he is?'

'I couldn't say,' said the voice. 'She says she'll only talk to you.'

'Okay.' He sighed. 'I'll be down right away.'

Wearily he dropped the phone back onto its cradle.

'Apparently there's someone downstairs who wants to talk to me about Ian Woods. Do you want to come, Norm?'

'No. That's okay,' said Norman, frostily. 'You deal with it. I've got these statements go through.'

A few minutes later it was Norman's desk extension that was ringing.

'Yo!' he said into the phone.

'It's me,' said Slater.

'I've just found proof Ian Woods paid for his meal at seven forty-five that evening,' said Norman. 'That would almost be a perfect fit if he went straight from murdering Diana.'

'It wasn't him,' said Slater. 'Come down here and I'll prove it.'

'What? What do you mean you'll prove it?'

'Woody has an alibi. Come down here and hear it for yourself.'

'Shit,' said Norman, as he put the phone down.

'Problem?' asked Jolly.

'It seems Ian Woods might have an alibi,' said Norman, disappointment washing over him.

'Well,' said Jolly, smiling. 'I don't want to say I told you so-'

'So don't,' interrupted Norman. 'Just don't, right?'

She gave him her sweetest smile and poked her tongue out as he stomped his way through the doors.

W hen Norman found Slater, he was talking to an attractive woman, aged around fifty, who turned out to be Jim Brennan's wife, Susie. Slater introduced her to Norman and then invited her to tell Norman what she had just told him.

'Ian Woods was at my house from three o'clock until about five on the day Diana Woods died,' she said. 'And before you jump to any conclusions, no, we're not having an affair.'

'So how come he was at your house?' asked Norman.

'I do the books for my husband. I work three days a week over there so I know all the guys who work there. They often sit in with me and have a cup of tea and, as a result, I tend to hear their problems. I suppose I'm a bit of an agony aunt to some of them. Anyway, Woody was a very unhappy man when he was with Diana, and he used to confide in me a lot. He used to talk to Jim as well. He's a friend as well as a driver so I think he trusted us.

'Between us we've been a bit of a shoulder for Woody to lean on over the last three or four years, but since he upped sticks and moved away, I've hardly seen him. And then, the other day he called to say he was going to be passing and would it be alright if he called in for a cup of tea.'

'So why didn't he tell us this himself?' asked Norman.

'Probably because he didn't want to get me involved.'

'Why would that be a problem?'

'Why do you think?' she said. 'Look at your own reaction. Straight away you assumed we're having an affair. How do you think my Jim would react?'

'Does he have reason to be suspicious?' asked Norman.

'No. Woody was passing so he came by to say hello, that's all. But my husband tends to be a bit suspicious, just like you are.'

Norman wanted to protest his innocence, but his red-faced embarrassment made it obvious he was guilty as charged, so he chose to let it go and pursue a different approach.

'But the murder was committed at around six,' he argued.

'Yes, I know that,' she said, calmly. 'But there's no way Woody could have got from my house and back to Diana's in time.'

'And what makes you so sure about that?' asked Norman.

'Because I live in Newbury.' She smiled. 'It's the best part of an hour away from here.'

'Can anyone corroborate this story?'

'Actually, yes, someone can,' she said. 'My next door neighbour was having a cup of tea with me when he arrived. I can give you her address and telephone number if you don't believe me.'

'Now do you believe him?' asked Slater, as they made their way back up the stairs.

'This alibi's very convenient, don't you think?' asked Norman.

'What? You think she's lying?' Slater shook his head, feeling slightly frustrated.

'I'm just saying she obviously likes the guy a lot,' argued Norman. 'I'm not convinced there's not something going on there.'

'Her husband likes the guy a lot. Are you going to suggest there's something going on there, too? How about you try to consider the fact that he's actually a nice guy? Wouldn't that explain why these people like him?'

'But if he left her house at five-thirty he would have been at the services by six-thirty. Yet he didn't pay for his meal until seven forty-five. If she's lying, it's still possible–'

'Oh come on, Norm,' said Slater, wearily. 'Give it up, mate. We've been focused on the wrong man. End of story.'

He pushed his way through the doors, Norman trailing in his wake.

'You were right,' said Jolly, as soon as she saw Slater. 'I checked back through the traffic reports. There was an accident causing big westbound hold-ups on the M4 that afternoon, starting from four o'clock, just in time for the rush hour. At their peak, the delays were getting on for two hours.'

Slater turned to Norman.

'Did you hear that? It explains why it took him so long to get from Newbury to the services, and he definitely couldn't have left Tinton at six and got to the services by seven-forty-five in that traffic.'

Norman looked crestfallen for a moment, but then he shrugged and smiled ruefully.

'Okay,' he said. 'I got it wrong. But you have to admit there was cause to suspect him. And don't think this gives you two an excuse to keep on telling me how you told me so. Right?'

'But I did tell you so,' said Jolly, with a wicked smile. 'You just wouldn't listen.'

Norman glared at her and then turned to Slater.

'So we're back to square one,' he said. 'Do you want to go and tell the Old Man?'

'Oh, I don't think so,' said Slater, grinning. 'I seem to recall him issuing a very definite instruction that "DS Norman will take the lead on this". And then there was something along the lines of "at least I know he'll do his duty," or some crap like that. Apparently I can't do as I'm told, so I think it's only right you should be the one to toddle off to give him the good news, don't you?'

Norman looked dismayed.

'Go on,' said Slater. 'It doesn't matter how big you make those brown eyes, you're still the lead. So, off you go and do your duty.'

'Yeah, but–' began Norman.

'Just go,' said Slater, his grin threatening to split his face as he pointed to the door. 'Now.'

'I always seem to get all the shit jobs,' mumbled Norman as he pushed his way through the doors.

'So how was it?' asked Slater, as Norman slumped back into the room half an hour later.

Norman turned and bent over.

'Can you see the boot mark on my arse?' he asked. 'That's where he kicked me when I told him the good news.'

'So he was pleased, then.'

'He went ballistic. He's still up in orbit right now,' said Norman, heading for his desk. 'Anyone would think we'd let Jack the Ripper slip through our fingers. Apparently we've just blown the chance for a quick result, wasted half the annual budget, and proved we're incompetent all in the space of just two days.'

'I thought we did that last week,' said Slater, laughing.

'No kidding, he went ape,' said Norman, unable to stop himself from smiling. 'Thanks for making me go. I've never seen him that bad before.'

'Privilege of leadership, mate. You get the glory, and the shite.'

'Well, you'll be pleased to know I've been relieved of that particular honour. Apparently now it seems I, too, can't be trusted to do as I'm told.'

'So who's in charge now?' asked Slater.

'He didn't say,' said Norman. 'By that stage he had gone purple and couldn't speak any more. I guess we'll just do what we usually do and make it up as we go along.'

They enjoyed the shared moment like a pair of Cheshire cats, grinning from ear to ear, until finally they both seemed to acknowledge it was time to get back to the job in hand.

'I guess we need to go back to the beginning and start again.' Norman moved across to the whiteboard and wiped it clean. 'So what do we know?'

'Diana Woods was killed by a single stab in the back with one of her own kitchen knives,' said Slater, slowly enough for Norman to keep up as he scribbled away at the board.

'Whoever stabbed her was either very lucky, or very skilled because the knife passed between her ribs and pierced her heart. There was no sign of forced entry, which suggests she knew her killer. Also, the fact she turned her back on her killer to fill the kettle would seem to suggest she invited the killer into her house and was comfortable enough to trust them. The pathologist feels the wound was inflicted by someone short. We have no fingerprints, and, so far, no forensic evidence, which again could mean someone was very lucky, or they were cool enough to clear up behind them.

'A small, white van was seen driving along Bishops Common lane around the time of the murder.'

Norman stepped and squinted at the board, before handing the pen to Slater.

'Your turn,' he said.

'So, what do we know about the victim?' asked Slater, taking Norman's place at the board.

'She's either an angel or a lying cheat, depending on who you listen to. She had sex with someone earlier, maybe lunchtime, on the day she was killed.

'She was wearing fancy underwear with the labels still attached. This suggests she could have been given the underwear as a gift, probably, but not necessarily, by the same person she had sex with earlier.'

They fussed around for another fifteen minutes adding little bits of information here and there until they were reasonably satisfied they hadn't missed anything.

'So what have we got?' asked Slater, stepping back from the board.

'Honestly?' asked Norman. 'Not much. In fact, now we've ruled out

Ian Woods we've got nothing really. We know what happened but we haven't got the first idea why.'

'We need to speak to Ian Woods again,' said Slater. 'But this time we need a bit more information about his wife and why they split up. Jim Brennan told me Woody caught Diana in bed with her boss. We need to find out a whole lot more about this guy.'

'Right.' Norman looked at his watch. 'We're supposed to be talking to Woods in a few minutes anyhow. Let's hope he's feeling amenable enough to help us out. It would also help if we could get hold of her mobile phone records.'

'Jane tells me they're on the way,' Slater assured him. 'Maybe they'll be here in the morning.'

'Let's go see what your friend Woody can tell us about Diana. And then I wanna go home. I feel like crap and I need an early night.'

Slater wasn't surprised Norman felt like crap. He certainly looked like crap. His face was an unpleasant shade of grey, and he had the appearance of a man who hadn't had a good night's sleep in weeks. He felt genuinely concerned for his friend, but he knew there was no point in asking if he was okay. Norman would say he was fine, and he'd be pissed off at Slater for asking.

CHAPTER EIGHT

'Good evening Ian, Mr Strong,' began Norman. 'I'm pleased to say we no longer consider Ian a suspect in the Diana Woods murder inquiry.'

Both Woods and Strong looked surprised at this sudden turn of events.

'How come?' asked Woods. 'What's happened?'

'Susie Brennan happened,' said Norman. 'She says you were at her house in Newbury until five that afternoon. You couldn't have got from there to Tinton in time to kill Diana.'

'My client told you all along he wasn't involved,' said Strong. 'I think perhaps we should consider making an example of you–'

'Your client could have told us this right from the word go,' interrupted Slater. 'As it is, we've wasted a lot of time on him when we could have been focusing our attention elsewhere.'

Strong looked suitably chastened and a little guilty.

'You knew about this didn't you, Mr Strong?' asked Slater. 'Shouldn't you have advised your client that wasting police time is a criminal offence?'

'He didn't want to drag Mrs Brennan into this,' said Strong. 'I can only advise a client. I can't force him to do what I suggest.'

'Oh great,' said Norman. 'So you're saying you think it was okay to let me think he was the murderer when you knew all along he had a cast iron alibi?'

'Look. I know how it must look.'

'You do?' said Norman, indignantly. 'Oh, good. In that case you might want to think about how you're going to apologise. We have a murderer who has now had forty-eight hours start on us, thanks to you.'

'Look,' said Woods, looking very uncomfortable. 'I wasn't trying to obstruct anyone. I was just trying to protect Susie. I did tell you I wasn't involved in the murder.'

'Funny enough,' snapped Norman, 'even the guys who are guilty tend to tell us that. If we believed everyone who told us they were innocent we'd never catch anyone.'

Norman was getting distinctly twitchy, so Slater thought it might be a good idea to step in and build some bridges before he really lost it.

'Okay,' he said. 'This isn't going to get us anywhere.'

He looked purposefully at Strong and Woods.

'I think DS Norman has every right to be pissed off with you two. Like he says, you've wasted a lot of our time when you could have sorted the whole thing out right at the start. However, we still need to find Diana's killer, and, if you're willing, Woody, I think you could be a big help to our inquiry.'

'How?' asked Woods. 'What can I do?'

'We've heard a lot of stuff about Diana from her friends,' explained Slater. 'They seem to see her as some sort of angel who never did a thing wrong in her life. Yet Jim Brennan paints a totally different picture.

'You're the guy who was married to her, so we could do with hearing your version of Diana. What was he really like? Why did you leave her? This would help us to build a much better picture of who she was, and that will help us find out who killed her. Surely you'd want her killer caught, wouldn't you?'

'Yeah, of course I would,' said Woods. 'I'll tell you whatever you want to know if you think it will help.'

'Is that okay with you, Mr Strong?' asked Slater.

'I don't think I'm really needed am I? If my client's no longer a suspect, he doesn't need to be represented, so I'm going home, if that's alright with everyone.'

'It's okay with me,' said Woods.

'It's certainly alright with me,' growled Norman.

And so for the next half hour, Ian Woods told them about his life with Diana, who he admitted had been a serial adulterer.

'She just couldn't seem to stop herself,' he said. 'I pleaded and begged, but she either couldn't, or wouldn't, stop.'

'So you knew all about it?' asked Slater.

'Well, not exactly,' said Woody.

He let out a huge sigh, and went quiet for a minute. Slater was beginning to think he was going to burst into tears, but then he managed to get control again.

'I loved her, you see. I loved her so much it hurt. When I first found out about her cheating on me I was going to leave her, but she pleaded with me, promised me she would change and that it wouldn't happen again. She said all the right things, so I forgave her and we agreed we'd try again. And it was alright for two or three years, but then I got the feeling she'd started again, you know? I had no proof, I just recognised the signs.'

'So what did you do about it?' asked Slater.

'Nothing.'

'But why? Why would you put up with that?'

'Because I didn't want to believe it,' explained Woods. 'I didn't want to believe she would want to hurt me like that, all over again. I just wanted us to be a happy loving couple, that's all. But she seemed to despise me for that. Somehow it wasn't good enough for her. I think that's why she did it – to punish me for being what she saw as weak. Is it a sign of weakness to love someone?'

'No,' Norman cut in, his voice sad. 'No, Woody, it's not a sign of weakness. In fact, I would go as far as to say it's a sign of great strength to be able to admit you love someone that much.'

Slater looked at Norman in surprise. Just a few hours ago he was ready to condemn Woods, and yet here he was empathising with him.

'So why do all her friends seem to think she's such an angel?' asked Slater.

'Ah yes,' said Woods, with a sad little smile. 'That was her magic trick, you see. She would do anything for anyone, but she never told any of them what she was really like. She'd sit for hours with one of her friends who was ill, for example, and then go and shag their husband on the way out. She must have had most of her friends' husbands, and just about all of my so-called "mates". They only got friendly with me so they could get a chance with her. And she was clever about when she did it too. I mean, no one thinks people go off shagging at lunchtime, do they? Diana realised that and took full advantage of it.'

'She'd had sex earlier on the day she was murdered,' said Slater.

'That will have been at lunchtime, then.'

'The day you caught her it was lunchtime, wasn't it?'

'Yeah,' said Woods, wistfully. 'I couldn't pretend it wasn't happening after that, could I? That was the day I decided enough was enough. I packed my bags and moved out that very same day.'

'So tell us what happened.'

'I had a wasted morning over at Jim's, waiting for this job to come in,' explained Woods. 'Then the customer called to say the job wasn't going to happen. I was well pissed off. Anyway, Jim sent me home to get some lunch. As soon as I got there, I knew something was up. She never comes home at lunchtime, but her car was outside. I thought maybe she had been taken ill, and come home, so I let myself in really quietly so I wouldn't disturb her.

'As soon as I was inside I could hear them. They were up in our bedroom, in our bed, grunting away like a pair of prize pigs. So I walked up the stairs, and still they didn't hear me. The bedroom door was wide open, and all I could see was this huge hairy arse humping away between her legs. So I just walked up behind them and I slapped his arse as hard as I could.'

He was smiling at the memory as he looked up at them.

'It didn't half make my bloody hand sting,' he said, laughing. 'But I tell you what, it hurt his arse a bloody sight more. He certainly squealed like a pig when I hit him. And he damned near shat himself when he realised her husband had come home and caught him in the act.'

'What happened then?' asked Norman.

'I threw his clothes out of the window. Out onto the drive. I told him I was going to see his wife and tell her to look for a big, hand-shaped bruise on his arse.'

'And did you?' asked Slater.

'Nah,' said Woods. 'I really thought about it, but then I thought better of it. Yeah, it would have been good to ruin his life, but somehow it didn't seem right to spoil her life, even if she is living a lie, you know what I mean?'

'But what did Diana do?' asked Norman.

'Oh, she went spare, of course. Told me it was all my fault. How I was a useless idiot, and how I had no right to tell her who she could shag. That's how she saw it you see. To her it was "just a shag". That's exactly what she told me. "What's the big deal," she said. "It's just a shag."'

'Jeez,' said Norman. 'And this is the angel we keep hearing about.'

'Yeah,' said Woods, sadly. 'And I had the misfortune to fall in love with her. Maybe she was right about me being a useless idiot. I certainly was where she was concerned.'

'So what's this guy's name?' asked Slater. 'I think we need to speak to him.'

'Bruce. Bruce Rossiter. He was Diana's boss.'

CHAPTER NINE

The offices of Rochester & Dorset (Marketing) Ltd. were housed in a huge, rambling old house on the outskirts of Tinton. The five-acre grounds included a swimming pool, two tennis courts, and more than an acre of woodland. There was even an old coach house which had been converted into a small gym, complete with changing rooms and showers.

Compared with the sparse facilities at Tinton nick, Slater and Norman agreed this was most definitely how the other half worked. Even their pool car managed to look totally out of place among the shiny, squeaky clean vehicles that filled the enormous car park off to one side.

'We're definitely working for the wrong side,' said Norman, from the passenger seat. 'This looks more like a luxury hotel than a workplace.'

'Marketing's not against the law,' said Slater.

'No. I didn't mean to suggest it was. It's our working conditions that are a crime.'

They climbed from the car and followed the direction indicated by an antique signpost inscribed with the word 'Reception'.

'What does this woman we're here to see do?' asked Norman.

'She's the HR director,' said Slater.

'What's that in old money?'

'It's Human Resources.'

'What was wrong with calling it Personnel?' grumbled Norman. 'Everyone knew what that meant. It was good enough for years and years.'

'I suppose someone in marketing decided they needed a trendier name,' said Slater. 'They have to justify their existence somehow.'

'This place sure looks pretty justified to me.'

A spotless path, bordered by neatly clipped, knee-high box hedges, wound its way towards the side of the building and a magnificent, ancient oak door. A small sign invited them to 'Please ring for attention'. Slater rang the bell and stared up into the CCTV camera that was focused upon them.

'Good morning, how can I help you?' asked a voice from a loudspeaker set in the wall.

'DS Slater and DS Norman from Tinton CID,' he replied, holding his warrant card up to the camera. 'We've an appointment to see Celia Rowntree.'

'Just push the door and come on through.'

The door buzzed and Slater pushed it open to reveal a corridor of polished wood topped with a very expensive-looking rug. At the end of the corridor they could see an open doorway leading into a large office.

'I feel like a pauper in the king's castle,' muttered Norman.

'It's a bit rich isn't it?' agreed Slater. 'And they say there's no money in marketing anymore.'

'They do? Well, it looks like they're wrong, whoever they are.'

They walked along the corridor and into the reception office. An enormous desk was set at an angle in one corner in such a way it seemed to stretch almost from one side of the room to the other. A small woman jumped up from behind the desk and beamed a warm, welcoming smile in their direction.

'Good morning, gentlemen,' she said. 'Mrs Rowntree will be with you in just a minute. Please take a seat.'

'Good morning, Millie Gibson,' said Slater, reading the badge on her lapel, and ignoring the invitation to sit down. 'We've come to ask some questions about Diana Woods. Did you know her?'

'Everybody here knew her,' said Millie. 'In her position she was sort of key to how the whole place worked.'

'She'll be missed, then?

'More by some than by others,' she replied, noncommittally.

'I thought everyone liked her, didn't they?'

But before Millie could say any more, her eyes darted to the side and her mouth clamped firmly closed. Slater followed her gaze over his shoulder where he saw a door swinging open as a tall, elegant, smartly dressed woman entered the room.

She glided smoothly across the floor, hand extended towards Slater.

'DS Slater?' she said as Slater took her hand. 'I'm Celia Rowntree. We spoke earlier.'

'Yes, of course,' said Slater. 'This is my colleague DS Norman.'

She shook Norman's hand and then took a step back.

'Won't you come through to my office?' she said. 'Millie will bring us some coffee, won't you, Millie?'

Millie nodded her assent.

'I take it you do both drink coffee?' she asked.

'Coffee will be just fine,' said Slater.

They followed Celia Rowntree through the door, up a short flight of stairs and then along yet another corridor until she pushed her way into her own office. Norman's mouth dropped open when he saw the size of the room.

'Wow,' he said. 'This is some office.'

'It's very grand, isn't it,' she said. 'It's one of the benefits of working in such a big old house. Of course, on the downside the running costs of a building like this are enormous.'

She led them across to an informal area where three armchairs had been arranged around a coffee table, and indicated where she wanted them to sit.

'I'm sure you can understand this is a very difficult time for all of us here,' she began. 'Diana was a very popular member of staff. She'll be sadly missed.'

'How long had she worked here?' asked Slater.

'She had been with us for almost five years. She actually started as my assistant, but it soon became clear she was wasted in here so we moved her over to one of the advertising teams. She soon impressed everyone with her all-round ability. Now she provides support to all the teams, travelling here, there, and everywhere.'

'That sounds like quite a meteoric rise in just five years,' said Norman. 'It's almost like someone's been pushing her along.'

'We're a company that likes to reward achievement with promotion.'

'So who did she work for after you?' asked Slater.

'She joined Bruce Rossiter's team. He's our number one man. In fact, she's still with him. Bruce and Diana head all our client meetings.'

'They sound like quite a couple,' said Norman. 'Do they travel together? Stay in the same hotel?'

'I'm not sure what exactly you're suggesting,' she said, bristling. 'But I can assure you this is a highly respected family company. We do not encourage our employees to be anything other than professional in their relationships.'

'Yeah, I'm sure you don't encourage it. But that doesn't mean it doesn't happen, does it?'

'I don't know what you mean. What's going on here? The poor woman's only been dead a couple of days and here you are dragging her name through the mud.'

'Diana's not just dead, Mrs Rowntree,' said Slater. 'She was murdered. Now you may think we're being insensitive, but if she was having an affair with her boss it could have a huge bearing on why she was murdered.'

She stared back at Slater.

'As I've already stated,' she said. 'We don't encourage that sort of behaviour.'

'Right. Of course you don't. So you're saying you didn't know Diana and Bruce were caught in a rather compromising situation by Diana's husband, and that as a result her husband subsequently left her?'

Celia Rowntree was beginning to look very uncomfortable.

'I'm sure that can't be right,' she said. 'That sort of behaviour would be regarded as gross misconduct within this company. Anyone guilty of such behaviour could lose their job.'

'Anyone?' asked Slater. 'Even your top marketing man?'

'It wouldn't matter who-'

'So why do you think Diana Woods and her husband split up, Mrs Rowntree?' asked Norman.

'That's none of my business,' she said. 'What happens in someone's private life is their business.'

'But surely such an event could affect a person's performance at work,' suggested Slater. 'Isn't it your job, as human resources director, to look out for the welfare of your employees?'

'Diana Woods was a very independent woman with a mind of her own, Sergeant. As I understand it her husband didn't walk out, he was kicked out. And she probably kicked him out because she outgrew him. Just as her star was rising, his was fading fast. He was a waster who was bringing her down and holding her back.'

'And she told you this?'

'Yes, she did. And after that conversation I concluded Diana's work performance was not going to be affected.'

'Did she also tell you her "waster" of a husband made over a hundred grand last year?' asked Norman.

Celia looked shocked, but said nothing.

'I didn't think so,' said Norman, smiling. 'And that kinda makes me wonder what else she forgot to mention.'

Celia Rowntree squirmed uncomfortably in her chair.

'So when was the last time you kicked someone out for illicit sex?' persisted Norman.

'I've been here nearly twenty years,' she said, haughtily. 'And in that time it's never been necessary to even mention it.'

There was an icy silence as she stared back at Norman.

'Is Mr Rossiter here?' asked Slater, breaking the silence. 'Because we need to ask him a few questions.'

'I'm afraid that won't be possible. He's up in London with clients today.'

'I did tell you I needed to speak to him when I called.' Slater felt exasperated.

'And I said I would see what I could do,' she replied. 'I didn't realise he was going to be out for the day when we spoke.'

'And you couldn't call me back when you found out?'

'I only found out shortly before you arrived. I'm sorry I should have checked earlier.'

'Come on,' Norman said to Slater, as he climbed to his feet. 'I think we're done here.'

He glared angrily at Celia Rowntree.

'But we're not finished yet,' he said to her. 'We'll be back tomorrow, and we'll keep on coming back until we speak to Rossiter. Perhaps you'd like to pass that message on, and tell him we're quite happy to call at his house and speak to him in front of his wife if he'd prefer it.'

'Don't get up,' Slater told her. 'We'll see ourselves out.'

They marched from the room and made their way back down the stairs and through the door into the reception area. Millie Gibson was just finishing a phone call.

'That was quick,' she said, as she put the phone down. 'I haven't even had time to make the coffee yet.'

'That's okay, don't worry,' said Norman. 'We didn't exactly feel the warm welcome up there that we got down here.'

'She can be a bit of a cow,' said Millie, with a grim smile. 'They don't call her Frosty Knickers for nothing.'

'You can make us coffee tomorrow, if you like,' Slater said. 'We'll be coming back to speak to Bruce Rossiter.'

'Oh. You mean God's gift to marketing. That'll be nice for you.' Millie pulled a face.

The phone buzzed on the desk in front of her. She picked up the handset and listened for a moment.

'Yes, Mrs Rowntree,' she said. 'They're just leaving. Right. I'll get on with it straight away.'

She put the phone down and grinned conspiratorially at the two detectives.

'Looks like I'm not supposed to be fraternising with you two,' she said. 'I just got my wrists slapped.'

'We're just going anyway,' said Slater. 'But before we do, maybe you can do us a favour.'

He fished a card from his pocket.

'This card has got my number on it. Perhaps you can ask around and see if anyone might know anything that would help us with our inquiry. I'm always on the end of that mobile number.'

She took the card, slipped it into her jacket pocket and winked at him.

'I'll see what I can do.'

'What's that woman's name again?' asked Norman as Slater started the car.

'Who? Frosty Knickers?' said Slater, chuckling.

'Yeah, that's her. There's no doubt she knew they were having an affair. I bet it's like one of those open secrets. Everyone knows about it but no one ever mentions it.'

Slater nodded his head.

'Yeah,' he agreed. 'But why doesn't anyone mention it? And how can the director of human resources so blatantly ignore something that's supposed to be company policy?'

'That Millie in reception,' continued Norman. 'I reckon she'll know everything that goes on in there, and she looks the sort who would know wrong from right. We need to speak to her.'

'She looks pretty sharp to me too. And I reckon you're right. I bet she doesn't miss a thing. But didn't you feel there was a bit of an atmosphere, like she was almost afraid to say too much? And it certainly looked like Frosty didn't want us talking to her.'

'And I thought Frosty herself was very careful what she said, didn't you?' said Norman. 'It was almost like she was reading from a prepared statement.'

'Yeah. She knew what we were going to ask. That more or less confirms our suspicions about Rossiter for me. All we've got to do now is prove he's involved.'

'Even then it doesn't prove he killed her.'

'No,' admitted Slater. 'But it can't just be a coincidence. It's got to be relevant to her murder, even if we don't yet know why.'

'Maybe Diana wasn't Rossiter's only bit on the side,' suggested Norman. 'Maybe Frosty melts in his arms too.'

'You think?' asked Slater, in surprise. 'I reckon she could fly close to the sun without melting.'

'It would explain why she's protecting him,' offered Norman.

'I got the feeling she despised him,' said Slater. 'Like maybe he makes a habit of shagging the female members of staff and she has to sort the mess out when it goes pear-shaped.'

'But if it's like that, why do they let him get away with it?'

'Now that, my dear Watson,' replied Slater, 'is the reason we're detectives.'

'Well, Holmes, in that case we'd better get on back to the office and do some of that there detecting. I'll start by going through the Rochester & Dorset website.'

When they got back to their incident room, Jane Jolly had a broad smile on her face.

'PC Jolly, you look like the cat who got the cream,' said Norman, following Slater in with coffee and cakes. 'Come on, out with it. What have you done?'

'Diana Woods' mobile phone records,' she said, holding aloft a fistful of papers.

'I fall at your feet, once again,' said Norman, bowing low.

'That's great!' Slater reached for the papers. 'Now perhaps we can make some progress.'

'While you're doing that I'm going to study this website,' said Norman. 'Jane, can you get onto Companies House and check out their profit and loss for the last three or four years?'

'They're just about breaking even,' announced Jolly, twenty minutes later. 'But I think that's because most of their profits go into maintaining their headquarters and paying over-inflated salaries.'

'As I suspected,' said Norman. 'So here's my theory. What if old

Brucie boy is the only one there who keeps bringing home the bacon? That receptionist called him "God's gift to marketing", and looking at this website it seems he's the one with all the big clients.

'If they're all on fancy salaries but rely on him to keep the company successful, I bet he's allowed to do what he likes, and no one dares to speak out against him for fear of the consequences. You know the sort of thing, speak out of turn and you find you're straight out the door with your arse on fire.'

'Yeah, that figures,' said Slater. 'The working conditions there are pretty fantastic, and if the salaries are big as well, who wouldn't be prepared to turn a blind eye to a little bit of sexual harassment?'

'Well, I bloody well wouldn't, for a start,' said Jolly, indignantly.

'Okay, let me re-phrase that. Let's call it a little bit of consensual sex between co-workers.'

'Yuck. That almost sounds worse.'

'But you know what I mean,' said Slater. 'These two people might be bonking each other senseless, but as long as they're not actually doing it in front of anyone else, and the work's still getting done, why complain and risk losing a nice fat salary? And besides, if one of those doing the bonking is the person who keeps the company afloat, would you really want to get him sacked? You'd all lose your jobs then.'

'Well, I wouldn't put up with it,' said Jolly. 'I'd leave.'

'But not everyone has your standards, Jane,' said Norman. 'You'd be surprised what people are prepared to not see in exchange for a good salary, especially these days when well-paid jobs are scarce.'

'Well, it all sounds very seedy to me. Surely the people at the top wouldn't allow it.'

'They can pretend it's not happening. Unless someone makes an official complaint, but we already know no one ever will. The company stance is quite simple – if it was happening, someone would make a complaint. No one has made a complaint, therefore it's not happening.'

'That's awful,' said Jolly.

'That's life.' Slater shrugged.

'But what if he made a pass at someone who wasn't interested?' persisted Jolly. 'If it was me I'd complain.'

'Yeah, but it would be your word against his,' said Norman. 'And which side do you think the company would take? The irreplaceable star player, or the backroom staff?'

'But that's just wrong.'

'Of course it's wrong. And I'm not trying to defend it. But to the company it's not about right or wrong, it's about profit. And in the case of this particular company, it's about survival.'

'I'm obviously not cut out for business,' said Jolly, gloomily.

'You're just fine where you are, Jane.' Norman patted her on the shoulder. 'You'd be wasted anywhere else.'

'What else have you learnt about them, Norm?' asked Slater.

'They were started back in the sixties by Jonathon Rochester and Ian Dorset. They quickly got a reputation for creating effective advertising campaigns and went from strength to strength through the seventies and eighties. They currently employ nearly fifty people and have some real big clients. Both the original partners are retired now, and although they maintain a large shareholding they no longer have anything to do with the day-to-day running.

'I reckon, back in their heyday, they would have been as moral as Jane would like them to be, but the people who run the business now are only interested in profit. Mind you, from what Jane just said about profits it looks like they have no idea how to make money. Their main asset seems to be Bruce Rossiter. Apparently he wins awards on a regular basis, and his clients love him.

'There's talk of a takeover by a US company, but assuming they just want to get their hands on the best clients, all they need to do is poach Rossiter.'

'What you've said certainly backs up your theory,' said Slater. 'A US takeover would be interesting. I've heard these US companies can be a bit narrow minded when it comes to that sort of behaviour. They might not be quite so keen on turning a blind eye.'

'So that's my news,' said Norman. 'What about those mobile phone records?'

'Very interesting,' said Slater, smiling. 'She obviously used her mobile a lot more than the landline. I've taken out all the numbers that only get called once in a while and concentrated on the more frequently called numbers. One of those numbers is Ian Woods.'

'Really?' asked Norman. 'Did she call him a lot?'

'She bombarded his mobile with calls and texts a few months back, around the time when he walked out. If those calls were begging him to come back, it would back up what he told us. The calls get less frequent as time goes on, but that makes sense too.'

'Okay. So who else is there?'

'There's a landline number I recognise as her parents, but apart from that it's all mobile numbers,' said Slater. 'I haven't had a chance to check them out yet, but there's one number she sends a hell of a lot of texts to, Monday to Friday, mostly during office hours, but rarely in the evenings or at weekends. I'm guessing that could be Rossiter's mobile number.'

'But they work together. Why would they need to text each other?' asked Jolly.

'They often work in a group, or with clients. Perhaps it was their way of being discreet. Let's suppose they wanted to arrange a little lunchtime nooky. Doing it by text means they can arrange whatever they want, in a roomful of people, without anyone else knowing what's going on.'

'Or maybe it was just for the thrill,' suggested Norman. 'A bit of secret dirty talk right under the clients' noses.'

'That sounds distinctly smutty, and extremely juvenile,' said Jolly.

'I'm sure you're right, but apparently that's what turns some people on. I guess there's no accounting for taste.'

'Or a complete lack of it,' finished Jolly.

'Whether it's poor taste, bad taste, or no taste,' said Slater, 'it's my guess that's the sort of thing that was going on.'

'Is there something wrong with me?' asked Jolly, sadly. 'Perhaps I'm just naive, but I seem to be the only one who finds this shocking. You two seem to think it's quite normal.'

'There's nothing wrong with you, Jane, and no, I don't think it's normal. It's just that these people live by a different moral code. You might inhabit the same planet, but your world isn't their world, if you see what I mean,' said Slater.

'Maybe I'm some sort of prude.'

'Somehow I doubt that,' said Norman then, almost as an afterthought, he added quietly, 'but I sincerely hope you never have to work vice.'

'D'you want to help me check out these numbers, Norm?' asked Slater. 'There's only six. Three each, it shouldn't take long.'

'Okay,' said Norman. 'Last one to finish buys the coffees.'

'Right, slowcoach,' said Norman to Slater, twenty minutes later. 'You're buying. I've got Laura Pettit, Amanda Hollis, and Arthur Hanning. Not very exciting I'm afraid. What have you got.'

'She certainly likes Bruce Rossiter,' replied Slater. 'So far I've got his work mobile number, and his personal mobile number. The one that's holding me up is this mystery number she sends all the texts to during the day. It seems to be an unregistered pay-as-you-go number.'

'I'll bet my salary that's Rossiter's secret smutty text number.' Norman grinned. 'You have one mobile number anyone can use and one only your girlfriend uses. You never know when a suspicious wife might decide to take a peep at your phone. I bet his wife doesn't even know this phone exists.'

'You seem to know a lot about all this,' said Jolly, suspiciously.

'You seem to forget I wasn't always a provincial copper, out in the sticks, where nothing happens. I spent most of my career up in the big City where you can't help but get exposed to all sorts of shit you'd rather not know about. This stuff is nothing, believe me.'

'Why don't you just ring it and see if he answers?' Jolly asked Slater.

'I'm sure he's not that stupid. Probably only one person knows that number, and she's dead. If we ring it now, he's not going to answer it.'

'Dave's right,' added Norman. 'The chances are he's already got rid of it, but if he hasn't, and we call him, we could spook him into dumping it.'

'So how do we prove it's his number?' asked Jolly.

'Like Norm says, he's probably already got rid of it,' said Slater. 'But if he hasn't I've got an idea that might just catch him out. It's a long shot, but it's worth a try.'

'Well, come on then, Baldrick.' Norman looked at him expectantly.
'Let's hear this cunning plan.'

'I hope it's better than one of his,' muttered Slater.

'Yeah, so do I.'

'Well, we're going to see him tomorrow, right,' began Slater. 'Now
I'm going to insist we see him at eleven o'clock...'

CHAPTER TEN

They arrived at Rochester & Dorset's offices shortly before eleven o'clock the next morning. Once again they were warmly greeted by Millie Gibson in reception, but then things quickly cooled down as Celia Rowntree, aka Frosty Knickers, who had obviously been waiting for them to arrive, appeared on the scene.

'Why, good morning, Mrs Rowntree,' said Slater. 'Anyone would think you were waiting for us.'

'I just happened to be passing.' Her lips were set in a tight line. 'I thought you might like to meet Mr Rossiter in my office.'

'Oh, did you?' replied Slater. 'I'm afraid you got that wrong. Perhaps you weren't listening when I spoke to you yesterday. I distinctly said we'd like to see him in his own office, and I also said we'd like to see Diana's desk. And I understand they shared an office...'

'Perhaps we could discuss this in my office,' she said, through gritted teeth.

Slater made a big deal out of looking at his watch.

'Okay,' he said. 'We can spare you five minutes before we meet Mr Rossiter, in his office.'

They followed her up the stairs, along the corridor, and through the door into her office.

'That'll be four minutes left,' said Slater, studying his watch as they entered her office.

'Are you naturally arrogant, and rude, or do you have to practise?'

'Oh he hasn't started yet,' interrupted Norman. 'And I can assure you I can be much worse. But let me ask you a question. Are you naturally obstructive to any police inquiry, or is it just this particular one you have a problem with? I wondered what you were up to yesterday, but it didn't take too much working out once I did a little research.'

She looked momentarily horrified.

'Oh, sorry,' he said. 'Were we supposed to be too stupid to check things out? Oh dear. Now who's guilty of being arrogant? The thing is we have been doing our homework, and it seems very clear to us that this whole company relies on Bruce Rossiter to keep it afloat. Ergo, he can get away with near enough anything he wants, and you're happy to mop up any mess he leaves in his wake, just as long as he keeps on bringing in the clients to fund your salary. And let's face it, you have to do something to justify that huge salary you earn, and that nice company car you drive.'

Celia Rowntree had gone very pale.

'Now,' said Slater. 'You can step back out of our way, and allow us to do our jobs, or we can get seriously rude and come back with a search warrant and a dozen clumsy coppers with big boots and bad attitudes.'

There was a distinct look of alarm on her face at this suggestion.

'This is police intimidation,' she said.

'Did you hear any intimidation, DS Norman?'

'I certainly did not,' said Norman. 'Perhaps Mrs Rowntree didn't hear you right.'

'This is a disgrace.'

'Obstructing a police inquiry is none too clever,' said Norman, smiling pleasantly at her. 'And I should remind you this a not some petty crime we're talking about; this is a murder inquiry.'

Slater looked at his watch again.

'Time's up,' he said. 'What's it going to be, Mrs Rowntree? The two of us in Bruce Rossiter's office? Or twelve pairs of big boots going through the entire building?'

. . .

'I think you'll find you've made the right choice,' said Slater as they followed her from her office, and along yet another corridor.

'Yeah,' said Norman. 'Some of those PCs are all thumbs. They're so clumsy.'

She swung round to face them, eyes blazing.

'Alright,' she snarled. 'You've got your way, and you've made your point. Can we just leave it at that?'

'Sure,' said Norman, with an amiable grin. 'Whatever you say, Mrs Rowntree.'

'You can rest assured I'll be having words with your superiors.'

'For doing our jobs?' Slater raised an eyebrow. 'Then you'll need DCI Murray. He's probably waiting for your call, right now.'

'Don't forget to mention how you've been obstructing our inquiry,' added Norman.

'He's in there.' She pointed to a door just ahead of them.

'That's very kind of you,' said Slater, but she was already stomping back down the corridor, and she definitely wasn't listening.

'I wonder what's upset her,' said Norman, grinning.

'Maybe it was something we said.'

'C'mon,' said Norman, reaching for the door. 'This is turning out to be much more fun than I thought. I could even get to like this place.'

'You think?' asked Slater, sceptically.

Norman paused for a moment and then turned back to Slater.

'No, you're right,' he said. 'I'm just getting carried away by the moment.'

He gave his colleague an exaggerated wink and then, with a theatrical flourish, he swung the door open and stepped into the office.

It was a large open-plan office with a cluster of six occupied desks at the far end and two desks much closer to the door. One of those desks was a normal size and was clearly empty, the other was enormous and obviously belonged to the king of this particular territory.

Rossiter was facing them as they entered, casually leaning back against the enormous desk, arms folded across his chest. Slater wasn't quite sure what he had been expecting, but the man who stood before them certainly wasn't it. He had pictured a handsome, roguish womaniser, but what he saw before him was a be-spectacled fifty-something who looked as if he would easily beat Norman at a weigh-in.

However, that's where any similarity between Norman and Rossiter ended. Whereas Norman looked worn out by life, and his suit appeared to have been stolen from the nearest clothes bank, Rossiter looked as though he didn't have a care in the world. By contrast, his suit had obviously been expensively tailored, and probably cost more than Norman had ever spent on clothes in his entire life.

Rossiter looked them both up and down, smiling – although Slater thought it bordered on a smirk. He oozed confidence and gave the impression he was used to dominating the proceedings, getting his own way, and enjoying the very best of everything life had to offer. The gold Rolex watch on his wrist glinted as the light caught it.

'Can I help you, gentlemen?' he purred. 'Only you look a little lost, and I'm expecting two detectives at any minute.'

'That's very good, Mr Rossiter,' said Norman. 'I'll try not to burst my sides laughing.'

He produced his warrant card and waved it vaguely at Rossiter.

'I'm DS Norman, and this is my colleague DS Slater, as you already know. You also know we're here because of the death of Diana Woods.'

'I'm not sure I can help you much,' said Rossiter. 'I was up in London addressing clients most of the day she died. By the time I got back she had already gone home.'

'What time was that?' asked Slater.

'About five-fifteen.' Rossiter yawned loudly.

'And what did you do after that?'

'I was tired, so I dumped all my paperwork and went home.'

'And you got home when?'

'About five-forty-five,' said Rossiter, irritated.

'Can anyone vouch for that?' asked Slater, enjoying the effect his questioning was having.

'Yes,' said Rossiter. 'My wife will. I think you'll find that's an alibi. I know what you're trying to do.'

'I'm just doing my job,' said Slater. 'Trying to establish facts. Didn't anyone ever tell you? It's what police officers do.'

The other occupants of the office were far enough away they would have had difficulty hearing the conversation, but it was obvious Rossiter was keeping his voice down to make sure.

'I understand you and Diana worked together quite closely,' said Norman. 'You must have got to know her quite well. I wonder if perhaps she had mentioned anything that might have had a bearing on why she died.'

'We had a very productive, efficient, and professional relationship,' said Rossiter, haughtily. 'Diana was probably the best PA I have ever had work for me. But we didn't become such a good team by sharing our private lives. If she had any problems, she didn't discuss them with me.'

'Oh,' said Norman, raising his voice. 'We must have got it wrong. We were under the impression you and Diana were very close.'

'Can you keep your voice down?' hissed Rossiter. 'There's no need for everyone else to hear this, is there?'

'We can make it quiet, or we can make it louder still if you want,' said Slater. 'It's up to you.'

Rossiter scowled at him and opened his mouth to speak, but Norman interrupted him.

'Well? Were you close?'

'I don't know where you got that idea from,' said Rossiter. 'It's preposterous.'

'Actually we got it from Diana's husband,' said Slater. 'He seems to think you caused his marriage to break up.'

'That had absolutely nothing to do with me. Like I said, my relationship with Diana was purely professional.'

'Really?' said Norman. 'Ian Woods seems to think it was you he caught in bed with Diana, and that was why he walked out on her.'

Rossiter's face had gone an interesting shade of red, and he didn't seem quite so confident all of a sudden.

'I can assure you that's rubbish,' he spluttered. 'I think you'll find Ian Woods is a dreamer, a fantasist who seems to think he can make money staying at home messing about on the internet. The man talks a lot of nonsense.'

'And you found this out how?' asked Slater. 'I thought you said you and Diana didn't discuss personal problems.'

'And I should tell you we find we are inclined to listen to what Ian Woods says,' added Norman. 'You might think he talks a load of rubbish, but he's actually making a living "messing about on the internet", as you call it.'

Rossiter looked genuinely surprised to hear this piece of news and seemed briefly confused. Diana had obviously convinced him her husband was a totally useless waste of space.

'Look. I know nothing about any of that, and I bet you don't have a single witness other than Woods, do you? So it's just his word against mine, and I deny it.'

'How many mobile phones do you own, Mr Rossiter?' asked Slater.

'I don't see how that's any of your business.'

'It's our business,' said Slater, firmly, 'because your secretary has been murdered, and her mobile phone records show several numbers she called and texted regularly. Obviously we need to figure out who these people are and eliminate them from our enquiries. I would have thought you'd want to help us, Mr Rossiter.'

'Of course,' said Rossiter, contritely. 'Of course I want to help. I have two mobile phones. One is provided, and paid for, by the company for company business, and I have a personal mobile that I pay for.'

'Do you mind if I see them?' asked Slater.

'If you must.' Rossiter sighed impatiently, but he made no effort to move.

'Maybe we need to start talking real loud,' Norman suggested to Slater. 'Perhaps that'll make him more co-operative.'

'Oh, for goodness sake,' snapped Rossiter. But he moved around his desk and produced two mobile phones from his top drawer. He tossed them onto the desk.

'Here, help yourself,' he said. 'I'm telling you now there's nothing to see. I have nothing to hide.'

Slater smiled a false smile at Rossiter.

'I'm glad to hear it,' he said. 'Thank you for your co-operation. Sir.'

He took the phones in turn and checked the contacts. He knew from Diana's phone records that he was unlikely to find anything incriminating, but he was curious to see if she was listed under his contacts.

'Thank you,' said Slater, returning the phones to the desk. 'You don't seem to have Diana Woods' number listed in either phone. Surely you must need to call her sometimes?'

'Her number was in my work phone,' said Rossiter. 'But it seemed a bit pointless now, so I removed it.'

'So you didn't have her number on your personal phone?' asked Norman.

'Why would I? I have already told you our relationship was purely business.'

Slater checked his watch. It was eleven thirteen. Two minutes to go.

'We haven't managed to find Diana's mobile phone,' he said. 'You wouldn't have any ideas would you, Mr Rossiter?'

'I seem to recall she took it everywhere with her,' said Rossiter. 'She was very secretive about it. She didn't want other people to get their hands on it.'

'Maybe she left it in her desk.'

'We didn't find it.'

Slater gave him a hard stare.

'We had to make sure there was no outstanding company business,' Rossiter said, holding his hands up. 'We didn't find any personal stuff.'

'Who's we?' asked Norman.

'Well, it was just me, actually,' said Rossiter.

'That's a bit of a menial task for you, isn't it?' said Slater.

'She worked closely with me. I was the best person to know what was what.'

Slater looked at his watch again. It was eleven fifteen. From somewhere close by, the muffled sound of a mobile phone ringing could be heard. He watched Rossiter, and saw his eyes dart to his desk and then back to them.

'Can you hear that sound, Norm?' asked Slater. 'Don't you think it sounds like a mobile phone ringing?'

'You're right,' agreed Norman. 'It sounds like it's coming from Mr Rossiter's desk.'

Slater looked hard at Rossiter.

'Aren't you going to answer that?'

'Answer what?' asked Rossiter, looking distinctly uncomfortable.

'You look a little peaky, Mr Rossiter,' said Norman, smiling. 'Are you sure you're okay?'

'That's not my phone,' said Rossiter. 'Look, both of mine are on my desk.'

'Well, it certainly sounds like it's coming from your desk,' said Slater. 'Maybe I should take a look.'

'That desk is private.'

'Well you answer it then. Only it's driving me mad, and it doesn't look like it's going to stop.'

'But-,' began Rossiter.

'Here,' interrupted Slater, marching around the desk. 'Let me help you.'

He pointed to the right hand bottom drawer.

'It's coming from in there,' he said. 'I can hear it clearly now I'm round this side.'

He reached for the drawer, expecting to be challenged, but Rossiter just stepped back out of the way.

'Someone must have put it there,' he spluttered.

'Well, it certainly can't have got there on its own,' said Norman.

Slater pulled on a pair of latex gloves and slid the drawer open. There, sat in a charging cradle, was a mobile phone.

'Well, well,' said Slater, lifting the phone from the drawer. 'Look at that. Whoever hid the phone here installed a charging kit, too.'

Slater pressed a key and raised the phone close to his ear.

'Hi, Jane,' he said. 'Right on time. Well done. Oh yes. Perfect.'

He ended the call and looked at the contact list.

'Only one contact number listed,' said Slater. 'Care to tell us whose it is, Mr Rossiter?'

'How would I know? I've never seen that before in my life,' mumbled Rossiter. 'Someone has put it there.'

'Yeah. You already told us that,' said Norman. 'And you reckon Ian Woods talks a load of rubbish. It's Diana's mobile number isn't it?'

'You can't prove that phone is mine. Someone's planted it there.'

'And why would anyone do that?' asked Norman.

'To make me look guilty, of course,' spluttered Rossiter.

'Well, it's done that alright,' said Slater.

'I think you have some explaining to do, Mr Rossiter,' said Norman. 'Don't you?'

'I've done nothing wrong.'

'My, my,' said Slater, looking at the sent and received text messages on the phone. 'Look at these messages. There's a lot of X-rated content here. They all seem to be from someone called D and they all seem to have been sent to someone called B. Now I reckon D is Diana Woods, but d'you know I just can't seem to think of anyone who has the initial B. Can you think of anyone, Norm?'

'I'm wracking my brain,' said Norman. 'How about you read one of those messages out? Maybe that will help me think.'

'Here you go,' said Slater. 'There's a word here that my mum says I should never use so I'll just use the first letter. I'm sure you'll know the one I mean. It goes like this: Hi B, Fancy a lunchtime "f"?'

He looked at Rossiter.

'Wow. Not much doubt about what that can mean, is there? Explicit and straight to the point. And it's signed D and there's two little xs. D'you think they're sort of kissey, kisseys?'

'It sounds like a real romantic lovey-dovey message to me,' agreed Norman. 'So yeah, I think you're right. Kissey, kisseys. It's gotta be.'

With a theatrical flourish he put his hands up.

'Oh my, wait a minute!' he said. 'I've just realised. Mr Rossiter's initial is B. How's that for a coincidence?'

'Now, you know I'm not one for coincidences,' said Slater. 'But, how about you, Mr Rossiter? Do you think it's a coincidence?'

'I've told you I don't know how that phone got there. And if you want to ask me any more questions you'll have to do it in front of my solicitor.'

'Are you volunteering, Mr Rossiter?' asked Slater.

'It'll be down at the station,' said Norman.

'Right.' Rossiter seemed to have restored some of his lost confidence. 'I'll phone him right now and we can make an appointment.'

'I'll take this phone in and get it checked for fingerprints,' said

Slater. 'That should tell us who planted it in your drawer. Of course we'll need to take your prints too, just for elimination purposes. I'm sure your solicitor will explain how that works if you have a problem.'

I t was no real surprise to find Rossiter's solicitor was also the company solicitor, a weary looking man called Brian Humphreys who didn't exactly seem to be overjoyed at the prospect of getting involved when he walked into the room two minutes later.

'What the bloody hell have you done this time?' he asked as he marched in, barely glancing at Slater and Norman.

'These two police officers would like me to answer some questions,' said Rossiter, hastily. 'I've told them I'm happy to do so, but that I wish you to be present.'

'I'm DS Norman, and this is DS Slater,' said Norman.

Humphreys acknowledged them before turning his attention to Rossiter.

'Well, I'm afraid I can't do it now, Bruce,' he said, testily. 'I'm not here solely at your beck and call. I do have other duties besides representing you. I'm busy right now. You'll have to wait.'

'Err, I was thinking maybe tomorrow morning at Tinton police station, Mr Humphreys,' said Norman.

'Oh. Right. I see,' said Humphreys, scowling at Rossiter. 'But I need some time with my client. If I have to represent his interests, I need to know what he's supposed to have done.'

'We're not saying he's done anything,' replied Norman. 'We're conducting an inquiry into the murder of Diana Woods, and we need Mr Rossiter to answer some questions to help us out, that's all.'

'Can't you do it here?'

'We tried that,' said Norman. 'But Mr Rossiter has indicated, quite clearly, that he prefers to come to the station. It's probably the right thing to do in the circumstances. It'll be more discreet. If you see what I mean.'

Humphreys looked distinctly annoyed at this development, and he glared at Rossiter.

'Mr Rossiter found this phone in his desk,' Slater told him, holding up the phone. 'He says it's not his, and that someone must have planted it there. We're going to take it with us to check it for fingerprints. Obviously we'll need Mr Rossiter to allow us to take his fingerprints for elimination purposes.'

Rossiter squirmed unhappily and turned to Humphreys.

'Of course,' said Humphreys, with a grimace that could have been a smirk. 'That won't be a problem.'

Humphreys seemed to be enjoying the fact that Rossiter was firmly on the back foot.

'Would ten o'clock tomorrow morning be convenient?' Slater asked the solicitor.

Rossiter opened his mouth to say something, but Humphreys beat him to it.

'It'll be a pleasure,' said Humphreys, grinning. 'I think we should all do our bit to help the police, and I'm sure Bruce agrees, don't you Bruce?'

But for once, Bruce Rossiter didn't seem to have anything to say.

CHAPTER ELEVEN

'I'm sorry,' said Ian Becks, calling up from the tiny forensics lab in the basement at Tinton police station. 'But this mobile phone's been wiped clean. There's not even a partial print anywhere on the case.'

'Bugger,' muttered Slater down the phone. 'I should have known the slimy sod would be too clever for that. I know it's his bloody phone, and I bet no one else has ever used it, but he's going to argue it's not his until he's blue in the face.'

'So, let him argue,' said Becks. 'Because, you see, he's not actually as clever as he thinks he is.'

'How do you mean?'

'You're saying he bought this as a pay-as-you-go phone, so he could communicate with his bit on the side without anyone ever knowing, right? So, it would figure he's the only person who's ever handled this phone.'

'Yes,' said Slater, slowly, trying to guess where this train of thought was going, but not succeeding. 'And?'

'Well, think about it,' said Becks. 'When you buy a mobile phone it comes in a box, but the battery and SIM card aren't usually already in the phone, are they? If he's the only one who knows about this phone, it means he must have put it together.'

'Come on Becksy, get to the point. What are you saying?' asked Slater in exasperation. 'Don't make me follow you all round the houses, mate. Just spit it out.'

'What do you think I'm saying? I've found some fingerprints on the inside of the case and on the battery.'

'You're kidding me. Really? Oh, Becksy, that's brilliant.'

'It's just what we do down here,' said Becks. 'You've got a problem? Just send it down here, and the real brains will solve it for you.'

Slater couldn't argue with that one. Well, not this time, anyway.

'He's coming in tomorrow morning,' said Slater. 'If we get him printed before we interview him, do you think you can give us a result while he's still here?'

'I don't see why not,' said Becks. 'It should be a piece of cake.'

Slater was relieved to find Ian Woods was still in town when he called him just before lunch. He seemed quite keen to come in and talk to them again, but then, as he said, he didn't really have anything else to do.

'Thanks for coming in again, Ian,' said Slater, a little later that afternoon. 'I wasn't sure if you'd still be in town.'

'Well, I was going to stay around for the funeral,' said Woods. 'But it's been made pretty clear I'm not going to be welcome. Besides which, they need a body, don't they?'

'Yes,' said Slater. 'I don't know for sure when it will be released. I heard they were considering a memorial service in the meantime.'

'I'd like to go, really I would,' said Woods. 'But her parents will only cause a scene and I wouldn't want that.'

'I'm sorry,' said Slater. 'Would it help if I talk to them?'

'Ha! I don't think so,' said Woods. 'They've made their minds up. You could come up with the real killer, but I don't think it would make any difference. Diana seems to have done a great job of discrediting me since I left, but I'm not surprised. Accepting responsibility for her actions never was her strong point.'

'You have good reason to feel bitter,' said Norman.

'But I don't, really. I'm more disappointed than bitter. And anyway, being bitter isn't going to change anything is it? What's done is done.'

His sad face showed he wasn't really quite as happy about the situation as he was trying to make out, but then he seemed to snap out of it and perk up.

'Anyway, I'm making a new start down in Wales, so it really doesn't matter what anyone up here thinks. I know the truth, and I don't have any problem sleeping at night.'

He offered them a brief smile.

'Anyway, what can I do for you?' he asked.

'When we spoke to her parents, we got the feeling Diana's mother wasn't quite so sure Diana was a saint,' replied Slater. 'Her father was adamant, but we felt your mother-in-law wasn't convinced.'

'That's because she knew about the first affair. No one told the old man, so he's totally unaware, but she knew.'

'How did she react?' asked Norman.

'She never actually said anything to me. But I overheard her telling Diana how disappointed she was, and how she thought I didn't deserve to have that happen. Diana blamed it on me being at work all the time, you see. But like her mum said, I was only doing that to pay for all the improvements to the house. How else could we afford to get it all done as quickly as Diana wanted?'

'So who was the guy involved in this earlier affair?' asked Norman.

'There was more than one,' said Woods. 'Diana thought nothing of moving on if a better offer came along.'

'A better offer?' asked Norman.

'The first guy flattered his way into her knickers and plied her with free gin and tonics. He was young and worked behind a bar, see. Then this older guy started hitting on her, and she quickly discovered older men have money. The young barman couldn't compete with that, so he was ditched and she got used to having nice clothes bought for her. I was so thick I didn't realise she was spending his money on those things. I even told her to stop spending all our money on that stuff.'

'So you knew?' asked Slater.

'You'd have thought, wouldn't you?' Woods sighed and shook his head. 'But I trusted her, you see, and it wasn't as if she was going out at night to see these blokes. She realised very early on that no one suspects a lunchtime affair. She used to rush out of work at lunchtime, run around the corner and jump into the old guy's car. Five minutes later they'd be stripping off in his bedroom, then he'd drop her back at work when they'd finished. It was great for him. He was nearly forty and she was barely twenty. And she was beautiful.'

'Jeez,' said Norman. 'She was quite a piece of work.'

'Not just deceitful, but cunning, too,' agreed Woods.

'Can you name any of these guys?'

'Why? What difference will it make now?'

'It will help us to corroborate your story,' explained Slater. 'And it will confirm the picture we're building of Diana. We're going to need it because all her friends are going to stand up in court and say she was nothing like that. And they will probably also say that if she was like that it's because of the mental torture and physical abuse you subjected her to.'

'But I never did,' said Woods, emphatically.

'Easy, Woody, easy,' soothed Norman. 'We're not accusing you, this is what we're hearing from them.'

'If I was so evil, why did she write to me telling me how much she missed what she called the "mental support" I used to give her? And why did she keep asking me to come back?'

'Do you still have those letters?' asked Slater.

'Yeah, I think so,' said Woods. 'She didn't know where I was living, but she knew Jim Brennan was in touch with me so she asked him to send them on to me.'

'D'you think we could see them?'

'If I've still got them they'll be back at home. But I'm sure I know where they are.'

'Why did you keep them?' asked Norman.

'I don't know.' Woods sighed heavily. 'I suppose because they proved that, despite everything, I had actually meant something to her.'

'Maybe you should show them to Diana's father,' said Slater.

'He'd probably say I'd written them,' said Woods. 'It would be a waste of time.'

'It would be really useful if you could let us have them,' said Norman.

'I'm going back tomorrow. I'm not welcome around here, so there's not much point in hanging around. I'll post them to you.'

'Take then down to your local station,' Norman told him. 'They'll make sure they get to us.'

'And if you can give us those names,' asked Slater.

'Sure,' said Woods. 'I'll write them down for you, but I don't know if they still live around here.'

'I'm sure we'll be able to find them,' said Slater.

It was seven-thirty. Slater was slouching in an armchair, trying to enjoy a can of lager, as he flicked through the TV channels trying to find something he actually wanted to watch. The best bet so far seemed to be a match from a pre-season friendly football tournament, but the fact it was a friendly match suggested it would be a passionless affair and he was clinging to the vain hope that surely there must be something better. He wondered what was the point in paying to have over a hundred channels to choose from if they were all showing crap?

This had become his habit over the last three months, and he found he was becoming increasingly apathetic about life outside of work. He knew exactly why he felt that way, and when it had started, yet he seemed powerless to snap out of it.

It had begun about a week after he had split from his girlfriend Cindy. When he had first got to know her, he had actually thought he might have found the woman he had been looking for all his life. They had quickly become close, and he had been spending more and more of his time living at her house. But Cindy found it increasingly difficult to share Slater with the demands of his job, and they'd decided to take a break while she decided what it was she really wanted.

For the first week after she had left he had felt a sort of guilty relief, but then he had been so busy he had no time to think about what he'd lost. Now, however, he'd had plenty of time to think about it and he was keenly aware of the big empty space that seemed to fill his life away from work.

The agony was made worse for him by Cindy's decision to fulfil an ambition and go travelling. She was keeping in touch with the occasional email. The one waiting for him when he got home announced her arrival in Thailand, but there was no suggestion she would be coming home anytime soon.

It probably didn't help that he was spending so much time in her house. He had offered to keep an eye on it while she was away, but he found he was spending more and more time there, as if being there somehow made him nearer to her. He was there now, flicking through her TV channels.

He was aware that this was rather sad and pathetic behaviour, but such was his apathy, he just didn't care about that. He wondered if perhaps he should take some leave and go and find her. But then, suppose she didn't want him to find her. He'd never felt like this about anyone before, and he was struggling to cope with the possibility of losing her for good. How did other people cope? How did you stop thinking about her?

Then his mobile phone began to ring. He tossed the remote control onto the settee and reached for the phone. He squinted at the incoming number but it wasn't one he recognised, not that it mattered, he had to answer it just in case it was something important.

'It's Millie Gibson. From Rochester and Dorset. You said I could call.'

'That's right, I did,' said Slater, sitting up much straighter. 'What can I do for you?'

'It's more what I might be able to do for you,' she said mysteriously. 'Only I've been thinking about what you said the other day. About if anyone had any information?'

'Oh, right. And does someone have some information?'

'We all know what's been going on between Diana and old Porky Rossiter. Diana thought no one knew what they were up to, but we'd all have to be blind and stupid. The thing is, I don't think anyone's brave enough to come forward and risk their job.'

'Oh, that's a pity.'

'Oh it's alright,' said Millie. 'I heard today I've got another job. So I don't care. They can't sack me now, can they?'

'So what do you want to tell me?'

'It might be better if you were to come to my house. This could take quite a while. There's a lot to tell.'

'Okay. Whatever suits you. When do you want us to come?'

'You can come now, if you want to.'

'I'll pick up my colleague DS Norman, on the way,' said Slater. 'Now what's your address?'

'This had better be good,' said Norman, five minutes later, as he climbed into Slater's car. 'I'd just got settled with a couple of cans of lager.'

'Oh, it's good,' said Slater. 'Millie Gibson wants to spill the beans about Diana and Rossiter.'

'In that case, the lager can wait. Let's go!'

After a moment, he spoke again.

'You were at Cindy's again, weren't you?' he asked.

Slater couldn't think what to say. He was embarrassed that his pining was so obvious.

'I know you were, so don't deny it,' said Norman. 'You couldn't have got from your own house to my flat that quickly.'

'Okay,' said Slater, with a heavy sigh. 'It's a fair cop. I was just checking the post and making sure everything's okay.'

'Are you sure you don't keep going round there just to feel a little closer to her?'

'What? No, of course not.'

'I know it's hard,' said Norman. 'But you've got to be patient. You have to give her as much time as she needs. In the meantime, you have to stay positive about the outcome.'

'I am,' said Slater.

'Yeah, right. Anyone can say the words, but if you don't believe them...'

'I just didn't realise it was going to be so bloody hard,' said Slater.

'I know. I've been there. At least you still have hope.'

'I'm sorry. I don't mean to-.'

'Hey. I asked the question, didn't I?' interrupted Norman.

'Well, yeah, but even so.' Slater felt guilty; he knew how much Norman missed his wife, and she had assured him she was never coming back.

'It's because I know how hard it is, that I worry about you,' said Norman. 'But I can promise you, sitting there allowing yourself to get depressed doesn't help. Trust me, it's easy to get down, but it's damned hard to get back up again. You can't just flick a switch and turn your happiness back on.'

'That's easy to say,' said Slater.

'It's the truth. If Cindy came back tomorrow, and found you like that, she'd think she was making a big mistake. How's that going to help?'

Slater thought about what Norman had said. When you thought about it, it made a lot of sense.

'You know,' he said, with a wry smile, 'for an old "has been", you talk a lot of sense.'

'The thing about an old "has been" like me,' said Norman, smiling, 'is my experience. You name it, I've probably been there, done it, and got the tee shirt. Therefore, I know what works and what doesn't, and I can offer sound advice.'

They were parked outside Millie Gibson's house now.

'You're right,' said Slater. 'I need to stay positive.'

'It's difficult to get down when you're positive about things,' said Norman. 'It works for me, and it'll work for you, just as long as you believe it.'

'Getting this new job is such a relief,' said Millie Gibson, once they were all settled in her lounge. 'I enjoyed working for Rochester's for the first month, then it all started to go sour.'

'How come?' asked Norman. 'You seemed pretty happy to us?'

'I put on a brave face. Most of the girls in that place are the same. The problem is the money's so good no one can afford to leave.'

'But why would they want to?' asked Slater.

'Sexual harassment,' she said, bluntly. 'Celia Rowntree knows it goes on – in fact he's probably tried it on with her – but she won't do anything about it, because that revolting man brings in all the money. Without him the company would sink like a stone.'

'You mean Rossiter, right?' asked Norman.

'Porky the Pig, the girls call him. He thinks we're some sort of harem and he can have anyone he chooses. He's propositioned every girl who works there.'

'All of them?' asked Slater, appalled.

'Oh yes. Married, single, old or young. He doesn't care. He seems to think he's God's gift to women and we'd all want to. Of course most of the girls think he's disgusting. But then there was Diana. I suppose in a way she did all of us a favour. At least once she said yes he stopped hassling the rest of us.'

'So he's a sex pest,' said Norman.

'He just wants no strings sex,' Millie said. 'Or, at least that's what he's told us all. The problem is he also wants to be able to cop a feel anytime he's passing. How she put up with it I just don't know. Just thinking about those fat, podgy fingers groping through your under-wear, well, it's just horrible.'

She shivered.

'So he's actually been groping her in the office?' asked Slater.

'Oh yes. They think no one can see what they're up to, but it's a hand up her skirt here, a grope of her boobs there. Honestly it's like watching two teenagers who've just discovered sex for the first time. But he's in his fifties, and she was well into her forties.'

'So why hasn't anyone ever complained about him?' asked Norman.

'Apparently someone did, once.' She sighed. 'They were escorted off the premises and told never to come back. No one can criticise the company's top asset, you see. And, of course, for the last three years he's also had Diana by his side, telling everyone what a paragon of virtue he is.'

'Now let me get this straight. You're saying he's made the same offer to everyone?' asked Slater.

'Oh yes,' Millie said. 'He worked his way through every woman in the company, having his revolting offer turned down, and then he found Diana. She was the only one who was willing. Apparently he approached her when a group of them were on some sort of business trip up in London. They stayed in some fancy hotel. He made his offer to Diana in the bar on the first night. They were there for three nights in all. Rumour has it Rossiter didn't sleep in his own room once. I'm told you could hear him grunting from his efforts all night long.'

'So what's the attraction?' asked Norman.

'Well, it's obviously not physical, is it? Sex in exchange for presents, I believe. It's been suggested he liked buying underwear for her, as long as he could put his hand up her skirt and see what it felt like. Every time he goes abroad he makes sure she gets a bottle of her favourite perfume, or a bottle of expensive gin, anything like that.'

'He's more or less buying it, then?' Slater asked.

'There's no "more or less" about it.' She sniffed, primly.

'Aren't you worried about any repercussions from talking to us?' asked Norman.

'Not now I'm leaving. Anyway, someone has to stick up for that poor husband of hers. Have you heard some of the stuff that's been said about him since he left her? And all because she wants to portray herself as some sort of innocent victim. It's disgusting.'

'But all her family and friends and neighbours make her out to be some sort of saint,' said Slater.

'Oscar-winning actress, more like,' Millie replied.

'Now that rings a bell,' said Norman.

'Some people see things as they really are and some people see things how they want to see them. Diana knew that and she played people accordingly.'

'But how could she be conducting an affair without anyone noticing?' asked Slater. 'The neighbours claim she never had men calling on her, and she hardly ever went out without her husband.'

'How many of her neighbours are home at lunchtime? And twice a week Porky has an empty house at lunchtime. And they're not secretive about it. They jump in his car together and off they go. They quite often come back late as well. Everyone despised Diana for it, but no one had the guts to say anything out in the open.'

'You really didn't like Diana, did you?' asked Slater.

'I despised her for behaving like some cheap tart,' said Millie. 'We all did, men as well as women.'

'What about Rossiter's wife?' asked Norman. 'Does she know what he's like?'

'Who, Angela? I'm not sure if she really doesn't know, or if she's one of those women who keeps pretending it's not happening as long as the money keeps pouring in.'

'What do you think will happen now Diana's gone?' he asked.

'I suppose he'll try to find someone else who's willing, or failing that he'll employ someone who's willing.'

'What if his wife had walked in, one lunchtime, like Woody did?'

'I think she would take him to the cleaners,' said Millie. 'She might be prepared to trade her lifestyle for his philandering, but trust me, if she was to catch him doing it right under her nose I think she'd ruin him.'

'What do you think would happen if we showed up at his house asking questions about his relationship with Diana?' asked Slater.

'I just told you,' she said, with an evil grin. 'She would take him apart, bit by bit.'

'I'm really tempted to go round Rossiter's house right now,' said Norman, as they drove away from Millie Gibson's house. 'Just to suggest he might have had a relationship with Diana in front of his wife, and then watch what happens.'

'Yeah, I know what you mean,' said Slater. 'I thought the guy was a creep when we met him, but he's something else, isn't he?'

'Yeah, he certainly is. But does that make him a murder suspect? I mean they were consenting adults. Why would he want to do away with his sex partner?'

'Who knows. Maybe she wanted to become more than just a bit on the side. Perhaps she thought she could become Mrs Porky but he had other ideas.'

'It might be worth slipping that into the conversation when we talk to him tomorrow,' Norman said. 'Sort of shake the tree and see what falls out.'

CHAPTER TWELVE

When Bruce Rossiter arrived at Tinton police station next morning, he had the appearance of a man who hadn't slept the previous night. By contrast, Brian Humphreys looked as bright as a button.

The first indignity for Rossiter was having his fingerprints taken. Humphreys seemed to be positively enjoying Rossiter's discomfort, though. Slater and Norman were watching through the observation window of the interview room.

'I got the feeling this isn't the first time he's had to represent Bruce Rossiter,' said Slater, as Humphreys stood back with his arms folded, a grin playing around his lips. 'Maybe getting dragged into a murder inquiry is a step too far for him and he's had enough.'

They watched as Ian Becks took Rossiter through the procedure.

'Rossiter doesn't seem to be as bothered about having his prints taken as I'd expected,' said Slater.

'That's probably because he knows he's wiped that phone clean. Wait until you tell him we found prints on the inside. That should get a reaction.'

They waited until Ian Becks had finished before they entered the interview room.

'Did you get your fingerprints taken?' asked Norman.

'You know damned well I did,' snorted Rossiter.

'Well, you'll be pleased to know it hasn't been a waste of time,' said Slater, smiling. 'Because we found some fingerprints inside the phone on the battery. That should tell us who put the phone together in the first place.'

He was watching Rossiter's face as he spoke, convinced he was going to get a good reaction, but Rossiter didn't bat an eyelid.

'Well, I've already told you it wasn't me,' said Rossiter. 'And my fingerprints will prove it.'

'You're very confident about that,' said Norman, and Slater could tell he was surprised. He was too.

'Yes, because I know I'm right,' said Rossiter, smiling calmly at them.

And at that moment, Slater began to think that maybe he wasn't bluffing. But surely he must have been lying about the phone. There was no way it had been planted. It had to be his phone. Didn't it?

'We'll have confirmation of that soon enough,' said Norman. 'Our little forensics team are very good. They'll be working on it right now. In the meantime, we have some questions we'd like you to answer.'

'Yes,' said Rossiter, impatiently. 'That's why I'm here when I should be at work. Now, can we get on with it, please?'

'When we spoke yesterday, we asked you if you had an intimate relationship with Diana Woods-'

'Ah. Yes,' said Rossiter. 'I may not have been very honest when I gave my answer.'

'You may not have been very honest,' echoed Slater. 'Does that mean you lied to us?'

'I prefer to call it being economical with the truth. Now I've spoken to my solicitor I can see that was the wrong thing to do.'

'So you did lie to us,' said Norman. 'So how about you tell us the truth now.'

'The thing is my wife mustn't get to hear about this. I'm sure you can see this would be very embarrassing for me if it did get out. You will make sure she doesn't hear about it, won't you?'

'We can't guarantee that, Mr Rossiter,' said Norman. 'It may be that we'll need to speak to your wife during our enquiries.'

'But why would you need to do that?'

'Maybe we won't need to,' said Slater. 'We can't say for sure. We just follow the evidence where it leads and question people accordingly.'

'But my wife isn't involved in Diana's death. That's an absurd idea,' said Rossiter.

'It doesn't sound so crazy if she knows about your affair,' said Norman.

'But she doesn't. And it was hardly an affair. It was more of a flirtation that went a bit too far.'

Norman gave a huge, weary sigh.

'I thought you were going to tell us the truth, Mr Rossiter. 'From what we've discovered, your "flirtation" has been going on for almost three years. It started in a hotel on a business trip, and it's been going on ever since. Now, that's a bit more than a flirtation, wouldn't you agree?'

Rossiter paled slightly.

'Every Tuesday and Friday lunchtime,' said Slater. 'At your house when your wife's at work.'

'There's no law against two friends having lunch together.' Rossiter's eyes darted around the room.

'That's very true,' said Norman. 'There's also no law against two consenting adults having sex every Tuesday and Friday lunchtime.'

Rossiter looked at Humphrey pleadingly, but the solicitor sat staring straight ahead, his lips curled slightly.

'We're not here to judge your morals, Mr Rossiter,' said Norman. 'We're just here to try and get to the truth of what happened to Diana Woods. The fact you were conducting a long standing affair with her could be very significant. Your lies are preventing us from getting a clear picture of her life.'

'You're obstructing a police inquiry,' added Slater. 'I'm sure Mr Humphreys can explain the consequences.'

'Alright! Yes we were having an affair. But we were discreet, and weren't doing anyone any harm.'

'Discreet?' said Slater. 'Every employee at Rochester & Dorset knew what you were up to. They used to watch you getting into your car together. They knew where you were going and what you were doing. How the hell is that discreet?'

'That's rubbish.'

'Is it, Mr Humphreys?' Norman asked the solicitor.

'Everyone knew,' was all he said.

'Ian Woods knew as well,' said Slater.

'He's just a waster,' said Rossiter, bitterly. 'How Diana ever got tied up with him I'll never know. He's been bringing her down for years.'

'Or perhaps it was her behaviour with men like you that was bringing him down for years.'

'She has supported him for years,' said Rossiter. 'What sort of man is that?'

'Maybe it's a broken one,' said Slater. 'But if he was such a bad person, why did she want him to come back to her after he left. It doesn't quite add up, does it?'

'Did he tell you that? That's just another one of his fantasies I'm afraid.'

'Like the fantasy about him earning a good living "messing about on the internet"?'

'I know for sure she didn't want him back,' insisted Rossiter.

'You do?' said Norman. 'And why was that? Did she have plans for her future?'

'What do you mean "plans"?'

'Well, maybe she wanted to turn your relationship into something more permanent,' said Norman. 'Perhaps she was planning on taking your wife's place.'

'No way,' said Rossiter. 'She knew right from day one that was never going to be an option. I just wanted a partner for sex, nothing more.'

'But perhaps she didn't see it like that anymore. Was she leaning on you? Trying to pressure you to get rid of your wife? Maybe she had threatened to tell your wife about your affair. I mean that would put you in a difficult position, wouldn't it? You might even feel you had to do something about it'

'Wait a minute. What are you suggesting?' asked Rossiter. 'You think I killed Diana? But that's crazy. She didn't threaten me with anything. We were both quite happy as we were.'

'Are you sure about that?' asked Slater.

'Yes, I am. Quite sure.'

'And are you quite sure your wife doesn't know about you and Diana?' asked Norman.

'What? Now you think my wife killed her? Rossiter shook his head vigorously. 'Now that's just a crazy idea. My wife couldn't do anything like that. She liked Diana. She thought Diana was wonderful, the best PA I had ever had.'

'In which case the betrayal would hurt even more,' said Norman.

'I'm telling you she doesn't know, and I don't want you telling her.'

'It might be difficult for us not to talk to your wife now, Mr Rossiter,' said Slater. 'In view of the circumstances she would have to be considered a possible suspect.'

'Can you account for your movements on the day Diana died?' asked Norman. 'We know you were up in London, but what time did you get back to Tinton?'

'I got back to the office just after five, and then I went home.'

'Can anyone confirm you were up in London all day?' asked Slater.

'I think you'll find there are about thirty witnesses who were with me from ten in the morning right through until we wound things up at around three,' said Rossiter.

'So you weren't in Tinton at lunchtime?'

'I just said I was in London, didn't I?'

'Diana had sex with someone at lunchtime on the day she died,' said Norman. 'Do you have any idea who that might have been?'

'None at all,' said Rossiter. 'But if she was with someone else it rather proves she wasn't trying to get closer to me, doesn't it?'

'When it comes to people like you and Diana, I think the only thing we can say it proves is that she was having sex with someone else that day,' said Slater. 'Normal rules don't apply, do they?'

'You can think whatever you like about my morals,' said Rossiter. 'The fact is I haven't broken any laws, have I?'

'We're not sure about that yet,' said Norman.

There was a knock on the door. Slater got up and went across to answer it. He stuck his head out and there was a short, hissed conversation, before he came back across to the desk with a sheet of paper which he placed in front of Norman. A frown spread across Norman's face as he studied the sheet of paper. Finally, he looked up at Rossiter.

'You'll be pleased to know the fingerprints we found inside the mobile phone aren't yours,' he said.

'I think you'll find I told you that yesterday.' Rossiter smiled broadly, his confidence and smugness now evidently fully restored. 'I don't know how that phone got into my desk.'

'Yeah, right,' said Slater. 'Of course you don't.'

'I think we're done here, don't you? Come on, Brian. I think I've answered enough questions for one day.'

'You said it would be a piece of cake,' Slater complained down the phone, ten minutes later.

'And I was right,' argued Becks. 'It was a piece of cake. I got you a result in less than twenty minutes.'

'Yeah, but you proved it wasn't him.'

'That's not my fault. I can't prove they're his prints when they aren't, can I? That's the thing about fingerprints. They're unique, or didn't they teach you that at detective school?'

'But we've had to let the bugger go now,' said Slater.

'Well don't blame me, mate. I can only report what I find, and in this case I find the fingerprints don't match. End of story.'

'I was sure they were going to be his fingerprints, If they're not his, who the bloody hell do they belong to?'

'We're running them through the database now,' said Becks, testily. 'That's the best we can do.'

'Okay Ian, I know it's not your fault,' said Slater, trying to pour some oil on the waters he had just stirred up. 'Let me know if you find anything.'

Slater felt like throwing the phone through the window in frustration, but he resisted the urge and placed it carefully back on its cradle.

'It's no good bollocking him,' said Norman. 'It's not his fault.'

'Yeah, I know,' Slater said, sighing. 'I was just so sure.'

'So we need to think again,' said Norman.

'And who the hell was she bonking that lunchtime if it wasn't Rossiter?' asked Slater.

'Now there's a good question.' Norman looked thoughtful. 'She certainly seems to have liked sharing it around. It could have been anyone. Did she have anyone working on her house, or her garden?'

'There wasn't any sign of that,' said Slater.

'Can I offer a suggestion?' asked Jane Jolly. 'Only I'm sitting here listening to you two talking doom and gloom, and I think maybe you're missing something.'

'Go on,' said Slater. 'What's your suggestion?'

'Now I don't know anything about having affairs,' she began. 'But I do know something about men, and I know if I wanted my husband to get a mobile phone so I could contact him secretly I would probably have to wait a very long time for him to get around to doing it.'

'No offence, Jane, but I don't think you can compare your husband to an animal like Rossiter.'

'Certainly not in terms of his morals, but most women will agree – if you want a man to do something it's often best to do it yourself.'

Slater wasn't sure what she was getting that.

'What I mean is, I would have to buy the phone myself,' she said, slowly.

'Ah. I see what you're saying,' said Slater. 'You think Diana would have got the phone for Rossiter.'

'She was his PA. She would have been used to doing stuff for him. I bet she bought the phone and set it up for him. All he had to do was use it.'

Slater grabbed his phone and dialled Ian Becks' number.

'Hi, Ian? Can you check if those prints inside the phone belong to Diana Woods?'

'Great minds think alike,' said Becks. 'I've just realised they're a woman's prints. I was just going to check hers first.'

'Now we're getting somewhere,' said Slater, as he put the phone down. 'Ian reckons they're a woman's prints. It has to be Diana.'

'Well it helps in one way,' said Norman. 'But then you have to remember she would have had access to Rossiter's desk, so in a way it strengthens his argument that he didn't know the phone was there. He'll say she put it there and he knew nothing about it.'

'Yeah, but what about those texts from D to B? If we can manage to prove they're from her to him, we've got him.'

'Is that all we need to do?' asked Norman. 'Oh, great. It's a piece of cake, then.'

'D'you think there's any doubt?'

'No, of course not. There's no doubt the texts are from Diana to him, I just don't think it's going to be so easy to prove it without her phone.'

'I do keep ringing it,' said Jolly. 'I've set up my computer to call it at random intervals. But whoever took it has either destroyed it, or they're clever enough to keep it switched off.'

'Keep on trying with that,' said Slater. 'I'm beginning to think it's been destroyed, but you never know.'

'Rossiter travels a lot, doesn't he?' Jolly said, suddenly. 'You could try seeing if the text messages tie up with any events in his diary.'

'He's not going to help us out by giving us his diary,' said Norman. 'We'll need to get a warrant.'

'Before we do that, we could try asking our pet receptionist,' said Slater. 'Maybe she can help.'

'Perhaps. And how about we track down some of the other men Diane Woods has been "seeing" at lunchtimes?'

CHAPTER THIRTEEN

'Mr Stephen Grey? My name's DS Slater from Tinton CID, and this is my colleague DS Norman.'

The man was obviously startled to find two detectives on his doorstep asking awkward questions about his past. A small boy appeared at his side, but was quickly ushered back inside.

'Go and help mummy,' said Stephen Grey, steering the little boy back inside. 'I'll be there in a minute.'

Once the boy had gone back inside he pulled the door closed behind him.

'What's this all about? I haven't seen Diana Woods for years.'

'As I said when I called,' said Slater, 'we're investigating Diana Woods' murder. I understand you were in a relationship with her.'

'Yes, I was,' said Grey. 'But that was a mistake I made over fifteen years ago. I haven't spoken to her since, and I don't even know where she lives now.'

'But you did have an affair with her?' asked Norman.

'Yes, but keep your voice down, can't you? That was before I met my wife and she doesn't know about it. I'd like to keep it that way, if you don't mind.'

'Did you know Mr Woods?' asked Slater.

'Yes. He used to drink in the pub where I worked.'

'Did you get on with him?' asked Norman.

'He'd buy me a drink now and then,' said Grey. 'I suppose he was alright.'

'And when did you conduct this affair?' asked Slater.

'What? What do you mean "when"?'

'Well, was it at night, in the morning, or when?'

'Usually it was lunchtime,' said Grey. 'She used to reckon no one would ever guess she'd be going like a train all lunchtime and then back at work afterwards. And she was right.'

'And you didn't have a problem facing Ian Woods and accepting a drink from him while this was going on?' asked Norman.

'Look, Woody was alright, but he was stupid. At first I used to worry he'd find out, but he thought the sun shone out of her backside. He was so dazzled by it he couldn't see what was going on right under his nose. Poor sap.'

'Maybe he just made the mistake of trusting people,' said Norman. 'Like his mates.'

'Oh, for sure. And the biggest mistake of all was trusting his wife. Like I said, poor sap. They were queuing up to give her one and he still couldn't see it.'

'What's going on?' called a woman's voice from behind Grey, whose face suddenly turned ashen.

A small, aggressive-looking woman pulled the door open and elbowed her way in alongside him.

'Who are these men?' she asked, looking hard at Slater and Norman.

'We're police officers,' said Norman.

'What do you want?'

'We're just following up some enquiries about an accident,' said Norman, thinking fast. 'We were told Mr Grey might have seen it, but it seems we were misinformed.'

Grey let out an audible sigh of relief.

'Yes. Thank you for your time, Mr Grey,' said Slater. 'Sorry to have disturbed you. We'll be off now.'

They turned and headed for their car.

'That was very noble of you, getting him out of that hole,' said Slater, when they were out of earshot.

'Noble?' said Norman. 'I don't know about that. I just think it was a long time ago, and he seems to be married to a little terrier who would happily tear him apart at the drop of a hat. Why spoil things for them by telling her about something her husband did before he even met her?'

'My point entirely. That was a noble act. You could have dropped him right in it.'

'Yeah. But I doubt she bought that excuse I invented off the top of my head, so now we've given her cause to be suspicious. My guess is she'll keep chipping away at him to try and find out what he's really been up to, and I reckon that's going to drive him mad.'

'Noble, but devious with it,' said Slater admiringly. 'A slow, agonising, form of torture. And all because his wife doesn't trust him.'

'It seems appropriate somehow, don't you think?'

'Remind me never to get on the wrong side of you.' Slater grinned, shaking his head.

They reached their car and climbed in.

'Being serious now, did we actually learn anything new?' asked Slater.

'Not exactly. But it confirms what Ian Woods told us about her past, and we also confirmed Diana's liking for lunchtime nooky. Whether that really helps us in any significant way I'm not so sure.'

'So what do you think, Norm? Are we getting anywhere? Because I'm not convinced we are.'

'I'll give you my best guess,' said Norman. 'Diana was pushing Rossiter about leaving his wife, and he had to stop her. Or, as an alternative, his wife found out, and she killed Diana.'

'That's two theories,' said Slater. 'I think I'm more inclined to agree with the first one.'

'But you have to agree the second one works, and we haven't spoken to his wife yet. We don't have any idea what she really knows, but I find it hard to believe she's unaware of what's been going on if everyone else knew.'

'Maybe she's like Woody used to be, and just doesn't see it.'

'There's only one way to find out,' said Norman. 'Tomorrow morning, we'll just have to go and ask her.'

CHAPTER FOURTEEN

There had been hardly any mention of Angela Rossiter during the investigation to date, so Slater and Norman had no idea about her background, what she looked like, or what she did. Basically all they knew was that she was married to Bruce Rossiter, so they had requested Jolly to carry out some background research for them. It hadn't taken her long to gather a few pages together, which she presented to them before she went home.

'I sometimes wonder how Jane does this so quickly,' said Slater to Norman as he read through the information. 'It would have taken me all day yet she did this in a couple of hours. How does that work?'

'For one thing she presses the right buttons, at the right time, and in the right order,' said Norman.

'What's that supposed to mean?'

'I'm referring to the way you use that PC of yours. You need to learn how to type properly. I've watched you fumbling your way around the keyboard. It's just as well we're not still on typewriters. We'd have to buy correcting fluid by the gallon.'

'Rubbish,' said Slater. 'My typing's just fine.'

'Then why do you swear so much when you use your PC?' asked Norman, innocently.

'That's just my style, okay?'

'Is clumsy classed as a style? Or should it be called all thumbs and no fingers?'

'Arsehole,' muttered Slater. 'Since when have you been so good?'

'I can do forty words a minute. It's not high speed but it's not bad. It's certainly beats the twenty cock-ups a minute that you manage.'

'Alright, so I admit you can type better than me. All I said was I thought Jane was bloody brilliant at this stuff.'

'She knows where to look, as well as being quick,' said Norman. 'I guess it's because we give her lots of opportunities to practice.'

'Do we ask too much?' asked Slater.

'Sometimes. But I think you'll find she enjoys being part of the team. And let's face it, she's not shy about saying what she thinks, is she? I wouldn't worry about it. I'm sure if she thought we were being unreasonable she'd say so.'

He flipped a page and looked at the photo in front of him.

'Wow,' he said. 'Angela Rossiter is a bit of a looker, don't you think?'

'Makes you wonder why old Bruce would need a bit on the side, doesn't it?' said Slater. 'I guess some guys are just greedy.'

'Or they just don't appreciate what they have. Or maybe she's been with him so long she despises him as much as I do.'

'It says here this photo was taken at some marketing awards ceremony five years ago,' said Slater. 'She's fifty-three now, so she must have been forty-eight when this was taken.'

'She looks more like thirty-eight,' said Norman, admiringly. 'And I have to admit I do like small, slender women. Oh well, at least we know she'll be nice to look at when we're asking questions.'

Slater thought so too.

T he Rossiters' front door swung open, and Norman opened his mouth to introduce himself and then stopped, speechless, as what could only be described as a female version of him filled the doorway.

'Err, we've an appointment to see Mrs Rossiter,' said Norman, uncertainly.

'That's me,' she said, with a cheery grin.

'It is?' he said, unable to stop the words spilling out.

'Is there something wrong?'

'Oh no,' rallied Norman. 'No not at all, it's just, ah, I was just, err..'

'I'm DS Slater, Mrs Rossiter.' Norman breathed a sigh of relief that Slater had stepped in to save the situation. 'And this is DS Norman.'

'Your young lady said there would be two of you when she called yesterday. Don't you have to show me your badges, or something?'

'Oh, right. Yes,' said Norman, fumbling in his pocket and producing his card.

She studied his warrant card, and then did the same with Slater's.

'Well, come on in,' she said, turning on her heel. 'Come through to the kitchen and I'll make some tea.'

Norman wondered what had happened to the small, slender woman in the photo. It looked as though she had arrived at her fifties and then given up for some reason. Then she turned and gave him the most beautiful smile and he had a rush of guilt. *It's not what's on the outside that matters, it's what's on the inside that really counts*, he thought. *And anyway, look at me. Who am I to criticise?*

As he walked into the kitchen, Norman's eyes alighted on the fancy coffee machine on the worktop. His envious look must have been obvious, as Angela Rossiter followed his gaze.

'If you'd prefer coffee, it won't take a moment to fire up the machine,' she said.

'Are you sure?' he asked her. 'Only we don't get to drink decent coffee very often.'

'Of course,' she said. 'My pleasure. Sit yourselves down.'

She waved them towards the breakfast bar under a window looking out onto the garden.

'This is a nice place, Mrs Rossiter,' Norman said, looking out at the garden. 'I bet this cost a tidy penny.'

'That's the benefit of being married to a money machine,' she said. 'We can afford a nice house in a nice area. Of course the downside is he's away a lot.'

'Can't you go with him?' asked Slater.

'Good God, no,' she said, laughing. 'I wish he went away more often, pompous pig that he is.'

Norman and Slater exchanged a look. This wasn't what they had expected.

'Well, you've met him,' she said, with another flashing smile. 'Don't tell me you liked him? If you did, you're the only ones.'

'Err, well,' said Norman. 'He did seem to be a little-'

'Up his own backside?' she interrupted. 'Yes, that's him. Thinks he's the only one in the world who has an opinion that matters. Fat sod.'

Norman saw Slater try to stifle a grin – not successfully, as Mrs Rossiter noticed and let out a roar of laughter.

'I know,' she said. 'How can I call him fat? Its pot and kettle, isn't it? The thing is, I know I've let myself go. He, on the other hand, thinks he's God's gift to women.'

'It can't have always been like that,' said Norman. 'I saw a photo of you from five years ago and you looked pretty good to me.'

'Why, thank you,' she said, going slightly pink. 'I used to have to work at it though. It didn't come naturally to me. I had to be really careful what I ate, spend hours at the gym, didn't drink, all that sort of crap. And for what? Just so I could be displayed in public like some sort of possession. And then, just to top it all, I'd have to put up with that fat pig climbing all over me.'

She stopped talking for a minute while she poured two coffees. Norman and Slater sat in silence, waiting for her to continue.

'And then, one day, I realised what a bloody fool I was,' she said, handing them each a steaming mug. 'So I stopped doing it. I thought if I made myself less attractive he'd leave me alone.'

'And did it work?' asked Norman.

'Not at first. But he finally got the hint when he came home one day and found we had separate bedrooms. That was nearly four years ago now. Best thing I ever did. The only pity is he still comes home. I haven't managed to drive him out completely yet, but I'm still hoping.'

'That sounds like irretrievable breakdown,' said Norman, carefully.

'Oh it is,' she agreed.

'So how did it get that bad?' asked Slater.

'My husband has a roving eye and finds it impossible to keep his todger where it belongs,' she said. 'So now we have an understanding. I don't care what he does, as long as he doesn't try to do it with me, doesn't do it here in my house, and he doesn't embarrass me.'

Norman hadn't been expecting that, and he found it impossible to keep it from his face.

'I know,' she said. 'You probably think I should divorce him. But what's the rush? I have a good life here, I don't want for anything, and now I can keep him at arm's length.'

'It wouldn't suit everyone,' said Slater.

'I'm biding my time. One of these days he's going to slip up, and then I'll have him for every penny I can, believe me.'

Slater looked confused, and Norman knew he was considering how best to approach the subject of Diana Woods. They had no time for being sensitive, though.

'I'm sure you're aware of the death of Diana Woods, your husband's PA,' said Norman. 'We're trying to create as broad a picture of her as we can. Did you know her?'

'Oh yes,' Mrs Rossiter said. 'I met her at various functions to do with my husband's work, and of course as his PA she called here occasionally. She was a lovely girl. She always had time for everyone. She even found the time to help me with one or two fundraisers. In fact, we were planning another one in a couple of months.'

'What fundraisers are these, Mrs Rossiter?'

'I volunteer at the St Anne's children's hospital.'

'That's miles away, isn't it?'

'We used to live near there,' she said. 'That's how I got involved originally. I was soon on the fundraising committee. When we moved here I thought I would have to give it all up, but I actually enjoy it, so I'm still doing it now. I work in the shop there on Tuesdays and Fridays. It keeps me busy and gives me something to look forward to.'

'Can you think of any reason why anyone would want to murder Diana Woods?' asked Norman.

'Absolutely not, Sergeant. She was a lovely person. It makes no sense to me.'

'One more thing. Can you tell us where you were on Monday afternoon between five and six o'clock?'

'I drove down to the post box to catch the last post at five-fifteen,' she said. 'I almost didn't make it because the postman was already there.'

'So he saw you there?' asked Norman.

'Oh yes.' She smiled. 'He held the bag open for me so I could put my letter straight in. Then I came back here to prepare a trough for Porky to come home to.'

'What time did he come home?' asked Slater.

'Late,' she said. 'It was gone seven by the time he got here.'

'Don't say a word,' said Norman, as Angela Rossiter closed her front door behind them, and they headed for their car.

'What do you mean?' asked Slater, in surprise.

'You're going to ask me what I think. And right now I'm not ready to tell you.'

'Why not?' Slater was perplexed.

'I need ten minutes to consider, that's why,' said Norman. 'You rushing me isn't going to help.'

'What do you want me to do, then?'

'Drive,' said Norman. 'It'll take about ten minutes to get across town to that burger van. We'll stop there. Then I'll tell you what I think.'

'You mean you want an early lunch, right?'

'Now you're talking,' said Norman. 'That's a seriously cool idea. I always think better when I'm eating.'

'Of course,' said Slater, sighing. 'How could I have forgotten?'

As Norman had requested, they drove in silence across town. Twice Slater went to speak, and each time Norman held a finger to his lips as a reminder.

'There. That wasn't so hard, was it,' said Norman when they reached their destination. 'As a reward for keeping quiet you can buy me a burger and a large coffee.'

'How is that a reward?' asked Slater. 'I'm always buying you lunch.'

'And you should be proud of such charitable acts. It's very humbling for me to be in the presence of someone with such a big heart. I'm hoping one day I can be like you.'

'There are givers, and there are takers,' said Slater, sighing, as he walked across to the burger van.

As he climbed back into the car five minutes later, Norman held out his hand.

'I want answers first,' said Slater.

'Aw, come on. It'll be cold by then. Anyway, I said I think better when I'm eating, not when you're holding my lunch to ransom.'

'Bloody hell,' said Slater in exasperation. 'You really do have an answer for everything, don't you?'

'Listen and learn,' said Norman, grinning. 'Listen and learn.'

For the next three minutes, Slater sat brooding while Norman devoured his burger, and then, finally, he delivered his opinion.

'I think I preferred her without the excess weight,' he said.

'Oh, for f-' began Slater.

'Alright, I'm sorry. Okay. I'll be serious. I'm actually confused. I'm not sure if I just met the dumbest woman ever, or the cleverest.'

'I know what you mean,' said Slater. 'How can she have known what he was like and yet not know about Diana?'

'And I just cannot believe he was bringing Diana back to his house and they never left a trace of evidence for her to find,' said Norman.

'They did have separate bedrooms.'

'Yeah, but even so. I just can't see it. I mean, she comes across as quite intelligent, and she's obviously got old Brucie sussed out for what he really is. Yet she expects us to believe she can't see what he's doing right under her nose? Jeez, he's almost rubbing her nose in it taking Diana back there.'

'And what about that Diana?' said Slater. 'She helps Angela out with fundraisers, and humps her husband at the same time! She was even more of a piece of work than I thought.'

'In my opinion we shouldn't trust Angela Rossiter,' said Norman emphatically. 'She was way too nice, and way too helpful for my liking. Look at all that stuff she volunteered about her old man and their relationship, and that was before we'd asked her a single question.'

'So you reckon nobody's that stupid?'

'Correct.'

'What about Woody? It was going on under his nose for years, and he didn't see it.'

'Yeah,' said Norman. 'But once he realised he didn't get fooled again, did he? Angela Rossiter is asking us to believe she's missing all the signs even when you know what they look like. I don't buy it.'

'There's a difference, though,' insisted Slater. 'Woody still loved Diana. Angela Rossiter gave up doing that years ago. She's just waiting for our friend to fail big time so she can take him to the cleaners.'

'But that's what's wrong here. If she's so keen to catch him out and clean up, surely she would be trying extra hard to see the signs, wouldn't she?'

'You have a point,' agreed Slater. 'But for now I'm keeping an open mind on that. However, I am intrigued about the apparent discrepancy in the times Rossiter arrived home. He says five forty-five, and she says after seven.'

'Yeah,' said Norman, a smile playing around his lips. 'And he was so confident about his alibi. I can't wait to see his face when we tell him he had plenty of time to drive out to Bishops Common before he came home.'

'It's a pity no one saw his car,' said Slater. 'That would be the icing on the cake.'

'Yeah. We've still not found out anything about this white van yet. If no one had a delivery of any sort, and no one was working down there with a white van, what the hell was it doing there? It has to be relevant to the murder.'

CHAPTER FIFTEEN

S later and Norman were back on the carpet in front of DCI Bob Murray's desk. He had demanded an update, and it was quite obvious he wasn't hearing what he wanted to hear.

'But why hasn't this Woods man been charged with his wife's murder?' demanded Murray.

'Because he didn't do it,' replied Slater.

'You told me he had the motive, the means and the opportunity. And you even have someone who saw a white van leaving the scene. Good God, man, what more do you need?'

'Err, we did inform you he had an alibi, Boss,' said Norman. 'I came up and told you myself. I would have thought you would have remembered – you weren't exactly in the best of moods when I left.'

'You told me it was a pack of lies,' roared Murray. 'Why haven't you proved it?'

Slater looked at Norman in surprise. He hadn't mentioned anything about telling Murray he thought it was lies.

'That's not what I said,' insisted Norman. 'I said I thought it was very convenient, but I also said we have no reason to believe Mrs Brennan isn't telling us the truth.'

'Well find a bloody reason,' snapped Murray. 'As far as I'm

concerned you have an open and shut case. Woods went round to see his wife, they argued, he lost his rag, and he stabbed her. End of story. You find the murder weapon and you'll see I'm right. This alibi will prove to be false, you mark my words. Now stop wasting time, and money, making irrelevant enquiries into the dead woman's past, and get on with closing this case.'

Slater could take criticism when he felt it was warranted, but this was getting ridiculous. It wasn't anyone's fault they hadn't solved this case yet; it was just how it goes sometimes. One thing was for sure – he had just about had enough of Murray and his foul temper.

'Oh, now I see where we've been going wrong,' he said, with heavy irony. 'We've been trying to find evidence to lead us to the killer, when what we should be doing is choosing a killer and then making the evidence fit. No wonder we waste so much money. Why didn't you tell us this before?'

Slater watched in fascination as Murray's face slowly turned purple. He was spoiling for a fight, and was prepared to give as good as he got. But Murray seemed to be so angry he couldn't speak. Norman shifted uncomfortably next to Slater.

'Err, right, Sir,' Norman said. 'Arrest and charge Ian Woods. We'll get onto it right away. Come on Dave. Let's go.'

He grabbed Slater by the arm and ushered him out of the office before Murray could stop them. And keeping a tight grip of his colleague's arm, he continued to frog march him down the stairs and out to their car.

'Just get in,' he ordered Slater. 'I'll drive.'

'Where are we going?'

'Anywhere that's not here. Now get in. And phones off. Let's just disappear for a while.'

'I don't get it,' said Slater once they were under way. 'Why is he so keen to pin the blame on Ian Woods? And why is he being so bloody unreasonable? It's not our fault it's not as straightforward as he wants it to be, is it?'

He looked across at Norman, before adding, 'And don't you stick up for him by telling me he's under pressure. Everyone on the bloody planet's under pressure. That is not an excuse.'

'Actually I wasn't going to defend him,' said Norman. 'I feel as aggrieved as you do, but provoking him the way you just did doesn't help. If we're going to solve this case, I need you here working with me. Fall out with the Old Man and you could end up directing traffic.'

'It's a matter of principle, Norm. I told you before I want to be able to sleep at night. I won't be able to do that if we stitch up Ian Woods.'

'Look, you're preaching to the converted here. I agree with you. But the way to deal with Murray is to humour him. Agree with what he says and then carry on doing the right thing. We do what we always do and follow the evidence wherever it leads. I just hope it doesn't lead us all the way round in a big circle and right back to Ian Woods, because if it does, we'll both be directing traffic.'

'You don't think it will, though, do you?' asked Slater.

'Nah,' said Norman. 'My money's on Rossiter.'

'So what are we going to do now?'

'We're going to stay out of the way for a few hours. We can start by going to see our new friend Bruce Rossiter. It's time he explained why there's a gap of over an hour between when he says he got home and when his wife says he got home.'

'What? D'you mean to say you're not expecting me to buy lunch again?'

'I don't remember saying anything of the sort,' said Norman. 'You buying lunch is a given. That's where we're going first.'

'But we had an early lunch just a couple of hours ago,' protested Slater.

'Ah yes,' agreed Norman. 'But it just so happens all that excitement in Murray's office has made me extra hungry. What we had before was just the starter. Now it's time for the main course.'

'You're fast becoming a one-man obesity epidemic. Don't you ever worry about your health?'

'What good did worrying ever do anybody?' asked Norman. 'Don't you know it's bad for your blood pressure?'

'So's all this fast food crap you eat,' said Slater. 'And I don't think I care to sponsor your personal obesity plan anymore. If you want to eat yourself to death, that's up to you, but don't expect me to help you. You're no good to anyone dead.'

'Wow. Where did that come from?' Norman looked stunned.

'You need to understand it's not all about you,' said Slater. 'Don't you ever think about your friends and how they worry about you?'

Norman didn't seem to have a reply. His face worked furiously, and then he sighed. Slater hoped he had got through to him.

'Okay,' he said, finally. 'But can we stop for coffee on the way? Coffee's okay, isn't it?'

The car park at Rochester & Dorset (Marketing) Ltd was half empty. Slater had a sinking feeling that this might prove to be a wasted trip.

'Park down this end of the car park, Norm,' said Slater. 'We can have a nose around on the walk up to reception.'

'Crap,' said Norman, looking around the car park. 'It looks like half the workforce is away today. I hope this doesn't mean Rossiter's not here.'

As soon as she saw them enter the reception area, though, Millie Gibson shook her head.

'I'm sorry,' she said. 'If you're looking for God's gift I'm afraid he's out for the day. You should have called first.'

'Yeah,' said Norman. 'I know, but this wasn't really planned. It was a sort of last minute decision to call in on the off chance.'

'There is something you might be able to help us with, though,' said Slater. 'Do you keep a record of people's movements.'

'You mean a diary of who's in and out, and where they are?'

'Yeah, that's exactly what I mean,' he replied.

'I have to,' she said. 'There's so much coming and going here I'd be putting calls through to people who aren't here, and that wouldn't be very professional, would it?'

'Could we have a look at it?' asked Norman.

'I'd be walked out of the door if anyone came in and saw you doing that. But I could copy it and email it to you. Just don't let on where it came from.'

Her smile suddenly changed to a frown.

'Oh, look out,' she said. 'Here comes Frosty.'

Slater looked over his shoulder in time to see Celia Rowntree pushing her way through a door into the reception area.

'There's an email address on that card I gave you,' he told Millie, quietly.

'Alright,' she said, out of the corner of her mouth. 'I'll do it later.'

'Gentleman,' called Celia Rowntree, as she approached. 'I'm sorry, but you're not welcome here. I must insist if you want to speak to anyone here again, you make an appointment, through me. Now, if you wouldn't mind leaving.'

'That's okay,' said Slater. 'We're just leaving anyway. Miss Gibson has just told us Rossiter's not here and it's him we wanted to speak to.'

'And we wouldn't want to stay where we're not welcome,' added Norman.

'I'm glad you understand. Now, if you wouldn't mind leaving...'

'He told us about his affair with Diana Woods,' said Norman. 'But then I'm sure you already knew all about that.'

She stared impassively at him.

'So how does that sit with your company's family values and terms of employment?' he continued. 'It seems to me it's against company policy, and as the HR director-'

'When I want your advice about company policy, and how to do my job,' she interrupted, 'I'll call you. Now, I've asked you to leave, but you still seem to be here.'

'We're going, but I'm pretty sure we'll be back, welcome or not,' Norman said. 'And next time we'll have a search warrant and perhaps a forensic accountant or two. You might want to discuss that with your company directors. I'm sure there's a whole host of things you'd rather we didn't find.'

He had definitely ruffled her feathers with his warning, but she stood firm and didn't back down.

Slater and Norman made their way back outside. The shortest way back to the car park was to the right, but a path led off to the left as well.

'Are you feeling nosey?' Norman winked.

'Oh dear,' said Slater, heading off to the left. 'We seem to have taken the wrong turning back to the car park. Never mind, this will probably take us all the way around the building to the car park, anyway.'

'Do you think she's watching us on CCTV?' asked Norman.

'I'm sure she'll be watching us every step of the way,' said Slater. 'But she asked us to leave, and we're leaving. What's she got to complain about?'

'Yeah, I didn't see any sign that said we couldn't come this way, did you?'

They followed the path around to the back of the building where they found an access road with a turning circle outside a pair of double doors, which allowed access for deliveries. Opposite the doorway, on the other side of the turning circle, was a small block of four garages with roller shutters. Three of the shutters were closed and padlocked, but the end shutter was raised. As they approached from the side they could see further and further inside, and more and more of what was parked inside.

'Well, well,' said Norman as the inside of the garage was revealed. 'Would you take a look at that!'

'I'll do better than look,' said Slater, fishing his mobile phone from his pocket and switching it on.

He focused the camera and took three photographs.

'This is one for the album,' he said.

'Hi, Jane,' said Slater into his phone.

'Where the bloody hell are you?' she said. 'I've had Murray down here raising merry hell. How do you think it makes me look when he asks me where you are and I don't have a clue?'

'Ah. Umm, Yes. I'm sorry about that-'

'You're sorry?' she snapped. 'You damned well will be when you get back here.'

'Aw, come on Jane. You know you love us really.'

'You're going to have to do a lot more grovelling than that. I can put up with a lot from you two, but this time you've really pushed your luck.'

He put his hand over the phone and turned to Norman.

'Jane's pissed off,' he said. 'She's had Murray on her case, looking for us.'

'Oh shit,' said Norman. 'I was so keen to keep you out of trouble I never even thought about him taking it out on her.'

'Yeah, me neither. But he has, and she's not very happy about it.'

He returned to his phone call.

'Hello, Jane? Are you still there?' said Slater. 'Look we're both really sorry. Norm says he's going to buy you dinner to make up for it. What's that? Yeah, I'll make sure his wallet's unlocked.'

He turned back to Norman.

'She says she's gonna put your wallet into shock,' he said.

'Yeah, right,' said Norman with a grin. 'Tell her I'm looking forward to that.'

'He says you can spend as much as you like,' Slater said down the phone. 'And you can bring the family. He'll pay for all five of you.'

'I said no such thing,' spluttered Norman. 'Here, gimme that phone.'

'Just drive. It's against the law to use a mobile phone while driving.'

'Anyway, Jane,' he said returning to the phone call once again. 'I need you to do something for me. I'm going to email you a photograph of a vehicle. I need you to check it out for me. Can you do that?'

'Is she really pissed off?' asked Norman when Slater had ended his call.

'Seriously,' said Slater. 'Apparently he was doing a war dance, and there was no one else to take it out on so he gave her chapter and verse, at full volume.'

'That's not on. His argument is with us. He had no right to take it out on her like that. Now I'm pissed off with him.'

'He has no right to treat anyone the way he does,' said Slater. 'I used to have a lot of respect for him, and he has helped me out of the shite a couple of times, but he's just about eroded all that away now. But how do we stop him?'

'I don't know,' said Norman. 'Maybe they'll grant his wish and make him redundant. That seems our best bet.'

'When I first heard about that, I thought it was all wrong,' admitted Slater. 'I thought he'd been such a good servant it wasn't right to be pushing him out of the door, but now I can't wait to see the back of him. I wish we could hurry it along in some way.'

'Yeah, that would be good. What we need is a bit of leverage, but he's pretty much squeaky clean, isn't he?'

'It feels disloyal, talking like this.'

'Yeah, I know what you mean,' said Norman. 'But there's a limit to how much shit people can be expected to take, and he's gone way past that limit now.'

Slater thought that was a pretty good assessment of the situation.

'Can I ask a question?' he said.

'That's what we do,' said Norman. 'Ask away.'

'Where are we going? We can't just keep driving aimlessly around all day. We're not going to solve anything that way.'

'Come on now,' said Norman. 'Give me some credit. I'm not driving aimlessly around. I'm driving back to the crime scene. Maybe another look into Diana's house will give us some fresh insight.'

'Oh, right. That actually sounds quite convincing. 'But what you really mean is if we stay away long enough the Old Man might cool down a bit.'

'Well yeah,' said Norman. 'And that, too.'

CHAPTER SIXTEEN

'Crap,' said Norman, as Diana Woods' house came into view.
'What?' asked Slater.

'How the hell are we going to get in? The guard's been removed and we don't have a key.'

'How come the guard's gone? Who authorised that?'

'Can't you guess?' Norman smiled grimly. 'As far as he's concerned the case is solved, remember? So having a guard on duty here is a waste of resources.'

'Oh, for frank's sake.' Slater shook his head in irritation.

'Is that a new curse? I haven't heard you use that one before.'

'I'm test driving it. It still means the same thing, but it doesn't offend anyone.'

'It might offend Frank,' said Norman.

'I'll try and remember not to say it in front of him.'

Norman pulled up outside the house and they sat in silence for a moment.

'Let me call Jane, see if she knows what's going on,' said Slater.

'I'll have a wander around the house,' said Norman. 'Maybe I'll find a window open.'

'But no breaking in. We don't want to have to explain a broken window, alright?'

Norman grinned at Slater, but said nothing as he climbed from the car and wandered towards the house.

Slater was just about to call Jolly when he noticed a movement in the wing mirror. A small woman was making her way along the lane towards the car. A large, hairy dog, of indeterminate breed, walked obediently alongside her. He didn't recognise her as one of the neighbours so he assumed she was just walking her dog and returned to his phone. He was just about to press 'call' when a rap on the window right next to his head made him jump. The small woman was glaring at him, so he wound the window down. The dog had sat down next to her, and he raised his head to take a sniff at Slater as the window came down.

'Can I ask you what you're doing here?' she asked him in a lilting Irish accent. 'And why there's a fat man wandering around that house. Is he something to do with you?'

'Police,' he said. He rummaged in his pocket for his warrant card and showed it to her. 'We're investigating the death of Diana Woods.'

'And that fat man's police, too?' she asked, eyebrows raised. 'He hardly looks fit enough to chase any villains.'

'He doesn't do chasing, he uses his brain instead and out-thinks them.'

'Well, I hope his brain's sharper than his suit. Anyway, why is he casing the joint? He looks like he's planning to break in.'

'You ask a lot of questions,' said Slater. 'Anyone would think it was your house.'

'That's my house, next door,' she said. 'So anyone acting suspiciously in this area is of interest to me.'

At the mention of the word suspiciously, the dog shifted his position so he could see Slater more clearly and cut off any attempt at escape.

'Is he going to tear my leg off if I get out of the car?' asked Slater.

'Only if I tell him too,' she said with a grin.

Slater looked at the dog again. He didn't look particularly vicious, but he seemed to have enormous teeth.

'Where did he get those teeth? They're not all his are they?'

'Oh for goodness sake,' she said. 'What are you a man or a mouse? Sure, he's as soft as you like, unless I tell him otherwise.'

Slater climbed gingerly from the car, all the while keeping a careful eye on the dog, which, in turn, kept a careful eye on him. It waited patiently until Slater closed the car door and couldn't escape before he made his move. In one quick movement he was all over Slater, slobbering all over him, and giving his suit trousers a liberal coating of free hair.

'There. See? He likes you,' said the woman.

'How come we haven't seen you before?' asked Slater.

'We've been away on holiday, the dog and me. We only got back yesterday. It's a pity I was away. I might have heard something, or seen something. I was shocked to hear what had happened. But, I'll tell you one thing, that woman wasn't the saint everyone around here would have you believe. I've lived here for years and during that time I've seen numerous men coming and going whenever Woody has been away. I often wanted to tell him, you know? He was such a lovely feller and she was treating him like shite all the time.'

'So why didn't you tell him?' asked Slater.

'How could I?' she said. 'He adored her. It would have broken his heart if he'd known, and he probably wouldn't have believed me anyway. He was the worst one for thinking she was perfect. But when she started bringing this latest one round here at lunchtimes, I always thought it would only be a matter of time before he found out.'

'Can you describe this man?'

'He was a big, fat, man. A bit like your friend there, but taller, and not as scruffy.'

'Can you hang on a minute?' asked Slater. 'I need my colleague to hear this, too.'

Norman was just heading back towards the car.

'Hey! Norm,' he called out. 'You need to come and hear this.'

The woman waited while Norman puffed his way over to them. The dog gave him the slobber and hair treatment, and then, satisfied he'd ruined a second suit, he retreated and sprawled out across the lane.

'There's no windows open,' said Norman.

'D'you want to get inside?'

'Well, yes,' admitted Slater, reluctantly. 'But we don't have a key.'

'I've got one,' she said. 'She gave me a key when Woody left. I kept an eye on the house for her when she was away. I've never had to use it but I don't suppose I need to now, do I?'

'This is, err, I'm sorry, I didn't ask your name,' said Slater.

'Mary O'Connell,' she said.

'Mrs O'Connell lives next door. 'She's been away. That's why we've not seen her before.'

He turned back to Mary.

'Could you tell my colleague what you just told me about the man who comes here at lunchtime,' he asked her.

'Big, fat, man,' she said. 'Built like you, but taller. Always wears a smart suit. Sometimes they'd come in her car, and sometimes they'd come in this little white van.'

'A van?' echoed Slater.

'It didn't seem to be the right vehicle for a man like that,' she said. 'You'd think he'd be driving a Mercedes or something similar, but no, he had this little van. It used to amaze me he could fit inside it, the size of him.'

Neither detective wanted to stop her talking, so they waited patiently while she stopped for a moment's reflection, but it was only a few seconds before she spoke again.

'I've had to live here watching that lovely man gradually being worn down by her,' she said. 'Sometimes I wanted to slap him, he was so blind to what she was doing. But then I think maybe he did know what she was up to but he never wanted to face up to it.'

'But all the neighbours say they've never seen anything untoward,' said Slater.

'Was Amanda Hollis one of those neighbours, by any chance? 'She ought to worry about her own shite husband before she starts running down poor old Woody. Now there's a man who could tell you all about Diana, but Amanda's as blind as Woody when it comes to her husband and what's going on right under her nose.'

'You mean him and Diana were-' asked Norman.

'You'd have to ask him,' she interrupted. 'But I can tell you this –

he's done several little jobs around the house for her since Woody left, and he doesn't do it for cash. And Amanda has no idea. She thinks he's just being a good neighbour. But I suppose that's part of the problem, isn't it? We usually see what we want to see, hear what we want to hear, and miss what's really happening.'

'That's pretty much how it is for a lot of people,' said Slater. 'It always amazes us how witnesses give different versions of things, but that's exactly the reason why. It's human nature to try to make events fit in with our beliefs and expectations.'

'That's exactly what I mean,' she said. 'If a small white van comes down the lane and turns into Diana and Woody's drive, everyone expects it to be Woody coming and going because he's been doing it for years. They assume it must be him, and because of that assumption, they don't take much notice. The result is they miss the details.'

'Such as?' asked Norman.

'Well, Woody's van is a Citroen. The one that used to visit before Woody caught them at it was a Peugeot. They're exactly the same van. Same shape, same style, same colour. It's just the badges and logos that are different, but if you don't look closely, you don't notice these things.'

'How come you noticed?' asked Slater.

'I like Woody a lot. I used to talk to him a lot. Every opportunity I got, to be honest. He told me about the difference last time he changed his van. He used to have a Peugeot you see, and I couldn't see the difference when he first got this van.'

'You talked about his new van?' asked Norman.

'I know. Sad, isn't it? But, like I said, I liked him. A lot. I really miss him. It would have been much better if he'd kicked her out, but even after he caught her red-handed he couldn't bring himself to make her suffer. She cheats and she gets to keep the house. How's that right?'

'But she's dead now,' said Slater. 'Do you think that's right?'

'If you play with fire, you know you risk getting burnt,' she said. 'What's happened to her isn't right, but if Woody's found guilty because of the crap she's told everyone about him since they split up, that won't be right either. She'll not be going to heaven that's for sure.'

She suddenly seemed to think she'd said more than enough.

'I'll just get you that key,' she said. 'I won't be a minute.'

'Now that was a very interesting conversation, don't you think?' asked Norman, once they were inside Diana Woods' kitchen.

'Yeah. We got more from her than we've had from the rest of them put together,' said Slater. 'It's a pity we couldn't speak to her before.'

'She definitely had the hots for Woody.'

'Sounds that way, doesn't it,' said Slater, absently sliding open kitchen drawers and peering inside.

'That could be seen as a motive for murder,' said Norman.

'Only if you want to put your money on a rank outsider. She's been in France for two weeks.'

'Yeah. I admit that would make it difficult,' agreed Norman. 'And it's certainly easy enough to check.'

'I'm more interested in the white van,' said Slater. 'That van we saw at Rochester's was a Peugeot, wasn't it?'

'It certainly was,' agreed Norman. 'And according to our new witness Rossiter used to drive one. Now that's a coincidence, don't you think?'

'It can't be a coincidence, can it?' Slater smiled. 'You know how much I hate them. I reckon Mrs Turner didn't see Woody in a white van. She assumed it was Woody, because that's what she expected, but we know it wasn't him because Susie Brennan says he was at her house and that's miles away. I reckon Mrs Turner saw Rossiter driving the white van. We already know there's a discrepancy between when he says he got home and when his wife says he got home. He had plenty of time to drive out here, kill Diana, take the van back, and then go home.'

'But we know he didn't have sex with her that lunchtime, because he was up in London, so who did?' asked Norman. 'We need to find out who that was, because whoever it was is still a possible suspect.'

'According to Mary, John Hollis had become a regular visitor,' said Slater. 'Now he told us the other day that he had been working the late shift. So, presumably he would have been at home for lunch.'

'And it's only a short stroll across the lane,'

'He fits the bill, doesn't he? Woody told us Diana liked to screw the husbands of her friends, and she especially liked having his mates. Hollis claimed to be Woody's best mate, so he fits the profile on both counts.'

Norman walked across to the front door, opened it and looked across the lane.

'He's got to be the prime candidate,' he said. 'And his car's over there. Why don't we go over and see what he has to say?'

Slater was staring intently into one of the kitchen drawers and didn't reply.

'Dave,' said Norman. 'I said, let's go and talk to Hollis now.'

'What? Oh, sorry,' said Slater. 'Yeah, sure.'

'You have that look,' said Norman, coming across to see what Slater was looking at. 'What have you found?'

'I don't know,' said Slater. 'Something just doesn't seem right.'

He slid the drawer shut.

'Maybe it'll come to me later,' he said.

'Mr Hollis,' said Norman, smiling pleasantly, when John Hollis answered his front door. 'We were hoping you might be able to spare us a few minutes. We have a couple of questions.'

'Oh. Err, right,' said Hollis, obviously caught off guard. 'Yes, of course, come on in.'

'Is Mrs Hollis here?' asked Norman, following Hollis inside the house.

'No, I'm afraid not. She works from ten until two. Did you need to see her?'

'Actually it's you we need to speak to, Mr Hollis,' said Slater. 'It's probably better that she isn't here.'

'Oh?' said Hollis. 'And why's that?'

'Because we want to ask you about your relationship with Diana Woods,' said Norman.

Hollis went a little pale and licked his lips.

'We are, sorry, *were*, just neighbours,' said Hollis. 'And friends, of course. Well, it was Amanda and Diana who were friends. Woody and I sort of became friends through the girls.'

'Oh yes,' said Slater. 'That's right. Didn't you say you were Woody's best friend?'

'I'm one of the few real friends he's got. Woody doesn't trust people easily.'

'And why do you think that is?' asked Norman.

'I think he's been let down a few times,' said Hollis. 'With Diana.'

'Have you let him down, Mr Hollis?' asked Slater.

'I don't think so,' said Hollis, uncertainly.

'You're sure about that, are you? 'Only we have a little problem. You see, Diana had sex with someone on the day she died. We thought we knew who that was, but now we know we were wrong.'

Hollis was looking worried, but he didn't say anything.

'But it's okay,' said Norman. 'Because whoever it was left us lots of evidence inside her, so we have his DNA, and of course, DNA is unique. So we're thinking it would be a good idea to take some DNA samples and do some comparisons. If we do that, are we going to find you're a match?'

'No you won't,' said Hollis. 'I always use a condom.'

'Ah! So you admit you've been there,' said Slater.

'But I only did it the one time,' blurted Hollis, desperately. 'Oh God, if Amanda finds out she'll kill me. You won't tell her will you?'

'We can't make promises like that,' said Slater.

'And you're sure it was just once, are you?' asked Norman.

'Alright, alright. But it was just an occasional thing. It wasn't serious.'

'Try telling that to your "best mate" Woody,' said Slater.

'But he's not even with her anymore,' said Hollis. 'What difference would it make to him?'

'I suppose you were just looking after her for him, were you?' asked Slater.

'So when did it start?' asked Norman. 'Was it after Woody left her?'

Hollis looked distinctly uncomfortable now.

'It was while he was still with her, wasn't it?' said Slater. 'Well, isn't Woody the lucky one? I'm glad you're not my best mate.'

'It wasn't like that,' pleaded Hollis. 'I didn't plan it. I didn't even like her that much. It just sort of happened, and once it had, I just had to come back for more whenever I got the chance.'

'Oh well, that's alright then,' said Slater. 'I wonder if Woody thinks you only "sort of" betrayed him. You do realise you're not the only bloke she's been doing it with, don't you?'

'Of course I bloody do,' snapped Hollis. 'I know she was just a sad old slapper. I wasn't under any illusions about that.'

'Don't tell me,' said Norman. 'It was just sex.'

'That's all it ever was for Diana. She had no need for love or affection, but she craved sex like some sort of addict. She didn't care who with, and she wasn't even that fussy about where she did it.'

'You mean to say you knew she was like that, and you still did it?'

'That's why I used condoms. I insisted, even though she didn't like them.'

'That was very noble of you,' said Norman. 'But I'd still go and get yourself checked out if I were you. And don't forget, if you have caught something, the chances are you've passed it on to your wife.'

'And good luck trying to explain how that happened,' said Slater, with an evil grin.

It was obvious Hollis had never even considered the possibility before, but now the ramifications were becoming crystal clear.

'Oh my God,' he said. 'She wasn't, was she?'

'I'm afraid we're not at liberty to divulge that information,' said Slater. 'I'll just say I'm glad it's not my problem.'

'Oh God, no,' wailed Hollis. 'What will Amanda say?'

'I reckon there could be another murder for us to investigate,' said Norman to Slater. 'Maybe we should wait.'

'No. I think you should get out, now. I've answered your questions, now leave, before she gets back.'

'We'll be checking out your story about being on the late shift on the day Diana died, Mr Hollis,' warned Norman. 'I hope, for your sake, it checks out, because if it doesn't we might have to consider the possibility your affair with Diana gave you reason to murder her.'

CHAPTER SEVENTEEN

Norman and Slater sneaked quietly into the car park at six-thirty that evening. They figured Murray would be long gone home, and sure enough there was no sign of his car anywhere. They planned to quickly look in to see if there were any messages from Jolly, and then to get out as quickly as possible.

There was a handwritten message on Slater's desk from Jane Jolly, demanding to know what was going on.

'We'll have to make up for it tomorrow,' said Norman.

There was a vehicle report from Jolly, confirming the small white van they had photographed at Rochester & Dorset was registered to the company, and they had owned it for two almost years.

'We need to find out who has access to it,' Norman said.

There was also a report from Ian Becks down in the forensics lab.

'Becksy says it's definitely Diana's prints inside that mobile phone we found,' he told Norman.

'Crap,' said Norman. 'That's gonna make it harder for us to prove he knew it was in his desk. We need her mobile phone more than ever now.'

Then, as soon as Slater checked his email inbox, he saw there was a message from Millie Gibson, with a file attached.

'Well, let's not give up hope just yet. Millie has sent a copy of their daily diary. Help me check it against these text messages. Maybe we can see some sort of pattern.'

It didn't take them long to find the first link.

'He flew out on the afternoon of Monday the fifteenth,' said Slater, reading from the diary. 'But he was out of office all day.'

'Okay, just a minute,' said Norman, scrolling through the stored messages on the mobile phone they had taken from Rossiter's office. 'Here you go. Received just before midday. It says "B. Fancy a quick f**k before you go. D xx." Then, he sends "MT house here" with a winky, smiley face. Then three minutes later there's another one received. "C U in 30. Xx."'

'What do you think?' asked Slater.

'It works for me,' said Norman. 'Sounds like she needed a seeing-to and he had an empty house.'

'Let's see how many more we can tie together.'

Over the next hour, they found another fourteen cases where the texts could be linked to Rossiter's activities.

'If there ever was any doubt, I think it's been removed now. This is his phone alright,' said Norman. 'But I still think we need to find her phone.'

'Okay,' said Slater. 'Let me just phone Millie Gibson to say thank you, and then we can get out of here.'

'Oh good. Because I feel a takeaway coming on. What do you fancy? Thai, Indian, or Chinese?'

'Hi, is that Millie?' said Slater into the phone. 'This is DS Slater. I just wanted to thank you for sending the email. I know you're taking a risk helping us out like that.'

'Not really.' She giggled. 'I'm leaving anyway, so they can hardly sack me, can they?'

'Even so, we do appreciate your help and I wanted to make sure you know it. That's why I thought it would be better to phone now and not phone you at work tomorrow.'

'It's a pleasure. And anyway, it's nice to have a little bit of excitement in my life. So what's going to happen now?'

'We're not exactly sure yet,' said Slater. 'And it's probably best that you don't know, then if we turn up you won't look as if you were expecting us. There is one more thing you might be able to help us with, though.'

'Go on,' she said. 'If I can help, I will.'

'We noticed there's a small white van parked in a garage at the back of the building. Can you tell me who uses it?'

'The Peugeot? It's like a company runabout. Basically anyone can use it. It's supposed to be for company business, like running errands, collecting stationery, and stuff like that, but you know how lax they are about things at that company. Just about everyone uses it. People go shopping in it, collect dry cleaning, and all sorts. Someone even used it to go and collect some compost from the garden centre a few weeks ago.'

'Is there a record of who uses it?' asked Slater.

'Well, there is a book. Anyone who uses it is supposed to say what time they went out, where they went, how many miles they did, and when they got back. But about one person in ten ever bothers to fill it in.'

'So it would be impossible to prove if someone had used it on a specific day and time?' asked Slater.

'Well, the book would be useless. But, how far do you want to go back?'

'I want to know if anyone used it the day Diana died,' said Slater.

'What?' she gasped. 'You mean you think someone from work killed her? Oh my God.'

'This is just between me and you, Millie. You mustn't discuss it with anyone else. It's a possibility we have to consider, because a small white van was seen in the area at the time she died. Now you asked me how far I wanted to go back.'

'The CCTV,' she said. 'We use CDs to store the footage from each day. They're used in rotation and recorded over every ten days.'

'So you always have the last ten days on file,' said Slater. 'And Diana died eight days ago.'

'So, if anyone used the van that day, you should be able to see when.'

'You're a real star, Millie,' said Slater.

'If I heard that right,' said Norman, when Slater had finished his call, 'they could have CCTV showing Rossiter driving off to Diana's in that van on the day she died.'

'It looks that way,' said Slater, smiling. 'We're beginning to build quite a case against Rossiter. I think it's time we dragged his arse back down here and asked him some more questions, don't you?'

'We need to organise a search warrant and get down there first thing tomorrow.'

They both jumped as a roar came from behind them.

'And where the bloody hell have you two been all day? I've been looking everywhere.' DCI Bob Murray was standing in the doorway, hands on his hips, face red.

Slater and Norman looked at each other in resigned dismay. Someone must have tipped Murray off that they had sneaked back into the station. They were caught and there was no escape. They were just going to have to take what was coming.

Murray seemed to rant on and on for hours, although in reality it was probably no more than two or three minutes. But in those two or three minutes he managed to bring up just about every little thing they had done wrong between them over the last few months. As he raved on, his face became more and more red, and then eventually, a vivid shade of purple. Finally, around about the time he was demanding to know why Ian Woods still hadn't been charged with murder, he seemed to run out of adjectives to describe just how useless they were and, most likely, breath with which to carry on his diatribe.

'Well,' he gasped to a finish. 'What have you got to say for yourselves?'

Slater had become more and more enraged as Murray rambled on and had been waiting for his chance to answer back, but before he could start telling Murray what he really thought of him, Norman stepped in.

'Alright, Dave, I've got this,' he said, stepping in front of Murray.

'Now just you listen to me.' He was right in Murray's face. 'We've just about had enough of you behaving like a bear with a sore head all the time. Has it ever occurred to you that you treat the people who

work for you like shit? Your job is to lead and inspire, but all you seem
to do is snap people's heads off and put them down.'

Murray looked shocked.

'Who do you think you are?' he roared at Norman. 'You want to
watch your tongue. If it wasn't for me, you'd still be wandering the
bloody moors up in Northumberland.'

'That's true,' said Norman. 'And don't you like to keep reminding me?
I know you gave me a lifeline, and I'm grateful for that, but I didn't come
down here to be constantly abused. Yes, I owe you, but that doesn't
mean I'm going to stand here and let you treat us like shit anytime you
like, just because it makes you feel better about your own problems.'

'The only problems I have are you two.'

'Oh. Is that right?' said Norman. 'I think maybe you need to take
another look at your crime figures. You know as well as we do that
we're most definitely not your problem. Your problem is you're still
stuck in the good old days when it was all about kicking arses,
knocking heads together and getting a result, even if it meant making
the evidence fit the result you wanted.'

Slater stood, in awe.

'You just haven't moved with the times have you?' Norman continued. 'You're so far behind you're still struggling to send an email
without making a balls up, and you're gradually drowning in a sea of
paperwork and modern thinking. That's why you've put in for voluntary redundancy, isn't it? Because, you just can't cope anymore.'

Slater could do nothing but stand back and listen. He sometimes
thought Norman sided with Murray too readily, but he couldn't accuse
him of doing that this time. Norman's words had actually taken all the
steam out of Murray who had gone quiet now, and was beginning to
look just a bit sheepish.

'I'm genuinely sorry you're struggling,' continued Norman. 'But you
can't carry on blaming everyone else for your own shortcomings. All
the guys that work here have the greatest respect for you and what
you've achieved. That respect has been earned over the years, but all
you're doing now is eroding it away. Carry on like you are, and they'll
have nothing but contempt for you. Do you really want that?'

Murray slumped back and parked his backside on the desk behind him. For a brief moment he looked utterly defeated, and it seemed he might even burst into tears, but then, with what appeared to be a monumental effort, he managed to pull himself together.

'You have no right to talk to me like that,' he said, quietly. 'You have no idea what I have to deal with right now.'

'I could argue that you have no idea what it's like for us, trying to carry out a thorough investigation, while we have you breathing down our necks trying to make us cut corners and arrest the wrong man,' replied Norman. 'But what would be the point? You've stopped listening to reason.'

'You don't know what it's like.'

'So tell us,' said Norman. 'Instead of treating us like little kids, how about you treat us like adults for once?'

'I don't think I can do that,' Murray said. 'I'm not one for sharing my problems. It's a weak person who can't deal with life on his own. It's my business and I prefer to keep it that way.'

'A problem shared is a problem halved,' said Norman. 'It's not weakness. It's bloody common sense, especially if you're not coping on your own and you're just making everyone else suffer. Just talking about it can help.'

'Maybe,' agreed Murray. 'But it's not my way.'

'And you think making everyone else's life hell is the right thing to do?' asked Norman. 'That takes away another slice of that respect I had for you.'

'No,' conceded Murray. 'I admit I'm in the wrong there. But I'm sure it's not that bad.'

'Not that bad?' echoed Norman. 'There isn't a single person in this station who wants to go anywhere near you at the moment. That's how bad it is.'

Murray's face hardened and he stared at Norman. It looked, for a few moments, as though he was going to start ranting again, but then his expression softened. It was hard to tell if he had taken on board what Norman had said, but at least when he spoke again it appeared he was no longer looking for a fight.

'Let's get back to this case,' he said. 'Explain to me why you haven't charged Woods.'

'Ian Woods has an alibi for the time of the murder,' Slater told Murray, feeling it was safe to speak now. 'And everything he's told us seems to check out. On top of that, we now have another suspect in her boss, and lover, Bruce Rossiter.'

'But does he have a motive?'

'We think Diana was pushing to take his wife's place, but all he wanted her for was sex. We've found a mobile phone which we think Diana gave him so they could keep in touch and arrange their sex sessions in secret. We've also discovered Rochester & Dorset keep a small white Peugeot van which anyone can use at any time. We believe this was the van seen leaving the scene of the crime.'

'And you think he had the opportunity?' asked Murray.

'There's a gap in his story,' said Slater. 'He says he was at home when the murder took place. His wife says he didn't come home until after seven. He had plenty of time to murder Diana.'

'You're sure about this?'

'It looks a better bet than Ian Woods,' said Norman.

'So why haven't you brought him in yet?'

'We've only just found out about the van,' said Slater. 'We're planning on getting a search warrant in the morning and taking a team over there. We want to bring him in and get Ian Becks and his boys to take the van apart.'

'You want to nick him at home, and search his house as well,' said Murray.

'I'm not sure I've got the clout to get the search warrants at this time of night,' said Slater.

'If you give me the information, I'll get the search warrants. You two organise the troops. I'd suggest Rossiter's house at six am, then on to Rochester's as soon as you can after that.'

Slater almost stepped back in surprise.

'Well, don't hang about,' said Murray. 'The clock's ticking. If I'm going to help you, I need that information, now.'

CHAPTER EIGHTEEN

At six o'clock the next morning, a small convoy of police vehicles drove through the gates and up the drive to Bruce Rossiter's house. If anyone was awake they didn't show themselves, so Norman took great delight in hammering upon the door.

'Police,' he yelled into the letterbox. 'Come on open up.'

He stood up and hammered on the door again.

'You enjoy this bit, don't you?' asked Slater.

'It's like this,' he explained, with a wicked grin. 'I had to get up extra early to be here at this ungodly hour, and I had to be really quiet not to wake my neighbours. Now I think the least the Rossiters could do is make the same effort and be waiting to let us in, but they don't seem to be awake yet, so I'm just letting them know we're here. And now I can make up for having to be so quiet earlier.'

'Ah. I understand,' said Slater. 'This is sort of restoring the noise balance in your life.'

'That's exactly right,' said Norman, grinning. 'Extra quiet before, extra noisy now, balance restored. Now I can spend the rest of my day at normal volume, knowing I don't have to worry about a noise deficit.'

'If you don't mind me saying,' yawned a weary looking PC waiting behind them, 'you're talking a load of bollocks. There's no such thing as noise balance.'

Norman looked around at the PC. He knew most of the PCs at Tinton well enough to address them by their first names, but this one was young and obviously new to Tinton.

'If you weren't so young I'd take issue with that statement,' said Norman, beaming a big smile at the PC. 'But I really can't expect you to understand these complex principles at such a tender age.'

'How can you be so bloody happy this early in the morning?' asked the PC, grumpily. 'It's not normal.'

'But you see that's exactly what I'm talking about,' explained Norman, cheerfully. 'My happiness is a direct result of caring for my noise balance. You should try it sometime.'

The PC looked puzzled, but there were sniggers from the rest of the assembled officers.

There was the sound of a bolt being slid back on the inside of the front door.

'Heads up,' said Slater. 'Someone's awake.'

They heard two more bolts being slid back, and at least two locks being undone.

'It sound like Fort Knox,' muttered one of the PCs. 'I'm glad we didn't have to break it down.'

'No problem. We could throw Norman at it,' suggested someone, to a series of loud guffaws.

'Alright, pipe down,' said Slater, as the handle turned and the door finally began to open, revealing a tousle-haired, bleary-eyed Bruce Rossiter in a pair of red tartan pyjamas.

'What the bloody hell's going on?' he cried. 'Do you know what time it is?'

'I certainly do,' said Norman, smiling. 'It's time for you to come and answer some questions.'

'At this time of the morning? Are you mad? And does it really need six PCs and two detectives to ask me these questions?'

'Oh, they're not here to ask questions, Mr Rossiter.' Slater was grinning. 'Two of them are here to escort you to Tinton police station, and the other four are going to search your house.'

'I know my rights,' said Rossiter, angrily. 'You can't search my house without a search warrant, and unless you're some kind of magician you're not going to get one at this time of the morning.'

'Oh, really?' said Slater. 'Well, it just so happens...'

He pulled the search warrant from his pocket with a flourish.

'Now, that's magic,' said Norman, slipping into a very poor impression of magician Paul Daniels.

There were sniggers all round from the six PCs.

'Give me that,' snapped Rossiter, snatching the search warrant from Slater's hand.

'It's genuine,' said Slater, leading the way through the front door. 'D'you really think we're that stupid? Come on lads, let's get on with it.'

'What's going on,' called a voice from the top of the stairs. 'Bruce? Why are there policemen in the hall?'

'It's DS Slater and DS Norman, Mrs Rossiter,' Slater called up to her as Norman began directing the search team. 'We have a search warrant to search the house. I think it might be best if you come down to the kitchen.'

'But why are you here?' she asked as she walked slowly down the stairs. 'What are we supposed to have done?'

'It's to do with the death of Diana Woods,' explained Slater. 'I'm afraid we need to ask your husband some more questions.'

'It's a bloody joke,' said Rossiter. 'They're trying to set me up. I've already told them I was here with you when she died.'

'Yeah,' said Slater. 'You did tell us that. But I'm afraid there's a bit of a problem there. You see, your wife says you didn't get home until after seven.'

'What?' Rossiter turned to his wife. 'What did you tell them that for?'

'I can't lie to the police, Bruce,' she said. 'It's against the law. I don't know what they think you've done, but I can't lie for you, can I?'

She turned her back on him and marched off into the kitchen, slamming the door shut behind her.

'Why are you doing this?' Rossiter called after her, desperately. 'You know I was here with you. We had dinner just after six!'

'I think that's enough questions for now, Mr Rossiter,' said Slater. 'We're going to take you down to the station where you will be formally interviewed.'

'You've put her up to this, haven't you? I don't know why, but she's lying. I was here before six o'clock that night, just like I told you!'

He made to lunge at Slater but the two PCs waiting to escort him away were far too quick for him and they easily held him back.

'I think you need to calm down, Mr Rossiter,' said Slater. 'Assaulting a police officer isn't going to help you, now is it?'

'This is a joke,' snarled Rossiter. 'You're making a big mistake. I already told you I had nothing to do with Diana's death.'

Slater nodded his head at the two PCs and they released Rossiter's arms.

'Yes, yes,' said Slater. 'So you did, but unfortunately for you we keep finding evidence that points to you being a whole lot more involved than you claim. And you're not averse to a bit of lying, are you? You lied about your affair with Diana, didn't you?'

'But I've already admitted that,' said Rossiter. 'Wait a minute. Is that it? You told my wife, didn't you? You told her about me and Diana. That's why she's lying for you.'

'If she knows about your affair, Mr Rossiter, she didn't hear about it from us,' said Slater. 'And she's not lying for us. I don't know what makes you think that.'

'Because she's not telling you the truth! I was here way before six, just like I told you. You have to believe me!'

'I don't have to believe anything, and I don't take orders from the likes of you,' said Slater. 'Now I think it's time you left. You can have five minutes to get dressed, before these two officers take you in, but they go where you go.'

'You can't do this. I demand to see my solicitor.'

'All in good time, Sir. You can call him when you get to the police station. Now do you want to get changed? Or would you like to go dressed as you are?'

'You'll regret this,' said Rossiter. 'You've got the wrong man.'

'That's what they all say,' said Slater.

'And I don't know what it is you're hoping to find,' continued Rossiter. 'But I can assure you it's not here.'

'They all say that as well.'

Slater nodded to the two PCs.

'Take Mr Rossiter upstairs to get changed,' he said. 'And then take him to the station. And remember he doesn't leave your sight, even if he wants to relieve himself.'

They moved towards Rossiter, but he turned and made his way towards the staircase. As the prisoner slowly made his way up the stairs, accompanied by his two new friends, Slater decided he ought to find out what Angela Rossiter was up to in the kitchen.

He found her, sipping tea from an oversized mug, staring out at her garden. She looked round as he came through the door. To his surprise the beginnings of a smile began to creep across her face, then, seeing his expression, she seemed to think better of it.

'What exactly is it he's supposed to have done?' she asked.

'It's to do with Diana's death. That's all I can tell you really.'

'But why search the house? What are you looking for?'

'Anything that might help us with our enquiries,' he said.

'You surely don't think he murdered her, do you?' she asked. 'Bruce is a lot of things that aren't very nice, but I don't think even he's capable of murder.'

'I really can't comment on that.'

'Oh my God,' she said. 'You do, don't you? You think he murdered Diana. But why would he do that? She was the best PA he ever had.'

'How well did you know Diana?' asked Slater.

'I told you before,' she said. 'I met her at a couple of work events. She was a nice person and we hit it off. I really liked her. She was very good with people. She even helped me out with a couple of fundraisers, and we were planning another one.'

'What about her relationship with your husband? Was it just professional?'

'She was his PA, end of story. Why are you asking me about her relationship with Bruce? What are you implying?'

Slater sighed. He really didn't want to have to tell her, but she knew what he was getting at.

'It's been suggested your husband and Diana were, well, let's say their relationship may have been more than just professional.'

'Well, whoever told you that is wrong,' she said, emphatically. 'Don't get me wrong, I know Bruce is no saint, but we have an agreement. I don't care what he does when he's away, but he doesn't do it in my backyard where I could end up getting humiliated.'

'And you're sure he sticks to that agreement?'

'Bruce loves his money, and his lifestyle, Mr Slater. If I catch him out, I'll divorce him, and take him to the cleaners in the process. And, trust me, I know enough about the way he works and who he's shafted over the years to be able to ruin his career. He wouldn't risk all that for a bit of nooky, would he? You don't shit in your own nest. That's the saying, isn't it? Besides, I'm quite sure Diana wouldn't have found him attractive physically. No one else does. Anyway, she was much too nice to sink that low.'

Slater didn't quite know what to say to that. Like Norman had suggested last time they spoke to her, he was finding it hard to believe what he was hearing. But he was spared having to say anything by a knock on the door. It opened a little way and a beaming face appeared. It was Norman. He held up an evidence bag.

'Looks like we hit the jackpot,' he said.

'What's that?' asked Angela Rossiter. 'What have you got? Is it a mobile phone? It's not mine, is it? Where did you find it?'

'Whoa,' said Norman. 'Too many questions, Mrs R. That's our job. I can tell you we found it in a drawer next to your husband's bed, and I can tell you it's not yours. But that's all I am going to tell you.'

'How's it going out there?' Slater asked Norman.

'We're just about done.'

Slater looked at his watch. It was just after seven. They were making good time. They might even be able to snatch a quick breakfast before they went on to Rochester & Dorset if they got a move on.

'We're going to leave you in peace now, Mrs Rossiter,' he said. 'I'm sorry we've had to do this, and I apologise for any mess we've left behind us.'

'No, no. It's alright,' she said. 'I know you're only doing your jobs. It'll give me something to tell the girls at the W.I.'

. . .

'She seemed to take that rather well,' said Norman, when they were back in their car. 'What happened to the usual indignant rage about over-zealous policing, human rights, and all that stuff?'

'It was pretty weird,' agreed Slater.

'Did you tell her why we were there?'

'Well, I had to. But she seemed to have more or less figured it out anyway.'

'Does she believe old Porky was sharing his sausage with Diana now?' said Norman.

'That's the strange thing,' said Slater. 'She insists they had this agreement. He was allowed to do whatever he liked when he was away, but he couldn't do it back here where he might embarrass her. She's adamant he wouldn't risk it, and she's equally adamant Diana was way too nice to do such a thing.'

'Was she for real?'

'Like you said before, I think she's either really intelligent, or really stupid.'

'So, come on, which one is it?' asked Norman. 'Sitting on the fence will only give you splinters in your backside.'

'I can't believe she's really that naive,' said Slater.

'Me neither,' agreed Norman.

It was a slightly different team that descended upon the headquarters of Rochester & Dorset (Marketing) Ltd at precisely eight o'clock that morning. Although they were quite sure there would be plenty to find, should they wish to look, they had decided to focus solely upon the things they knew related to the murder of Diana Woods. This included the Peugeot van, Rossiter's office and desk, Diana's desk, and the CCTV footage.

Slater led the way to the reception area. Of course, there were none of the usual staff around that early, but that was the plan. It took five minutes of ringing and banging on the door, but eventually the care-taker appeared.

'We're closed. There's no one here,' he mouthed through a window. 'Come back at nine.'

Slater slapped his warrant card and the search warrant against the window, making it clear he was in mood to be messed around. The caretaker squinted through the window briefly, and then started unlocking the door.

'Sorry,' he mumbled to Slater, as he opened the door and waved them into the reception area. 'Only I'm not supposed to let anyone in who's not staff.'

'Don't worry about it,' said Slater. 'We're in now. I have a search warrant here.'

'Yes. So I can see. What you looking for?'

'Have you got keys to the garage round the back? We need to get at the Peugeot van.'

'I've got them here in my pocket,' the caretaker said.

He took a keyring with four keys from his pocket and handed it to Slater.

'Will you need it for long? Only I'm going to the cash and carry this morning, to get some cleaning stuff.'

'I'd use another vehicle if I were you,' said Norman. 'We're going to take it away.'

'But I haven't got another vehicle,' said the caretaker.

'You could try the bus.'

'We also need the keys to start it,' said Slater.

'They'll be in it,' said the caretaker. 'None of the lazy buggers ever brings 'em back in here like they're supposed to.'

Slater handed the keys over to Ian Becks.

'Just follow the "deliveries" sign,' he told Becks. 'You'll find the garages opposite the back doors. The van's in the one on the left as you look at them.'

'Right,' said Becks. 'We'll do a quick check, then shove it onto the trailer and take it back to our workshops.'

'Good luck. We'll see you later.'

Slater turned back to the caretaker.

'We want the CDs the CCTV is stored on,' he said.

'They'll be in the TV room at the back of reception.' The caretaker pointed to a door in the far corner. 'Here, I'll show you.'

He led them across to the door, swung it open and led them inside. A desk faced a wall bearing several screens showing views from the CCTV cameras.

'They'll be in that top drawer,' he said, pointing to a desk with two drawers.

'And we want access to Mr Rossiter's office,' said Slater.

He slipped on a pair of latex gloves as he walked across to the desk and slid open the drawer.

'I don't know which office is which,' said the caretaker. 'But they're all unlocked so I could clean 'em. If you know which one it is, you can help yourself.'

'Yeah, we know where it is,' said Norman. 'We can find our way up there okay.'

'Is that it? Do you need anything else?'

'No we're good,' said Norman. 'You've been very helpful Mister?'

'Swan.'

'Yes, thank you, Mr Swan,' said Slater.

'Can I go now?'

'D'you think you could hang on until someone else gets here?' asked Norman. 'Just in case we need anything else.'

'I suppose,' agreed the caretaker, gloomily. 'I just hope it's not that snotty bitch from HR that gets here first. She'll chew my balls off for this.'

'For what?' asked Norman.

'Letting you lot in, probably,' he grumbled. 'Miserable cow. She's always moaning about something.'

'Let me guess. Mrs Rowntree, right?'

'Oh you've met her, then.' The caretaker grinned.

'Let's just say we're not her favourite people,' Norman said, grinning back

'You certainly won't be this morning, that's for sure,' Mr Swan said, letting out a laugh. 'Is it alright if I go and make meself a cup of tea?'

'Sure,' said Norman. 'Just hang around the reception area so we can find you if we need to.'

'Well, there's ten disks here.' Slater rummaged through the drawer. 'And they're marked with letters, but I've no idea which one is which.'

'Take 'em all,' said Norman. 'I've got a bag here. We can find out which is which later on.'

He opened a plastic bag and Slater placed the disks carefully inside.

'I didn't expect to see you two here this morning,' said a familiar voice from the doorway.

They looked round to see the smiling face of Millie Gibson watching them.

'Morning, Millie,' said Slater. 'D'you know how these CCTV disks are marked?'

'There should be a blue book, A5 size, in that drawer,' she said. 'It's a dead simple system. We just record the date, and the letter of the disk.'

'There's no book in here,' he said, turning back to the drawer.

She walked over and peered around him into the drawer.

'That's funny. It's always in there. It's not supposed to be removed.'

'Who's responsible for keeping the records?' asked Norman.

'Me and Frosty,' said Millie. 'I don't think anyone else is even aware we have CCTV. Most of them think the cameras are dummies.'

'When did you last see the book?' asked Slater.

'Yesterday morning. I usually change the disks when I come in.'

'Does anyone else have access to this room apart from you two?' asked Norman.

'Well, we don't keep it locked, so anyone could come in here if they wanted. But I've never known anyone else come in here.'

'What the hell's going on here?' Celia Rowntree marched fiercely through the doorway. 'What are you two doing here? I told you before you're not welcome. Who allowed you into the building?'

'This allowed us into the building,' said Slater, thrusting the search warrant towards her.

But she wasn't listening to him. Through the wonders of CCTV, she was watching Ian Becks loading the Peugeot onto his trailer.

'What's that man doing? Who said he could take that van away?'

'I did,' said Slater. 'This search warrant does, if you'll just stop carping long enough to read it.'

'How dare you speak to me like that!' she snapped, indignantly.

Then she suddenly realised Millie was in the room, watching the whole show.

'Don't you have any work to do, Millie?' she hissed.

'Yes,' said Millie, guiltily. 'Sorry. I'll get on.'

Celia waited for Millie to leave the room and then rounded on the two detectives again, but it was Norman who spoke first.

'If you'll just stop with the righteous indignation stuff,' he said, 'and listen to what he's telling you, you'll see we have a search warrant. We're taking the van for forensic examination, we're seizing the CCTV footage from the day Diana Woods died, and we're going to search Bruce Rossiter's desk, and Diana's desk.'

'Bruce won't allow you to do that,' she said.

'I don't think he's in a position to stop us,' said Slater, testily. 'And anyway, he doesn't have to allow it. This search warrant allows it, if you'll only stop and read it.'

'But there will be staff in that room–'

'There are no buts,' interrupted Slater. 'We have an officer posted outside that room turning staff away until we've finished. Now you can either co-operate with us, or we can get a much more extensive search warrant, come back with a small army, and turn the whole building upside down. Which do you prefer?'

She scanned the search warrant, and the air seemed to go out of her.

'Right. Well, that seems to be in order,' she said, awkwardly, when she had finished reading. 'So how can I help you?'

'Where's the book that goes with these CCTV CDs?' asked Slater.

'It should be in that drawer.'

'Yes. I know it should be in the drawer,' said Slater. 'But it's not, so where is it?'

'Perhaps Millie has it.'

'Millie says it was in the drawer last time she saw it, yesterday morning,' said Norman.

'Well, someone else must have it then,' she said.

'Millie says only you and her use the book or even know what it's for,' insisted Norman.

'What?' Celia Rowntree said. 'You think I've got it? Why would I want it?'

'Why would Millie want it?' asked Slater.

'I don't know,' she said, her patience wearing thin yet again. 'Why don't you ask her?'

'We have,' said Norman. 'She doesn't have it, and she doesn't know where it is.'

'Well, I'm afraid I don't know where it is, either,' she insisted.

'Perhaps we need to search everywhere, after all,' Slater said.

'You'll need another search warrant,' she said, with an icy smile. 'This one is very specific about where you can look.'

Slater couldn't argue with that. She was right. It had been a mistake to make it so specific, but they'd had to compromise. It was the only way they could get the search warrant granted late last night.

'We'll take these CDs anyway,' said Slater. 'I'm sure we'll be able to find what we're looking for.'

'We're going up to Rossiter's office now,' said Norman. 'If you want to come and watch what we're doing, you're more than welcome.'

'Mr Rossiter is going to be very upset when he comes in and finds out what you're doing,' she warned them. 'You're going to spoil his day.'

'We've already spoilt Mr Rossiter's day,' Norman said, grinning. 'He probably should be phoning in to say he won't be in for work today, but he's only got the one phone call at his disposal, and I'm pretty sure you won't be the first person he wants to call.'

'What do you mean?'

'Let's just say he's helping us with our enquiries, if you see what I mean.'

Norman winked at her as he followed Slater from the room and headed for Rossiter's office.

'Any problems, Jane?' asked Slater, as they approached Rossiter's office.

'Well, I'm not very popular with those people I've had to turn away from their office,' she said, smiling. 'But there's been nothing I couldn't handle.'

She stepped aside as Slater and Norman entered the office, and then followed them inside.

'So what are we looking for?' she asked them.

'Right.' Slater pointed to the two desks closest to the door. 'It's just these two desks. This one here was Diana's, and that one over there is Rossiter's. We're looking for anything that might prove they were in a relationship, and anything that might suggest they had fallen out.'

'That's a bit vague, isn't it?'

'You start on Diana's desk,' he said. 'You might not find anything because Rossiter has already been through it, but you never know, he might have missed something. Me and Norm will take his desk. It's twice as big, and we think we're more likely to find something in there.'

They quickly got to work at their respective tasks. Jolly soon drew a blank, but Slater and Norman were having a bit more luck.

'Wow!' muttered Norman. 'Look at this.'

He produced an expensive-looking carrier bag from one of the drawers.

'Drawers within drawers,' he said, as he produced a set of fancy underwear from within the bag and held them up. 'Do you think these are for him, or for her?'

'They'd have to stretch a hell of a long way to go around his arse,' said Slater, grinning.

He leaned across for a closer look.

'They're made by the same people who made the underwear she was wearing when they found her body.'

'How come you know so much about ladies underwear?' asked Jolly.

'You should see what he's wearing under that suit,' said Norman, winking.

'I recognise the label,' said Slater. 'It's not exactly run-of-the-mill stuff, is it?'

'Let's have a look,' asked Jolly, stepping closer so she could see.

'That's expensive stuff,' she said, admiringly. 'I certainly can't afford anything like that on my wages.'

'So it's not the sort of stuff your average girl wears?' asked Slater.

'Not if she's on an average salary.'

'But as a gift?' asked Slater.

'A girl would be very happy.'

'So now I know what to buy you for Christmas,' said Norman, with a wink.

'I wouldn't waste your money,' said Jolly. 'Because it couldn't possibly make me THAT happy.'

'Well, well, well,' said Slater reaching into another drawer. 'What did Millie say? A blue book, A5 size.'

He lifted something from the drawer and placed it on the desk.

It was a blue book, A5 size.

'If that's the right book,' said Norman, 'then it looks like all roads point to Rossiter.'

Slater opened the book and glanced at the first page. There was a list of dates and letters.

'This must be it,' he said. 'It's exactly as Millie described it. Dates and letters. Dead simple.'

As he thumbed through the pages the dates got closer and closer.

'Oh bugger,' he said. 'Would you believe it? The last page has been torn out.'

'So, how much more incriminating do we need it to be?' said Norman.

'I thought this bloke was supposed to be clever.' Jolly shook her head. 'First you find her mobile phone at his house, and now you find this book in his desk. That doesn't seem very clever to me.'

'He's arrogant,' said Norman. 'Arrogance makes people think they're much cleverer than anyone else. He certainly thinks he's too smart for us, but that's been his undoing. He thought we were too stupid to find anything.'

'You call it arrogance if you want,' said Jolly. 'But I think it's just plain bloody stupid.'

CHAPTER NINETEEN

'Before we start I would like to stress, for the record, that my client has repeatedly denied having any involvement in the murder of Diana Woods. Your continual refusal to accept this fact, and your behaviour this morning, amounts to persecution of an innocent man. I hereby inform you of my intent to pursue a claim for wrongful arrest and harassment.'

Brian Humphreys looked rather pleased with his performance as he sat down alongside his even more smug-looking client.

Norman shook his head slowly from side to side and went back to studying the notes in front of him.

'Thank you, Mr Humphreys,' said Slater, smiling broadly. 'Your intent is duly noted. Am I right in my belief that criminal law is not your particular area of expertise?'

'Can't be,' said Norman, without looking up from his notes. He said it just loud enough for Humphreys to hear.

The smug look on Rossiter's face faltered for barely a second, but Humphreys wasn't so good at hiding his feelings, and it was obvious he had no idea what Slater was suggesting. Slater stared impassively at Humphreys and gave him a few seconds to reply, but this just served to make the unfortunate solicitor even more uncomfortable.

'The reason we've invited your client here this morning-,' he began.

'I wasn't invited, I was bloody well dragged here,' snorted Rossiter.

'It's a question of perception I suppose,' said Norman, looking up from his notes. 'But I didn't see anyone place a hand on you until you made a move to attack DS Slater.'

He looked back at his notes. Rossiter glared at the top of Norman's head, but didn't comment further. Humphreys looked suitably alarmed. Slater bet his client hadn't mentioned that he'd almost assaulted a police officer.

'We just have a few discrepancies we need Mr Rossiter to clarify for us,' continued Slater. 'Once that's done to our satisfaction he'll be free to go. I think that's fair enough, don't you?'

'What discrepancies?' snarled Rossiter.

'We'll go through them one at a time. How about we start with the time you claim to have reached home on the day Diana was killed. You say you were home by five forty-five.'

'I said it because that's what time I got there.'

'But your wife says you didn't get home until after seven,' said Norman.

'Well, she's mistaken.'

'She's quite sure it was after seven. She even told us dinner was nearly ruined because you were late.'

'She must be thinking of another night,' insisted Rossiter. 'We had dinner at around six o'clock. It wasn't ruined at all.'

'So why does your wife say different?' asked Slater.

'Like I said, she must be mistaken.' Rossiter sighed, wearily.

'But she insists she's not mistaken,' said Norman.

'Well, she must be lying than,' snapped Rossiter. 'I assure you I was home by five forty-five.'

'Why would your wife be lying?' persisted Slater.

'I don't know,' replied Rossiter, angrily. 'Why don't you ask her?'

'We don't think you were home as early as you claim.'

'So where do you think I was?'

'We'll come to that shortly,' said Slater.

'How did you come to have Diana Woods' mobile phone in your bedside drawer, Mr Rossiter?' asked Norman.

'What?' Rossiter sounded genuinely horrified. 'I don't know what you're talking about!'

'Well, let me spell it out, as I'm the one who found it,' said Norman. 'You have a bedside cabinet next to your bed, yes?'

'Yes, that's right,' said Rossiter. 'Doesn't everyone?'

'Well, I searched it when we were there this morning,' said Norman. 'Second drawer down, tucked right at the back, under your socks, I found a mobile phone. Closer inspection showed it belonged to Diana Woods.'

Rossiter looked bewildered. He turned to Humphreys.

'I don't understand this, Brian,' he said, shakily. 'I don't understand what's going on.'

'We've been looking for that phone, since Diana's body was found,' said Slater. 'Perhaps you can explain to us how it came to be in your possession.'

Rossiter's earlier smugness and bravado had completely evaporated now. The colour had drained from his face, and sweat shone on his forehead. Humphreys had gone a strange colour, too. Slater thought the solicitor was rapidly realising he was out of his depth.

'So how did the phone come to be in your drawer, Mr Rossiter?' asked Slater, again.

'I have no idea how it got there,' he said, quietly.

'Is that the best you can do?' asked Norman.

'It's the truth. I can't tell you any more than that, can I?'

'I have to say, it's not looking too good for you, is it?'

'Why are you doing this to me?' asked Rossiter.

'Doing what?'

'Setting me up.'

'We're just doing our job,' said Norman. 'We don't need to set you up. The evidence is all pointing at you already.'

'But I haven't done anything. Why won't you believe me?' Rossiter's voice was pleading.

'Like DS Norman just explained,' said Slater. 'The evidence is all pointing your way.'

'And if we believed everyone who claimed to be innocent, we'd never catch anyone,' added Norman.

'What can I do, Brian?' asked Rossiter, turning to Humphreys. 'They won't listen to what I'm telling them.'

'I think you should probably keep quiet and not answer any more questions,' Humphreys said.

'That's not really gonna help him get out of here, is it?' said Norman. 'Because so far he hasn't managed to explain anything satisfactorily.'

'Do you ever use the Rochester & Dorset runabout vehicle, Mr Rossiter?' asked Slater.

'What?'

'Small, white, Peugeot van,' said Slater. 'Company runabout. I understand you all use it.'

'Well, yes, I've done a bit of shopping in it now and then,' said Rossiter.

'Have you ever used it to visit Diana Woods at her house?'

'No, I don't think I have,' said Rossiter.

'Are you sure about that?' asked Norman. 'Only we have a witness who claims to have seen someone matching your description visiting Diana in a small white van.'

'Well she's got the wrong man,' said Rossiter.

'She's seen you at lunchtimes,' explained Norman. 'She knows your routine. Diana arrives in her car, and then you arrive in the van a couple of minutes later. You stay for an hour or so, you leave, then five minutes later she leaves. Does that sound about right?'

Rossiter's mouth gaped open.

'Looks as if it's exactly right,' remarked Slater.

'I, err,' muttered Rossiter.

'If you're not going to follow my advice and keep quiet,' said Humphreys, quietly, 'you should at least stop lying and tell the truth. That sounds about right to me.'

'How the bloody hell would you know?' snapped Rossiter, turning on Humphreys.

'Everyone at Rochester's knows. You and Diana might have thought you were being clever, but it was obvious to all of us what was going on. And then someone followed you, just to confirm it.'

'You're supposed to be my bloody solicitor advising me here,' snarled Rossiter, 'Not a bloody witness for the prosecution.'

'I am advising you,' said Humphreys, testily. 'I advised you not to answer any more questions and you ignored me. As that's the case, I'm now advising you to stop being evasive and to start telling the truth.'

Slater watched happily as Rossiter and Humphreys argued about the rights and wrongs of telling the truth. He looked at Norman and raised his eyebrows. Norman smiled back at him. This was going very well so far.

'I hate to interrupt your little argument,' said Norman, affably. 'But you ought to know we have that company runabout in our garage downstairs. We have a forensic team going over it as we speak. If there's anything to find, they will find it.'

Rossiter looked blankly at Norman.

'Am I supposed to be concerned about that?' he asked.

'You tell me,' replied Norman.

'I can't see why it should worry me,' said Rossiter. 'I admit I have used it on occasion to visit Diana, but the last time I used that van was weeks ago.'

'Perhaps if I tell you we have a witness who saw that van driving away from Diana Woods' house, around about the time of the murder, you might be a bit more concerned,' said Slater.

'If someone did see that van,' said Rossiter, 'it can't have been me driving it. I was at home having my dinner.'

'Except your wife says you weren't,' said Norman.

'And I say she's wrong. Let me talk to her. I'll soon prove she's thinking of another night when I was late.'

'I don't think that's going to be possible,' said Norman. 'She says she doesn't want to talk to you at the moment.'

'But she's my wife. Why wouldn't she want to talk to me?'

'Maybe she's a bit concerned about what you've done.'

'But I keep telling you. I haven't done anything!' Rossiter shouted the last sentence and banged his fist on the table to emphasise his point.

'You have a bit of a temper there, Mr Rossiter,' said Slater. 'Is that what happened? Did you argue with Diana and lose your temper?'

'I've told you I didn't see Diana that day,' he said, wearily. 'How many more times do I have to tell you.'

'We should be getting some forensic results through soon,' said Norman. 'Do you want to save us all some time, and tell us what happened?'

'I have nothing to say,' said Rossiter.

'Hooray,' said Humphreys, sarcastically. 'You've finally decided to listen to me, although it's probably too late now.'

'Let me tell you what we think happened,' said Slater. 'We know you and Diana had a thing going. You were a couple of rabbits, going at it whenever you got the chance. On business trips, during your lunch breaks, and you even resorted to groping and touching each other up in the office.'

Rossiter actually looked embarrassed at the mention of the office groping.

'Oh,' said Norman. 'Did you really think no one could see what you were up to? Someone described frequently seeing you slide your hand up her skirt when she was stood at your desk. Your behaviour was described as "gross". I guess you were just checking to make sure she was wearing that expensive underwear you bought her. Like the feel of silk, do you?'

'Then one day, just a few short months ago,' Slater continued, 'you pushed your luck a bit too far and Woody came home and caught you at it. This wasn't the first time Diana had been cheating on him, and she figured he wouldn't do anything even if he did find out, but she was wrong. This time he decided enough was enough. He packed his bags and walked out.'

'But there was a problem for Diana,' continued Norman. 'She hadn't realised just how much she needed him. Oh, she despised him for letting her screw around all the time, but at the same time he was always there for her. He was her rock. But once he was gone, she suddenly realised what she was missing. So she tried to win him back. She even begged him to come back, but he was resolute. This time there was no going back.'

'This is sheer fantasy,' said Rossiter. 'I told you before she was glad to see the back of him.'

'That's right, you did,' said Norman. 'So how do you explain the letters he has from her, in her handwriting, telling him how much she was missing him, and asking him to come back?'

Rossiter obviously didn't quite understand what he was hearing.

'She didn't tell you about that? You seem to have forgotten Diana was practised in the art of deception. She was an accomplished liar. Do you really think she would have told you the truth about her and Woody? Come on, get real. She played you like she played everyone else.'

'So now Diana had a problem,' said Slater, continuing with his theory. 'She needed someone, and her someone had gone. We believe she then decided to make you her new someone. You were happy to have sex with her, so she figured it shouldn't be too hard to convince you to ditch your wife and install her as your new wife.'

Rossiter smiled and shook his head.

'More fantasy, I'm afraid,' he said. 'That was never going to happen.'

'Oh, we know that,' said Slater. 'You couldn't afford to give your wife grounds for divorce. She told us she'd take you for every penny you have, and then she'd ruin you, if that happened. But Diana wasn't prepared to accept that as your excuse, was she? She kept insisting, and in the end you decided you had to put a stop to it.'

'Then you got a lucky break and returned from London just after everyone had gone home. You took the company van, and drove out to Diana's house. Of course when she saw you at the door she was happy to let you in. You see, we know she let her attacker in. We also know she knew her attacker well enough to turn her back on him while she filled the kettle to make tea.'

Slater had stopped for breath, so Norman carried on.

'And that's when you saw your opportunity,' said Norman. 'You took a knife from her own knife block and stabbed her. Then you made your way back to Rochesters, parked the van back in the garage and went home. And that's why you were late home that day.'

Rochester didn't say a word. He just stared at Norman. It was as if he was in shock. Humphreys looked equally stunned, but he was now staring at Rossiter, with a look of horror at what he appeared to have done.

The silence was broken by a knock on the door.

Norman went across to the door and opened it. There was a whispered conversation and then he came back with a sheet of paper. He read it and then handed it to Slater who read it twice.

'It seems you're keeping our forensics team busy, Mr Rossiter,' said Slater, looking up from his reading.

'If you've found my fingerprints, that's hardly cause for celebration, is it?' said Rossiter. 'I've already told you I've used the van so I would be more surprised if you haven't found them. I expect you've also found another twenty or thirty prints besides mine. Are you going to ask the rest of the staff to provide fingerprint samples so they can be eliminated?'

He obviously thought he'd caught Slater out with this suggestion, and his natural superior smugness spread across his face once again.

'Already in hand as we speak,' said Norman, and the grin disappeared from Rossiter's face. 'You really do think we're stupid, don't you?'

'We actually worked out that there might be hundreds of prints on a van everyone uses,' said Slater. 'But that's not what I'm talking about. Someone's left a packet of condoms in the van, with one missing. And there's a receipt, too. They were bought the day before Diana died. Whoever had sex with her the day she died used a condom.'

'Than perhaps it was another male member of staff,' suggested Rossiter, slouching confidently back in his chair.

'The receipt ties up with a transaction made with your credit card,' said Norman. 'Exactly the right amount, at exactly the right time, and in exactly the right place.'

'And where am I supposed to have made this transaction?' asked Rossiter sarcastically.

'Local supermarket,' said Norman.

Now Rossiter sat bolt upright.

'This is getting ridiculous,' he spluttered. 'I haven't been to a supermarket in years. My wife does all the shopping. And anyway, what on earth would I want to buy condoms for? I've had a bloody vasectomy!'

This was something Slater hadn't considered.

'You have?' he said, unable to hide the surprise in his voice.

'Can you prove that?' asked Norman.

'I'm sure my doctor will confirm it,' said Rossiter, with a chuckle. 'Now that surprised you, didn't it? But the ladies like it, you see. It removes the need for condoms, and so many of them hate the damned things.'

'Not exactly a recipe for safe sex, is it?' said Norman. 'I hope you get yourself checked on a regular basis. Diana liked to share it around, you know.'

'Yes, I did know,' said Rossiter. 'I do the same thing myself. Never miss an opportunity, that was our shared ethos.'

'Oh, whoa,' said Norman, pulling a horrified face. 'That's information I really don't want to know.'

'But it might prove to be highly relevant in this case, don't you think?' sneered Rossiter.

'We don't think the condom was used for protection against pregnancy or disease,' continued Slater, ignoring the exchange between Norman and Rossiter. 'We believe it was used to avoid leaving any DNA evidence. Having a vasectomy wouldn't have been good enough to stop that.'

'How many bloody times do I have to say it,' spluttered Rossiter. 'I did not have sex with Diana on that day. I didn't even set eyes on her or speak to her. I was up in London at the time you say I was having sex with her, and I was at home when you say she was killed.'

Slater chose to ignore this latest denial and carry one with the forensic findings.

'They've also found traces of blood under the driver's seat,' he announced.

Rossiter simply stared down at the table in front of him.

'Where's the blood from?' Norman asked Rossiter. 'Is it Diana's? We'll find out when we analyse it. I suppose you hid the murder weapon under there until you dumped it, right?'

'I'm not saying another word. You seem to have made your minds up I killed Diana, even though it's obvious I'm being set up by someone. I'll save my breath for someone who wants to hear what I'm actually saying.'

Norman looked across at Slater, who nodded back to him.

'Well,' said Norman. 'If you're sure you don't want to speak to us anymore I think we're probably done here for now. I'm afraid you haven't cleared up any of the discrepancies we mentioned at the start, and now it appears we're finding more and more evidence pointing your way.

'I think you probably need a few minutes with your solicitor, and then I'll ask the PC outside to escort you back to your cell. Did the duty sergeant book you into the penthouse suite or the wedding suite?'

Rossiter didn't answer Norman. He just continued to stare at the table.

CHAPTER TWENTY

'Have you found anything else yet, Becksy?' asked Slater. He'd come down to the workshops where Ian Becks and his team were going through the van. He wasn't exactly sure why he'd come down here and not gone straight back to the incident room, but there was a growing feeling of uncertainty that was quietly nibbling away inside his head.

'I've found dozens of fingerprints,' said Becks, gloomily. 'There's no way we're going to be able to conclusively prove Rossiter drove the van to Diana's that day. We've got soil samples from the wheel arches that I'm pretty sure will prove the van has been driven down Bishops Common, but it's not going to prove when it was there, or who was driving it.'

'He admits he's taken it there in the past,' said Slater. 'But swears blind he didn't use it the day she was murdered.'

'And I don't think we can prove he did,' said Becks, gloomily.

'What about the packet of condoms?' asked Slater. 'Are there any prints on that?'

'Not even a partial. I've even tried the receipt and there's nothing there either. This guy was very careful where he put his fingers. He must have been wearing gloves all the damned time.'

'There has to be something,' said Slater desperately. 'At this rate we're not going to be able to prove anything.'

'We do have the blood under the seat. At least if it's Diana's blood it proves there's a link between her death and this van.'

Becks' phone bleeped quietly as he spoke. He snatched it from his pocket and listened intently to the caller.

'You're quite sure?' he asked.

He looked at Slater as he ended the call.

'Apparently there's a partial print on the ignition keys that doesn't match any of the prints we've taken from the staff at Rochester's,' he told Slater. 'It also doesn't match any of the prints we've taken from the inside of the van.'

'So what does that prove, and what does it mean? And how does it help? We need to prove Rossiter was in that van, not that someone, at some time, has been playing with the keys.'

'D'you want a theory?' asked Becks, with a glint in his eye.

'Will I like it?'

'I can't guarantee it. Because I can't promise it's going to fit in with what you're trying to prove.'

'Oh, don't say that,' said Slater, sighing.

'You've got doubts, though, haven't you?' asked Becks. 'You wouldn't be down here nagging me if you were sure, or if the guy had confessed.'

'Let's just say we've got two and two,' said Slater, unhappily. 'But I'm not convinced they actually add up to four.'

'I could make it worse.'

'Well, it wouldn't be the first time, would it? Go on, then.'

'When we did the crime scene, we didn't find any fingerprints,' said Becks. 'So we assumed the killer wore gloves. Now, we're pretty sure this wasn't a spur of the moment murder, right? We know the killer was quite careful, so it's not unreasonable to assume they wore gloves when they were driving the van. But what if they were just a tiny bit careless when they took the keys, and didn't put the gloves on until they were walking to the van?'

'Are you suggesting the killer could be someone we don't even have as a suspect,' asked Slater. 'That's a bit of a long shot, isn't it?'

'It's just a theory. And I did say you probably wouldn't like it.'

'But how are we going to prove it?' asked Slater.

'We're assuming it's only staff who drive this van,' said Becks. 'But what if they allow someone else to drive it?'

'I suppose it wouldn't hurt to ask.'

'I thought you'd got lost,' said Norman, when Slater joined him in the canteen. 'One minute you were following me, and then suddenly you were gone.'

'Yeah, sorry about that,' said Slater. 'I thought I'd go and see if Becksy had any real evidence yet.'

'And?'

'Zilch. He's got hundreds of fingerprints all over the van, but there's nothing to suggest Rossiter was driving it the day she died. All they've got is one partial print on the ignition key, and that doesn't match Rossiter, or anyone else at Rochester's.'

'Oh, great. Someone we haven't even considered yet. That's all we need.'

'It could just be from the guy who services the van,' said Slater. 'So don't hold your breath. Anyway, what's the verdict? Is he guilty? We seem to have plenty of circumstantial evidence but nothing concrete. And he's still denying it.'

'I'm a bit more convinced than you are,' said Norman. 'And I'd love for an arsehole like him to be guilty of something, but, if I'm honest, I'd like to be a whole lot more convinced.'

'It's not beyond reasonable doubt, is it?'

'We'd have to be pretty lucky, I think.'

They both stared gloomily into space, contemplating their next move.

'Okay. So let's start by taking a look at why we think it's not him,' said Slater.

'The pathologist suggested she was killed with an upward thrust,' said Norman. 'That suggests the killer is small. Rossiter is over six feet tall.'

'He couldn't have had sex with her at lunchtime on the day she

died. He was up in London. There's just no way it could have been
him. And, anyway, John Hollis has admitted it was him, and he has no
reason to lie that I can see.'

'And why would Rossiter buy condoms, and then leave them in the
van for us to find?' asked Norman. 'Our theory said he bought them to
avoid leaving any DNA, but that theory doesn't work now, does it?'

'We know he bought the condoms. But why? I can't figure out
where they come into it. Or, are they just a red herring?'

'Maybe some women insist on it,' said Norman. 'They can't all be
happy to risk an infection.'

'Okay,' said Slater. 'But why leave them in the van? I mean, anyone
could have found them. You'd have to be pretty stupid, right?'

'Yeah,' said Norman. 'He's an arrogant bugger, and he's got some
questionable morals, but he ain't stupid.'

'And then there's the thing with the mobile phones,' said Slater. 'He
would know they would link him to Diana and make him a suspect.'

'You're right. He woulda got rid of both of them, especially Diana's.
I mean, hiding it in the sock drawer? Nah. I don't buy it. He would
have dumped it. It's all a bit too convenient, isn't it?'

'Alright,' said Slater. 'So we're agreed it's all way too obvious. So the
next question is, who would want to set him up?'

'This could be a long list,' said Norman. 'He's not exactly Mr Popu-
larity, is he? You could probably start with everyone at Rochester &
Dorset.'

'Good point,' conceded Slater, with a smile. 'But let's try to focus
on those we know would have an axe to grind.'

'Well, Ian Woods, for one. The guy wrecked his marriage.'

'True,' agreed Slater. 'But he has an alibi for the time of the murder.
And how could he plant stuff in Rossiter's sock drawer, or in his office
desk?'

'Maybe he had an accomplice.'

'Rossiter's wife? I think she's a more likely candidate to be the
killer than an accomplice. First she denied Rossiter had affairs, then
she changed her story and claimed they had an agreement as long as he
kept it away from home. And we know Rossiter and Diana weren't just
doing it close to home, they were actually doing it in her home.'

'But she also said she didn't believe Diana was like that,' said Norman.

'Yeah, right,' said Slater. 'D'you think she was telling the truth about that?'

'She's been way too cool about the whole situation. I'm not sure she's told us the truth about anything so far. She's also small enough to have caused the stab wound that killed Diana, and she would have access to Rossiter's credit cards.'

'The more we talk about her, the more I see her as a suspect,' said Slater. 'But we should also consider Frosty Knickers, shouldn't we? I get the impression she spends a lot of time clearing up behind Rossiter, and she's definitely pissed off with having to do it. Perhaps she's had enough and decided to get rid of the problem once and for all.'

'She'd certainly have the opportunity to get at his desk, and the van,' agreed Norman. 'She's also small enough to be the killer.'

'Yes, but how would she get into his sock drawer?'

'What if she was working with Angela Rossiter?'

'That's another possibility,' agreed Slater, wearily. 'Or are we looking for a conspiracy where there isn't one?'

'I'm gonna be tearing my hair out soon,' said Norman. 'Maybe they're all in it together.'

'A three-way conspiracy,' said Slater, laughing. 'Now that would be something, wouldn't it?'

'Okay, okay,' said Norman with a smile. 'Woody has an alibi, so maybe not a three-way conspiracy. Whatever it is, I think we need to look a whole lot closer at Angela Rossiter and Celia Rowntree, don't you?'

'Definitely,' agreed Slater. 'But I think we should keep Rossiter where he is for now. If someone has set him up, it's better they think he's still our main suspect.'

'You still think we're missing something, don't you? Something was bothering you when we were at Diana's house the other day and you never did work out what it was. How about we go back there again? Maybe it'll come to you.'

'It can't do any harm, I suppose,' said Slater. 'But first we need to see if Jane's found anything on the CCTV disks.'

. . .

'I haven't found any CCTV cameras that can help us find out who used his credit card,' said Jolly. 'I've tried just about everywhere.'

'Damn,' said Slater. 'How about the CCTV discs from Rochester's? Did you find the one we want?'

'It's not there. I've been through them all twice. The dates and letters all tally with the book, but you take a look at this.'

She handed Slater a CD. He looked at it, turned it over and looked at the other side, then handed it to Norman.

'Right,' he said, doubtfully, not quite sure what he was supposed to see.

'Now look at this one,' she said, handing him another disk.

He looked at both sides of this disc, and then passed it on to Norman. It was as he handed it to Norman, and saw the two discs side by side, that he noticed what she meant.

'Wait a minute,' he said. 'That's a brand new disc, isn't it? The first one's covered in scratches.'

'Oh yeah,' agreed Norman. 'You can't miss it when they're next to each other. Let me guess which one's been replaced. Would it be the one we're looking for, by any chance?'

Jolly nodded her head.

'Rossiter?' she asked.

'Not necessarily,' said Slater. 'He doesn't have ready access to the discs and would have to risk being seen going into that room. It could just as easily be Celia Rowntree. She has access to these discs at all times.'

'So does the receptionist,' said Norman.

'I don't really see her as a killer, do you?' said Slater. 'And what would her motive be?'

'She does despise Rossiter,' Norman pointed out.

'I think that's a pretty universal feeling, don't you?' asked Slater. 'Especially among the women who work there.'

'I can't argue with that,' said Norman, with a wry smile. 'Anyway, we'd better get down there and find out why there's a disc missing.'

'Right. Take Jane with you. And find out if anyone outside the company uses the van. Then bring Jane down to Diana's house and meet me there. Maybe we need a woman's eyes to see what we're missing.'

'I spoke to that frosty cow,' said Norman, when they met up later. 'She claims she has no idea where the disc could have gone. She says she hasn't been near them recently and Millie Gibson is the only one who touches them.'

'Do you think she's lying?' asked Slater.

'Is the sky blue?'

'What about Millie? What did she have to say?'

'She says she hasn't thrown any discs away, or renewed any. She says anyone could have done it, and it could have happened any time she was out of the reception area. The discs are used in strict rotation so as long as it was put back in the right order she wouldn't even have noticed until she got to that disc.'

'D'you believe her?' asked Slater.

'For sure,' said Norman.

'What about the van?'

'Frosty says it's staff only. But I thought to ask Millie the same question. According to her, Rossiter arranged for his wife to use it for her charity work. She's used it several times, and she doesn't even ask. She just turns up and takes it like a member of staff.'

'Now that's very interesting,' said Slater. 'If we can find a way to prove Celia Rowntree knew about that, maybe your conspiracy theory isn't so far off the mark.'

'It works, doesn't it?' agreed Norman. 'They could easily have worked together to solve a shared problem. Diana gets bumped off, Rossiter gets put away, and the two women most affected by their bad behaviour get to live happily ever after.'

While they were talking, Jane Jolly was wandering around the kitchen.

'Are you sure it's in here?' she asked Slater.

'I can't say for sure,' he replied. 'But it's while I was in here that I felt I was missing something.'

'So it's a good place to start, then.'

She opened some cupboards, peered inside and closed them again. Then she did the same with some of the drawers, and it was one of these that finally caught her attention.

'What?' asked Slater.

'Look at these knives,' she said. 'They're real chefs' knives. They must have cost a fortune.'

'Yeah, but she was well known for her cooking,' said Norman. 'People like that tend to buy expensive stuff.'

'That's true enough,' agreed Jolly, but she continued staring into the drawer. 'Didn't we take a knife block in as evidence?'

'Yeah,' said Slater. 'The murder weapon came from it.'

'Maybe it's just me,' she continued, still staring into the drawer. 'But don't you think it seems a bit odd to have all these top quality, very expensive chefs' knives in the drawers and then have a cheap, run-of-the-mill knife block as well?'

'Was it that bad?' asked Norman. 'I can't really remember what it was like. But even if it was crap, perhaps she just used the crappy ones for everyday use, and kept the best ones for special occasions.'

'But everything in this kitchen is expensive. Just look around. There's nothing cheap anywhere else in here. In fact, there's nothing cheap in this whole house, apart from that knife block.'

'So, maybe someone gave it to her as a present,' said Norman. 'And she kept it out so she wouldn't hurt their feelings if they came round.'

'Somehow I don't see Diana Woods as the type to worry about hurting someone's feelings,' said Jolly.

'Ah, but don't forget she was like two people rolled into one,' said Norman. 'Maybe the heartless tart wouldn't care about hurting someone's feelings, but then the nice, angelic Diana wouldn't want to hurt anyone.'

'But you're not convinced, are you?' said Norman.

'No,' Jolly said. 'This woman does not like cheap tat in her house. She would have thrown away the cheap knife block or maybe given it to a charity shop. She certainly wouldn't have kept it out where everyone could see it.'

Slater had been listening carefully to the exchange between Jolly and Norman. It was telling him something, but what was it? And then it came to him.

'That's it!' he said. 'Jane's right. The knife block's wrong. It doesn't make any sense.'

'And nor do you right now,' said Norman, looking puzzled. 'I'm lost.'

'And I have been, too. Until now. All the time, we've assumed the killer came to see Diana, saw an opportunity, took a knife from the knife block, and stabbed her, right?'

'Yeah,' said Norman.

'But that's what's wrong, isn't it?' said Slater. 'When I was talking to Ian Becks earlier, he said about how the killer seemed to have made a point of wearing gloves and been really careful about not leaving a trace of evidence anywhere, all the hallmarks of a premeditated murder.'

'But then we're saying the killer used a knife taken from a knife block, which just happened to be in the kitchen,' said Norman, comprehension dawning on his face. 'Which is opportunist, and anything but premeditated.'

'Exactly,' said Slater. 'Would our killer really take so much care, and then rely on a piece of luck to provide a murder weapon? It doesn't make sense, does it? I seem to recall that knife block was brand new, or at least it looked new. So, what if the killer brought it with them?'

'It's an interesting idea,' admitted Norman.

'But why not just bring a knife?' said Jolly. 'Why bring the whole block?'

'To throw us off the scent,' said Slater. 'Or to get rid of it. If you just took one knife from it, you'd still have the rest of the knives and the block to dispose of. This way you don't have to dispose of it at all.'

'So, if we could find out who bought that knife block we might just find our killer,' said Jolly.

'It would be a big help.'

'Well, shopping is one thing I am quite good at,' she said, smiling. 'I'm pretty sure I can find out where it came from, and with any luck I might be able to prove who bought it. But first I need to see it again to make sure I know exactly what I'm looking for.'

CHAPTER TWENTY-ONE

Next morning, Slater, Norman and Jolly were in Slater's car, parked just around the corner from the market.

'Are you sure you'll be okay?' asked Slater.

'Of course,' said Jolly. 'The only problem I might have is if the guy isn't there today. He has one of those stalls that's here one week and gone the next. If you buy anything you never know if he'll be there again if you have problems with it.'

'Well, let's hope he is there, because we need one of those knife blocks. Have you got the photos?'

'Of course I have,' she said, with a forced smile. 'I have done this sort of thing before, you know.'

'I'm sorry. Just make sure you don't get into trouble. Any problems or doubts, you give us a call, alright? We'll be waiting in the car.'

'Are you sure you don't want us to come with you?' asked Norman.

'I'm just going shopping,' she said. 'What could be more innocent than a girl going shopping? I just want to see if my friend bought her knife block from him, and if he recognises her I want to buy one just like hers. If I walk around with two heavies for protection we're likely to scare the guy. I'll be fine, honestly.'

She pushed open the car door and slipped out.

'I'll be ten minutes,' she said, as she closed the door.

T rue to her word, it was almost exactly ten minutes later when she opened the door and slid into the back seat.

'Look what I've got,' she said, brandishing a carrier bag.

'Oh, great,' said Slater. 'Well done, Jane.'

'Is it the same one?' asked Norman.

'It's exactly the same. And we're in luck. He doesn't sell many of them so he tends to remember who he sells them to. I asked him if my friend had bought one, because I wanted one the same as hers. I told him it would have been ten days, or maybe a fortnight ago. He described a woman to me, I showed him the photograph of Celia Rowntree, and he identified her.'

'Brilliant,' Slater said, smiling broadly. 'Now we're starting to make some sense of all this. I think it's time we had a serious chat with Mrs Frosty Knickers, don't you, Norm?'

'For sure,' said Norman, beaming back. 'Houston, we have lift off.'

'S he doesn't look quite so full of herself now, does she?' said Norman, as he and Slater peered through the observation window at Celia Rowntree.

'How did she take it when you told her she was coming in for a chat?' asked Slater.

'She was the epitome of hostility when we arrived in reception,' said Norman. 'She told me I was wasting my time without making an appointment. Then she reeled off all this crap about how we were tres-passing, and how we were violating her human rights.'

'I bet you were *so* impressed.'

'Actually, in part, it was pretty impressive, to be honest,' said Norman, grinning. 'And she looked so pleased with herself, I just couldn't resist letting her ramble on and on. It's amazing how much she can say without stopping for breath. That was the impressive part. We probably ought to contact the Guinness Book of Records.'

'And then you got bored, I suppose.'

'Actually it was Jane who lost interest first,' said Norman. 'She interrupted old Frosty to tell her she could save all the bullshit for when we got to the station. That's when it got really entertaining. Frosty does indignity better than almost anyone I can think of. Apparently no one speaks to her like Jane did. But then Jane showed she can get pretty feisty herself.

'You should have been there. You would have loved it, especially the bit when Jane announced, at the top of her voice, that if the stroppy cow didn't shut up and come quietly she was going to be handcuffed and dragged out. That's when she started screaming about her rights all over again, and how she was entitled to a solicitor.'

'Is there a solicitor on the way?' asked Slater.

'Yeah.' Norman chuckled. 'It's that Brian Humphreys guy from Rochester's again. He actually came down to reception, while we were there, to see what all the noise was about. Man, he was not impressed to find another senior member of staff was being dragged into this investigation.'

'I bet he wishes he worked anywhere but Rochester's right now,' said Slater, laughing.

'Yeah, he kinda made that quite clear,' said Norman. 'But apparently it's written into his contract that he has to represent senior members of staff. At least that's what Frosty told him. I guess he never expected he would find it necessary to represent anyone for anything as serious as murder. Poor guy.'

'Good morning, Mrs Rowntree,' said Slater, with a broad smile, as he entered the interview room alongside Norman. 'Thank you so much for coming down to see us.'

'I don't seem to have had much choice,' she hissed.

'That's right,' said Slater, settling into his seat opposite her. 'You don't have any choice.'

He looked at her, but said nothing. She glared malevolently back at him.

'Let's get something clear, right from the start,' he said. 'This isn't some game we're playing here. We're conducting a murder inquiry, and so far you've been evasive, and downright hostile, towards myself and my fellow officers. At the very least we shall almost certainly be charging you with obstructing our enquiries, but I think it's likely we'll be charging you with something a lot more serious, don't you?'

'I don't know what you're talking about,' she said, uncertainly.

'You're sure about that, are you?

She didn't answer, preferring to study her nails instead.

Norman reached down under his seat and produced a carrier bag which he placed on the table. He pulled the knife block from the bag and placed it on the table in front of her.

'D'you recognise this?' he asked her.

'It's a knife block,' she said. 'Anyone can see that.'

'Have you ever bought one like this?'

'No. I don't buy cheap tat like that. I wouldn't give it house room.'

'What about buying it to give to someone else?' he persisted.

'I've never bought one of those in my life,' she said, adamantly. 'I wouldn't know where to find one.'

'Well let me help you out there,' said Norman. 'There's only one place you can get them around here, and that's the market in town.'

'I never shop there,' she said. 'You never know what you're buying in places like that. I prefer to buy quality goods.'

'Oh, really? Did you know you have a double walking around town?'

'What on earth are you talking about?' she asked, wearily. 'Is this why I'm here? So you can ask me where I do my shopping? Do you really think this is proper use of your time? And how on earth can it be relevant to your inquiry?'

'You know damned well why it's relevant, Celia,' said Norman. 'It's relevant because Diana was killed with a knife from a knife block just like this one. A knife block that you bought from the market about ten days ago.'

Celia Rowntree went very quiet, and her face seemed to turn a ghostly shade of white.

'The guy in the market sells very few of these,' said Norman. 'So he tends to remember who he sells them to. He remembered you because he thought you were nice looking, and because he didn't think you were the type to buy something so cheap. As a result, he was able to describe you perfectly. He also picked your photo out.'

'He must have been mistaken.' Her fingers tapped nervously on the top of the table.

'I should warn you there's CCTV overlooking the entrance to the market,' said Slater.

At the mention of CCTV, she seemed to slump in her seat, almost as if the stuffing had been removed from inside her.

'I bought it as a present for a friend,' she muttered.

'Not much of a friend,' said Norman. 'Or do you buy "cheap tat you wouldn't give house room" for all your friends?'

She looked around the room wildly, as if she hoped someone would appear and whisk her away.

'So who is this friend?' asked Slater. 'Maybe they can confirm you gave them the knife block.'

'Err, I don't remember. I didn't give it to them. It was just too tacky.'

'So you went to the market you never go to, to buy a knife block you wouldn't give house room to, to give to a friend you can't remember. Have I got that right?' asked Norman.

'Yes. No,' she said, and then she began to cry, quietly.

'No. That's not right is it, Celia?' said Norman, gently. 'You see you've been lying to us all along, haven't you? We think you bought the knife block as part of a plan to kill Diana Woods and frame Bruce Rossiter for her murder. We think you planted the mobile phone we found in his desk, and you removed the CCTV disc that shows who used the company runabout the day Diana was killed.'

She continued to cry quietly, her head in her hands.

'We could charge you with her murder, right now, Celia,' said Slater. 'But we don't think you were the murderer. That was someone else. You were just the accomplice. Are we right?'

At last she looked up at him, snot and tears dripping from her face. She shook her head.

'You don't understand,' she whined. 'You just don't understand.'

'But we want to understand,' said Slater. 'We want to help you.'

'Let's take a break for ten minutes, Celia,' said Norman. 'I'll go and get you a cup of tea while you get yourself together. Then maybe you'd better tell us all about it. Okay?'

She nodded slowly, then slumped forward onto the desk and began to sob quietly.

CHAPTER TWENTY-TWO

'Good evening, Mrs Rossiter. So nice of you to join us,' said Slater, back in the same interview room, a few hours later.

'What am I doing here?' she demanded. 'You've already arrested my husband for Diana's murder. What more do you want from me?'

'I'm afraid we have one or two things we don't quite understand,' said Slater. 'As Mr Rossiter's wife, we think you might be able to help us.'

'Was it really necessary to send a couple of goons?' she asked, bitterly.

'We find people tend to get here much quicker when we do that.' Norman smiled genially. 'We wouldn't want anyone getting lost on the way here, now would we?'

'And there are men crawling all over my house. Again.'

'That's what a search warrant allows us to do. But don't worry, they'll lock up when they've finished.'

She glowered at the two of them, but said nothing. They had thought she was likely to be a much tougher nut to crack than Celia Rowntree, and it looked as if they were going to be proved right.

'Does your husband ever go to the supermarket to do food shopping?' asked Norman.

'Hah!' She laughed. 'The fat pig doesn't even know where the super-market is. If it was left to him to put food in the cupboards we'd starve.'

'So he doesn't shop in supermarkets?' asked Slater.

'Never.'

'So you do all the supermarket shopping?' asked Norman.

'Yes,' she snapped impatiently. 'There isn't anyone else, is there?'

'So, were you in the supermarket on the Sunday before Diana died?'

'God. I don't remember.' She sighed. 'Does it really matter?'

'Yes, it does matter, so I'll tell you,' said Norman. 'You were there. We have your till receipt.'

'So why ask me if you already know? Anyway, what's this got to do with Diana's death?'

'Less than five minutes after you checked out, someone paid for some condoms using your husband's credit card,' said Norman.

'And what's that got to do with me?' she asked. 'If I'd bought condoms they would have been on my till receipt.'

'We believe you paid for those condoms, separately, at one of the self-serve check outs.'

'And why would I do that?'

'Because, that way, no one would notice you were using your husband's credit card.' Norman smiled, triumphantly.

'I didn't–' she began.

'I should tell you something, before you carry on lying,' interrupted Slater. 'One of our team is a mother of three. She spends a lot of time in the supermarket. She's also one smart cookie who notices all sorts of things. It's because of her that we know there are CCTV cameras on the self-serve tills.'

Angela Rossiter glared at him.

'And it's against the law to buy condoms, is it?' she snapped.

'Not as far as I know,' said Norman. 'But I'm curious to know why you paid for them with your husband's credit card.'

'Because they're for his use, of course. Why the hell should I pay for them? I stopped having sex with him years ago.'

'So why would he need them?' asked Slater.

'Why do you think?' she said, looking at him as though he were stupid. 'I might not want him grunting and snorting all over me, but it seems there are some women who aren't quite so fussy. I don't want to find he's fathered a child on our bloody doorstep again, do I?'

'Do you think he could, then?' asked Slater. 'Father a child?'

'Didn't they teach any sex education at your school?' she mocked. 'My God, what world do you live in?'

'Oh we did sex education, Angela,' said Slater. 'In fact it was one of my favourite subjects. But I always thought if a man had a vasectomy it meant he couldn't father children. Isn't that the whole point of it?'

Angela looked confused.

Norman tutted.

'Oh, my, my, you didn't know, did you? I knew you and old Brucie probably weren't the best communicators, but boy, things must be really bad between you if he had an operation like that and you didn't even know.'

'And they say romance is dead,' said Slater. 'Why on earth do you keep your marriage going if it's got that bad? Can it ever be worth it?'

'You wouldn't understand.' She sniffed. 'I have my position to consider.'

'Some people will do anything for money, I guess,' said Norman.

'Even frame their husband for murder,' added Slater.

Angela looked at him, enquiringly.

'We had Celia Rowntree in here earlier today,' he said. 'As a matter of fact she's still here, finding out what it's like inside one of our cells.'

Angela had jerked her head at the mention of Celia.

'You see, Celia's not as tough as you,' said Norman. 'So it didn't take long for us to expose the lies in her story. After that she became a lot more co-operative. So you might want to stop and consider whether you should continue with the lies, or do us all a favour and start telling the truth.'

'What did she tell you?' she hissed. 'It's all a pack of lies.'

'Is it?' said Slater. 'Well, it all seems to make sense to us, and it fits in very nicely with what we already know. But we want to make sure we get it right, so perhaps you'd better tell us your side of the story.'

'There is no story.' She sat back and folded her arms.

'You said you didn't want him to father a child on your doorstep again,' said Slater. 'What did you mean by that?'

'What did you think I meant? I'm sure Celia told you. He's always been cock happy, but she was the first one he actually got pregnant. He had to pay for her to have an abortion so her husband wouldn't find out. They might have got away with it, but she nearly died under the anaesthetic. There was no way they could keep that from her husband. He was gone within the week, and Celia's never been the same since. That was nearly ten years ago now.'

'So how come you didn't kick your husband out?'

'What? Give up my lifestyle? No way,' she said, with a wicked grin. 'I can make him suffer much more by staying and spending all his money. I made a deal with him. He couldn't ever touch me again, and he couldn't ever do it on our doorstep again.'

'But he has been doing it on your doorstep, hasn't he,' said Norman.

'With that cheap tart of a PA.'

'And you thought he might get her pregnant, too,' said Slater.

'I thought he was taking precautions. I didn't know he'd had a vasectomy.'

'But that's why the condoms were such a big mistake, Angela. If you hadn't bought them we might have been convinced your husband was guilty, but we knew that didn't add up, and it made us ask questions.'

'So you knew all about him and Diana,' said Norman. 'That's a very good motive for wanting her dead. And both you and Celia have good reason for wanting to frame your husband. But did you have to murder Diana Woods as part of your plan. Couldn't you have found another way that didn't involve murder?'

'Oh, but me and Celia didn't murder anyone,' she said with a smile. 'What do you take us for? All we did was try to frame my husband. That was all we set out to do, and we very nearly succeeded.'

'But didn't you drive the Rochester's runabout to Diana's that day?' asked Slater. 'Didn't you stab her in the back with a knife from the knife block you took with you?'

'Don't be silly,' she said, smiling. 'I was at home cooking my husband's dinner. We were having dinner at the time she was killed. My husband told you that several times, but you wouldn't believe him.'

Slater and Norman hadn't been expecting this. If Angela Rossiter hadn't killed Diana Woods, who had? They'd been convinced Celia wasn't capable, but maybe they'd got that wrong. They were so sure it was Angela they hadn't even asked Celia if she had an alibi.

'We'll still charge you with conspiracy to murder,' said Norman, trying to regain the high ground.

'But what did I do, that would prove to a jury that I was guilty?' she asked, sweetly.

'I think we'll adjourn this interview, now,' said Slater. 'You can go and try one of our deluxe rooms for a while, Angela.'

She smiled her acceptance of his offer, but didn't say a word as she was led off to a cell.

'What the hell happened there?' Slater asked Norman. 'She's as good as admitted she's involved, but she denies murder.'

'Whether she actually did the stabbing, or not, she knows exactly what happened. She's laughing at us.'

'She knows we have a huge gap in our story. And we should have known it, too. We thought we had it all worked out, but we didn't think this through properly. Rossiter gave her an alibi right from the start. How could she be stabbing Diana if she was at home cooking his dinner?

'Now I'm not even sure we can make the conspiracy charge stick. All we can prove is Celia went shopping in the company van, bought a cheap knife block and left it in the van. And she admits that much. It's not exactly cut and dried, is it?'

'We know Angela took the van out on the afternoon Diana died,' said Norman. 'But we can't prove it, because the CCTV evidence is missing, and the only witness we have insists she saw a man driving the van and not a woman.'

'And it's the same with the mobile phones.' Slater sighed, unhappily. 'We know how they got where we found them, but we can't prove it.'

'A good lawyer would argue there's more than enough doubt,' agreed Norman. 'Unless the search team find something, we're in trouble.'

'What are we missing, Norm?' asked Slater. 'There has to be something.'

'I guess we're gonna have to go over it all again,' Norman said, shaking his head. 'And we need to be quick. Right now we're holding three suspects and the clock's ticking. In fact, one of those isn't even a suspect anymore.'

'We'd better order a takeaway,' said Slater, grimly. 'This is going to be a long night.'

CHAPTER TWENTY-THREE

I t was just after nine o'clock the next morning when Slater made his way into the incident room. He looked jaded, as though he'd been up all night, but he managed to look pretty pleased with himself, too.

'I've just had a call from Wales,' said Jolly. 'They said to tell you your prisoner has been taken into custody and would you like to go and collect him.'

'That must have been a shock for him,' said Slater, smiling. 'I bet he thought he'd got away with it.'

'But I thought he was innocent and Angela Rossiter and Celia Rowntree were the guilty ones?'

'That's what we were supposed to think,' said Slater. 'But they knew we couldn't prove it because they both had alibis. Being stupid coppers, unable to find our own arses with both hands, we were supposed to give up at that point.'

'They got that wrong, then.'

'Instead of giving up we pulled an all-nighter. And so did Ian Becks. We might still be scratching our heads if it wasn't for him.'

'Where's Norm?' Jolly asked. 'Having a lie in?'

'He's just called me,' said Slater. 'He's on his way back from Newbury as we speak.'

'Come on then. Tell me the story.'

'It was Becksy who broke it. They found a pair of gloves in a bag of rubbish in the Rossiter's garage. When he got the gloves back here he found traces of blood which proved to be Diana's. We figured there would be DNA evidence on the inside of the gloves proving they were Angela Rossiter's, but we were wrong. The DNA was from Ian Woods.

'At around the same time, Norm found Angela Rossiter had Ian Woods' phone number. She also had his email address. She has a smart-phone so it was quite easy to access her email account where we found some very interesting messages.'

'Didn't he tell us he hardly knew her?' asked Jolly.

'Going by the messages, I'd say he knew her rather well,' said Slater. 'Very well, in fact.'

'Was he getting his own back on Rossiter, or did he genuinely like her?'

'That's a question we shall be asking him when he gets here,' said Slater.

'But what does he gain from killing her?' said Jolly. 'He doesn't seem to need the money, and if it was revenge, why wait until now? Why not do it sooner?'

'Perhaps it was Angela's idea and not his. Either way, they came up with quite an ingenious plan to get rid of Diana and frame Rossiter.'

'So what's Norm doing in Newbury?'

'It was bad work on our part, but we never checked out Susie Brennan's story about Woods being at her house. She told us her neighbour could vouch for her story, but we didn't follow that up. Norm's just done that. The neighbour confirms Woods was at Susie's house around three o'clock, but then she left to do the school run. She got back at four, and Woods had already left.

'We think he drove all the way back to Tinton where he met up with Angela Rossiter who had the Rochester's van. Woods drove the van to Diana's, killed her, and then returned the van to Rochester's. There was no one to see him, only the CCTV.'

'And Celia Rowntree subsequently removed the disc with that footage on it,' said Jolly.

'That's right,' said Slater. 'She bought the knife block at Angela's behest and left it in the van. And she also helped frame Rossiter by planting a mobile phone in his desk. Woods took Diana's phone when he stabbed her and gave it to Angela. That's how it came to be in Rossiter's sock drawer.'

'Did Celia know about Woods?'

'No. That's the clever part. She still thinks it was Angela Rossiter who stabbed Diana. She has no idea about Woody's involvement, so there's no way she could have told us about him. And it looks as though Angela Rossiter was so besotted she wasn't going to give him up come what may. He very nearly got away with it.'

'So let me get this straight,' said Jolly. 'We have two people conspiring to murder Diana Woods, and three people conspiring to frame Bruce Rossiter.'

'That's about the size of it,' said Slater. 'Norm said it was three-way conspiracy, and I thought he was having a laugh!'

'It's quite disappointing,' said Jolly. 'I had Ian Woods marked down as a nice man who wouldn't hurt a fly. Now it turns out he was little better than Bruce Rossiter where the ladies are concerned, and, on top of that, he's a murderer. Could I have been more wrong about him?'

'It could be he was even worse than Rossiter,' said Slater. 'Charm-less as Rossiter might be, he doesn't try to hide what he is. It's there for all to see. Woods, on the other hand, is very much the dark horse.

'When Norm called earlier he told me Susie Brennan had seen him this morning and asked him what he was doing. So he told her, and he also told her Ian Woods had been arrested.

'Now, if you recall, he's said all along that he thought there was something going on between her and Woods. He reckons her reaction confirms his suspicions.'

'Maybe you should tell Angela Rossiter,' said Jolly. 'She might not be quite so keen to protect him if she knew he was two-timing her.'

'Now there's a good idea,' said Slater, smiling.

EPILOGUE

'So you finally did as I suggested, and charged Woods.' Murray glared at Slater. 'I told you he was guilty, right from the start. Why the hell did it take you so long to follow a simple order?'

'We didn't have any conclusive evidence at the time, as you well know,' argued Slater. 'I thought we were supposed to ensure we have a case before we charge someone.'

'There was a case,' said Murray. 'You've just wasted a lot of time poking around unnecessarily.'

'Oh, I don't think so,' said Norman. 'I think it was time well spent. We would never have got Angela Rossiter to turn against Ian Woods otherwise. I have no doubt a half-decent lawyer would have got Woods off without us putting that time in.'

'So what was the big rush?' Slater asked Murray.

'It's quite simple. It was an open and shut case,' said Murray.

'But two people would probably have slipped the net if you had your way. And a good brief would have torn our case against Woods to shreds.'

'Yeah. We wondered if maybe you had some other reason for being in such a hurry,' added Norman.

'I don't know what you mean,' said Murray, uncertainly.

'Oh, is that right?' said Norman. 'So it didn't have anything to do with your name and number being in Diana Woods' contact list?'

'Really?' said Murray. 'I can't imagine how she got my number.'

Slater couldn't recall ever having seen Murray embarrassed before, but he was now. Slater and Norman waited while Murray struggled with his conscience.

'I only saw her a couple of times,' he mumbled, eventually. 'There's no need for anyone else to know about this. My wife would be deeply hurt if she found out.'

'That didn't worry you when you were shagging Diana Woods, did it?' asked Slater. 'Or when you went back for afters.'

'Just remember who you're talking to, Sergeant,' said Murray, bristling with anger.

'Oh I know who I'm talking to,' said Slater. 'I'm talking to the DCI who would have been happy to see the first face that came along charged with murder just to make sure we didn't stir the muck enough to bring his own indiscretion floating to the surface.'

'But I was right,' roared Murray. 'He did murder her!'

'But we didn't know that for sure, back then, did we?' said Slater.

He stood up and made his way across to the door.

'Where do you think you're going?' Murray's voice echoed around the room 'You come back here. I haven't finished with you yet.'

'But I have finished with you,' said Slater as he swung the door open. 'I used to respect you, but I'm afraid I'm going to find that a bit difficult in future. Sir.'

He marched out and pulled the door closed behind him, totally ignoring Murray's shouted order.

'Come back here!' roared Murray, but the door swung closed and Slater was gone.

'He'll pay for this,' muttered Murray. 'I'll show him.'

'I don't think so, do you?' asked Norman, who had been silently observing the exchange. 'We know your dirty little secret, and you wouldn't want it to leak out, now would you?'

'Don't tell me you're going to turn against me, too,' said Murray. 'We go back a long way. I helped you out when I brought you here.'

'That's true,' agreed Norman. 'You did help me out, but I don't remember ever saying I'd be prepared to repay you by perverting the course of justice.'

'Yes, but-,' began Murray.

'Don't you dare try to defend yourself,' interrupted Norman, raising his voice. 'There is no defence for what you wanted us to do. And, it was all because you couldn't keep your pecker under control.'

'You don't know what it was like for me back then,' pleaded Murray.

'You're right,' said Norman. 'I don't know what it was like for you back then, and you know what? I don't give a shit, because whatever it was like back then doesn't excuse what you wanted us to do now. '

He climbed to his feet and headed for the door.

'I suggest the next time you feel like taking your crappy temper out on any of the staff who work here you remember this conversation,' he told Murray, as he walked.

'Where are you going?' demanded Murray.

'There's a rotten smell in here, Bob,' replied Norman, as he stepped through the door. 'I need some fresh air.'

BOOKS BY P.F. FORD

ABOUT THE AUTHOR

P.F. Ford is the author of the Alfie Bowman Novella series, and the Dave Slater Mystery Series.

A late starter to writing after a life of failures, P.F. (Peter) Ford spent most of his life being told he should forget his dreams, and that he would never make anything of himself without a "proper" job.

But then a few years ago, having been unhappy for over 50 years of his life, Peter decided he had no intention of carrying on that way. Fast forward a few years and you find a man transformed by a partner (now wife) who believed dreamers should be encouraged and not denied.

Now, happily settled in Wales, Peter is blissfully happy sharing his life with wife Mary and their four rescue dogs, and living his dream writing fiction (and still without a "proper" job).

Learn more here:
www.pfford.co.uk

Printed in Great Britain
by Amazon

21230760R00129